- 1 DEC 200

GW00385463

Bat
18/3 75

THE SILVER BOWL

Historical Novels by Hugh Ross Williamson

Hugh Ross Williamson

THE SILVER BOWL

London

MICHAEL JOSEPH

First published in Great Britain by
MICHAEL JOSEPH LTD
52 Bedford Square
London, WC1
1948

This edition 1975

© 1948 by Hugh Ross Williamson

ISBN 0 7181 1326 8

Printed in Great Britain by
Hollen Street Press Ltd at Slough
and bound by James Burn at Esher, Surrey

TO

ALEXANDER MCINTOSH CANNELL

CONTENTS

★

Prologue

THE SILVER BOWL

ABOUT THE ORIGIN OF THE SILVER BOWL, WHATEVER MAY BE pretended, there is no certainty. Some say that Alexander the Great, in the year he crossed the Hellespont against the Persians, went one day hunting on the slopes of Mount Pagos. The chase ended, he came to the ruined Temple of the Nemeseis there, and, tired out, lay down to rest under the plane tree by the healing spring which wells up in front of the Temple. Here, in sleep, the Nemeseis appeared to him and bade him restore their glory by building a new city between the Temple and the sea. When he awoke he pledged himself to do them that honour and poured out a libation of water from the spring in token of his oath. For this he used the silver bowl which he carried with him and from which he was accustomed to drink. Afterwards ne caused it to be engraved with the figures of the Nemeseis as he had seen them in the vision and gave it to the priests of Serapis to guard as a palladium for the restored Temple and the new city of Smyrna.

There are, however, others, not wanting in scholarship, who contend that the Silver Bowl is centuries older than Alexander the Great and is a relic of the time when the first city of Smyrna was founded (at least a millenium before Alexander's birth) by the dreaded women-warriors of the double-headed axe, the Amazons. Here, from the mountain's height, these armed priestesses of the great Mother-Goddess ruled and made laws and offered the blood-sacrifice to the Nemeseis who, in answer to their prayers, came from

Mount Olympus, twelve miles away, to take up their abode among them on the hillside of Pagos.

Others again would seek to penetrate still further into that obscurity which veils the youth of the world and maintain that the Silver Bowl was already sacred when the Amazons came; that it was, in fact, connected with King Tantalus, Son of Zeus, whose country this was, and with Niobe, his daughter, whose children fell before the arrows of Apollo and Artemis. This, however, is idle speculation, Whether or not the Olympians and their children were concerned with the Bowl is not now likely to be known. Nor does it greatly matter. What is known beyond doubt is its connection with the Nemeseis and so with Smyrna.

For it was Smyrna which gave to the world the worship of the Nemeseis and it was in Smyrna alone that the true nature of these goddesses was understood and preserved. This is the more easily seen when it is remembered that, in the vulgar mind, Nemesis is imagined as a single figure. Absurd though this may be, it is the predictable result of man's addiction to pride and self-pity. When he is called on to pay for his happiness and his possessions, the pain of payment obliterates the previous joy of possessing. It is the nature of man that though he prays for bounty, once his prayer is heard, he considers the gift as his right and the divine exaction of dues for it as an act of capricious vengeance on the part of the gods. He says, when the reckoning is presented, that 'Nemesis has overtaken him,' forgetting that it was Nemesis also who came bearing gifts.

From this craven mistake the men of Smyrna remained free, since there was never a time when they did not worship the two Nemeseis —She who Gives and She who Exacts. They engraved proudly on their coins the Two, majestic in their gryphon-borne chariot. And the Two were also secretly engraved—though in what form exactly is known only to the initiate—on the Silver Bowl.

Essentially it was from this that its potency sprang. Not that any virtue inhered in the image, but that from at any rate the days of Alexander it had been handled for purposes which took account of the true nature of things. Both priests and people understood. They paid the dues of She who Exacts with the same equanimity as they accepted the favours of She who Gives. Thus they learnt a nicety of calculation, a discipline in asking, a sobriety in receiving. They perceived—though this was gradual—that many things which might be acceptable as a free gift were not worth buying. So the Silver Bowl was used less and less, and was in fact reserved for matters of high importance—matters usually of life and death, where a supernatural control of life was paid for by a premature surrender to death.

This is no place to chronicle the history of the peerless city and its palladium, but no one will forget that the greatest of the Magi, Apollonius of Tyana, came more than once to Smyrna, which he considered 'the most beautiful of all cities under the sun' and used the Bowl, so it is said, in restoring one dead to life. And at the same time came John, the Beloved Disciple of Jesus of Nazareth, who in his 'Apocalypse' has left on record, in the letter to the Christians of Smyrna, his horror of the initiates of the Nemeseis, whom he called 'the synagogue of Satan.'

The Christians won in the end, of course, though not before one of their bishops, Polycarp, had been burnt for his faith in the arena on the slopes of Pagos, and another bishop, Euktemon, had abjured Christ and made public sacrifice to the Nemeseis. And when, by decree of the Emperor Constantine, Christianity was at last established, the true worshippers of the Nemeseis were forced into silence or hiding and, with them, the Silver Bowl disappeared. It is said, however, that when the Templars came to Smyrna, there was a strange alliance between the devotees of the Old Faith and these arrogant and subtle Knights of the New and that the Bowl was secretly kept in their castle, which witnessed strange rites. It is also asserted that, when the Turks overwhelmed the city and the Crescent displaced the Cross, the last of the Templars hid the Bowl in the ruined tomb of Polycarp which stands on the slopes of Pagos above the city. But these are speculations only, and the truth, since it is known only to the initiates who are sworn to secrecy, is unlikely to be revealed.

Yet the persistent tradition that for some years in the seventeenth century the Bowl was actually in England lends colour to the suggestion that it may not have been unconnected with those mysterious and unexplained happenings in Gloucestershire which are known in history as the Campden Wonder.

CHAPTER I

★

The Disappearance of
William Harrison

THE BROTHERS WERE STANDING BY THE STONE GATEWAY INTO the meadow called the Conygree. Only a few moments of light remained to the burning August day. Not the least breath of wind, rustling the leaves, relieved the sultriness or the silence. The two Perrys neither moved nor spoke. Still as the landscape, they stood straining their eyes against the oncoming darkness. Richard, the elder, was looking fixedly down the road that leads to Ebrington and Charringworth. John, the younger, his back to the road, gazed south across the rough meadow towards the tall Banqueting House, framed in the narrow arch of the gateway.

That remnant of the ruined mansion stood lonely as a sentinel among the fields and gardens. About it hung a faint air of fantasy, as if it had pleased the caprice of an Eastern enchanter to drop it there—fantastic, not only by reason of its general improbability there, now, in that place, but in particular because its three tall chimneys, though less than fifty years old and made of good Cotswold stone, called strangely to mind by their shape, the minarets of the East. John Perry, however, who had seen it daily all his life, had in it only a severely practical interest. When, suddenly, the figure of a woman carrying a lighted lantern appeared on the balcony, he moved quickly behind the trunk of one of the beeches. The gesture was instinctive, since a moment's reasoning would have assured him that she could not possibly see him, even had she suspected he was there. He knew, moreover, that she had no reason to suppose that he had disobeyed her. Half an hour earlier she had ordered him to go to Charringworth in search of his master, who should have returned from his rent-collecting there hours ago. The lantern would be to guide them, should they come back through the fields instead of by the road. Mrs. Harrison was, he decided, more of a fool than he had always thought her if she imagined that her husband, with or without his aid, would attempt to return that way in the darkness.

But the road was empty still. Richard, when the impossibility of seeing more than a yard or two in front of him made him abandon his vigil, moved to his brother's side.

'You're certain he'll come?' he asked. His whisper, the first sound to break the strained silence, seemed unnecessarily loud.

'Yes, it's not nine yet.'

John's voice had in it a strange rasp of authority. Had a passer-by chanced to hear it there in the darkness, he would certainly not have ascribed it to a manservant of twenty-four. But Richard had been accustomed to it for years, too accustomed, indeed, to be particularly conscious of it. Neither, probably, was he conscious of the extent to which, in the ordinary traffic of life, he deferred to it. As the elder brother, six years older than John, he had been by turns admiringly and lazily acquiescent in his brother's habit of command. Though he had curbed it with blows when John was a boy, he found increasingly a vicarious satisfaction in it. It was like a family possession, some secret treasure, which could impress those who saw in the Perrys only a poverty-stricken family of Gloucestershire peasants.

At last, faint in the distance, came the sound of footsteps on the highroad. As they came nearer, the brothers, quiet as cats, left the gate and went a short way up the hill where, under the churchyard wall, they stood and listened. It was too dark to see, even faintly, the newcomer; but the footsteps stopped at the gate, the latch clicked, and the hinges screeched.

'That's him,' said John.

Richard hesitated. 'You're sure?'

'Of course. Who else could it be? Is mother there?'

'Yes.'

'Good; then you'd better go at once.'

'Aren't you coming?'

'In a moment,' said John. 'You go first; and don't say anything till you're in the middle of the Conygree. Voices carry on a night like this.'

When his brother had left him, he waited until he heard the gate open once more. But he did not follow. He went quietly on in the opposite direction, up the road and round the church. As he passed the church-gate, the clock struck nine.

Next morning—it was the morning of Friday, August 17th, 1660—a great mist enveloped Chipping Campden. From the upper storeys of the houses it could be seen advancing from the fields like a besieging enemy until it assaulted and took possession of the Street itself. Round the little hill on which the church stood it was so thick that the great tower was hardly visible even from the courtyard-gate of Campden House, at the bend of Church Street. Yet men and women on their morning business almost welcomed the clammy cold as a momentary relief from the heat of yesterday and the equal heat the mist presaged for to-day. By ten o'clock, however, when the sun scattered it, it was not the weather which concerned them. All Campden by that time knew that 'old Mr. William' had disappeared.

The news assumed more than the importance which the inexplicable disappearance of any citizen would have warranted. William Harrison was, indeed, much respected, both for his own person and in his official capacity as steward of the absent Lady Campden; but what made him almost a symbol in the place was that he was about the last real link with 'Sir Baptist.' The Chipping Campden of 1660 was still the town of Sir Baptist Hicks. The inhabitants had continued to refer to him as 'Sir Baptist' even though in the last year of his life he was created the first Viscount Campden, and they spoke of him in the same terms to-day, as if they might chance to meet him at any corner, even though he had been dead thirty-one years and lay quiet enough in the great marble tomb in the church. His coat-of-arms, the three *fleurs-de-lys*, could indeed be met with at every turn, carved on buildings he had given to the town of his adoption—on the row of almshouses across the road from his own mansion; on his squat lodge-gates, a stone's throw from the church; on the Market Hall in the High Street, the pride of Campden and the envy of less fortunate towns.

When he had bought the manor and first come among the proud, shrewd Gloucestershire folk as a stranger (albeit as a silk mercer of fabulous riches and a friend of King James) he brought with him William Harrison, then a mere youth of twenty, though experienced beyond his years. With tact and discretion, with charm and good-humour, Harrison had won the heart of Chipping Campden for its new lord. He had already served Sir Baptist in a difficult and confidential mission to the Levant, on whose trade so much of the merchant's fortune depended; and on his return he was charged with this so different yet hardly less difficult matter in the heart of England. In the new work he spared no pains. It was not long before he knew everyone in the town, their needs, their tempers, their ambitions. More importantly, everyone in the town knew him as the channel through which their case—were it alms or employment or a contract or a sale—would be presented promptly and with fairness to the new Lord of the Manor.

That was fifty years ago. And William Harrison, over seventy now, was still there in a changed world. The glory had gone. The fabulous pile of Campden House, which had cost Sir Baptist £30,000 to build, was a heap of charred ruins—burnt deliberately by order of Prince Rupert in the Civil Wars lest, when the Royalists left it, it should be used as headquarters by the Roundheads. Of the great three-storied mansion with its glass dome, in which a light always shewed at night for travellers lost on the wolds, there were left intact only some of the outbuildings—the two Banqueting Houses, which were connected by an underground passage running beneath the Terrace, the laundry, the stables,* and the lodges at the Great Gate.

And not only the House but the people were gone. Sir Baptist had no son. His daughter, Juliana, who inherited the Campden estate, had been widowed in the wars and had now, at seventy-five, taken up residence with her husband's family and her son in Rutlandshire. But William Harrison with his family stayed on to make the outbuildings among the ruins their home; and as long as he was there the past intruded into the present. His trim figure with its still upright carriage, the neat grey pointed beard, the kindly dark-brown eyes, the beak of a nose with its wide nostrils, all reminded the older generation of Sir Baptist himself as he had been in his last years. The resemblance may have been no more than a fancy, though, as Harrison had all his life moulded himself on his master, it was not an improbability. In his own person, he continued to discharge his appropriate duties. The somewhat rusty black coat, the neck-band always immaculately white, the hat set at a surprisingly jaunty angle, as if fifty years of the Gloucestershire countryside had not quite tamed the adventurous spirit of youth, was one of the familiar sights of Campden. Still he looked after the needs of the tenants of the estate, as he had done for half a century; still he collected rent punctually, but with discretion and sympathy, from the outlying farms. It was on such an errand he had gone yesterday, walking the two miles over the fields to Charringworth in the August heat. But this time he had not come back.

The first townsman to receive news of the occurrence was the oldest inhabitant of the almshouses, whose grand-daughter was in Mrs. Harrison's service. She managed to slip away and run over the road for the express purpose of telling him, because she had noticed on her last visit that he was becoming dull and moody and losing interest in life. Even the excitement of the happy Restoration of King Charles II earlier in the year had failed to move him to any-

---

* These were converted and enlarged in the eighteenth century and are now (1948) known as the Court House.

thing but the remark: ' 'Taint like 'twas Armada-year and 't'won't be, that's what I say, not whoever's King, now Bess has gone!' But now, when his grand-daughter, a little out of breath, shouted in his ear that Mr. Harrison had not come home the previous night and could not be found, he brightened perceptibly, nodded his head sagely and asked for particulars. Having mastered them and murmured that he really wasn't surprised, he asked her to give him her arm to lean on for the few yards from his almshouse to the new inn round the corner, *The Eight Bells*, where his news made him a contented centre of attraction.

From the inn it spread quickly into the town and down the Street—first, and as if by right, to Tom Barnes, the massive, knowledgeable, kindly blacksmith who, at seventy-three, was the local oracle; then, by way of the servants, to the Mosleys and the Izods and the Gilbys, the leading families of the place who lived in those fine mediæval houses which were still a reminder of Chipping Campden's importance in the past centuries as a wool centre. Outside the Woolstaplers' Hall, a group of old men, talking, had the news brought them from the inn and endorsed the opinion of the first hearer of it. They were not, they agreed, surprised, considering the curious goings-on up at the House recently. This was also the verdict passed by another and a more representative group of elders—for the young and ablebodied were now in the fields busy with the harvest—as they stood later under the cover of the Market Hall, grateful for its shade as the mist lifted and the sun came pitilessly through.

The 'curious goings-on' referred to an event in February which had never been satisfactorily explained. It so happened that one particular market-day had coincided with the visit of a preacher from Gloucester, who had the reputation of one greatly skilled in eliciting from and expatiating on those truths of Holy Scripture which seemed to apply to contemporary events. And in those early days of 1660, with the Cromwellian dictatorship over and General Monck marching on London, with every kind of rumour and uncertainty agitating the country, with threats of vengeance to those who had supported Oliver and reward for those who had remained true, if tactful, in their allegiance to the exiled Charles II, all men's minds were uneasy. It was not surprising, therefore, that the church at noon was crowded not only with those from Campden itself but also with many who had come in for the market and had concluded their business early so that they might hear the preacher's 'lecture.'

In the pews reserved for the Campden family were all the Harrisons—William and his wife Susannah; Edward, their eldest son, with his wife, very near the time of her first child-bearing; and William, the second son, with his wife, Hephizbah. Behind them Harrison's personal servant, John Perry, sat, a model of immobility, in charge of the domestic staff.

When the 'lecture' was over and Campden was its bustling, market-day self once more, it was discovered that, during the discourse, a ladder had been set up to the second-storey window of the larger Banqueting House, where Harrison lived, an iron bar wrenched away with a ploughshare (which had been left in the room) and £140 stolen. The robbers were never found, in spite of an intensive search in which the whole town co-operated. But the most curious feature of the affair was not that no one of those not in church had seen so public a daylight proceeding but that Mr. Harrison, though obviously very seriously worried, made light of the actual loss of the money and showed no disposition to press the inquiry as far as some of the townsmen—and particularly the Vicar, the Reverend William Bartholomew—were anxious to take it.

What many considered a sequel to the robbery occurred three months later, on the eve of May Day. The inmates of the almshouses and the casual passers-by in Church Street heard from behind the high garden-wall of Campden House the agonized screams for help of John Perry. Three men ran as fast as possible to the Courtyard-Gate of the House to be met by Perry himself in a state of obvious terror, a sheep-pick in his hand and his coat slashed about the pocket. The young man explained that he had been set upon by two men in white with drawn swords who would have killed him had he not defended himself with his sheep-pick—which indubitably bore marks of recent notches, as did also a large key in his pocket. He himself, however, was uninjured, nor was there any sign of the attackers. Yet those who saw Perry at this moment testified to the panic-stricken look on his face, nor did they waver in their assertion even when the scepticism of their fellow-townsmen might well have overwhelmed them. The whole affair—so common opinion ran—was a pretence of John Perry's. But no one suggested what motive he might have had.

The Perrys had never been popular in Campden. Richard, John's father, was a drunken ne'er-do-well who had left the town when the Royalist forces had gone, burning Campden House behind them, to join the King on his march to the North. He had been killed at Naseby, five weeks later, and his widow, Joan, was left to bring up his two sons, Richard, then fifteen, and John, who was nine. The daughters, Anne and Margaret, had both married, just before their father's death and had left the neighbourhood. Joan, Richard and John continued to live in their little cottage opposite *The Eight Bells*, dependent largely on the charity of Harrison who saw that they were charged only a nominal rent and were supplied from the Campden estate with any of the necessaries of life they lacked. Richard, a quiet, stolid youth, became a jack-of-all-trades at the inn opposite, and in due course, when he was twenty-four, married Anne Harris, a Campden girl. Now, in 1660, they had two girls, one five, the other nearly a year; and they all lived in the family cottage with old Joan who, with the advancing years, incurred the town's suspicion of being a witch.

John had had a different upbringing. From his childhood he had stood out from the squalid background. Stubborn and rebellious to his father, during his lifetime, he had a passionate devotion to his mother whom, in appearance, he now resembled. Mother and son had the same dark, smouldering eyes, the same wide brow and unbiddable hair, though whereas her mouth had a full sensuality, with humour in the upward curves at the corners, his was thin and straight as of one not much troubled, even in the heat of youth, with the insistence of the flesh. But with the coldness was allied a restless intelligence and a certain contempt of others which, sitting ill on one of his mean station, added to his unpopularity in the town. When his father was killed Harrison, realizing his latent abilities and wishing to rescue him from the life of a pot-boy or a farm-hand, had him sent to the Grammar School (which Sir Baptist had re-founded) and subsequently took him into his own service as a personal attendant, part clerk, part valet.

The gossips averred that Perry had repaid this kindness by ingratitude and incompetence, though nothing that Harrison himself had ever said could have formed the basis of such a judgment. The origin, for anyone who had troubled to trace it, was to be found rather in the remarks which Harrison's son, Edward, frequently let slip in conversation with all and sundry.

That John Perry and the 'young master' were on the worst possible terms was indeed patent for all to see; but it was an antagonism which provoked little partisanship. Campden liked Edward Harrison as little as it liked John Perry, though for different reasons. Edward, at forty, suffered from all the disabilities of a man of mature years still living in his father's house and allowed no real responsibility. The sense of frustration found its outlet in criticism of his father and over-bearingness to his tenants. He did not trouble to hide his opinion that his father should by now have relinquished the stewardship of the estate to him. He regarded the old man as out-of-date and sentimental in his methods, apt to be swayed in his judgments by yesterday's memories; and the tenants dreaded the day when Edward would take his father's place. Fortunately for them, William Harrison, who wore his seventy-two years lightly enough, showed no disposition to abdicate in favour of Edward; but unfortunately for the peace of his own family life he tended to give to Perry the confidences which Edward, properly enough, considered his right. Thus was widened the breach, which circumstances and temperament had already made wide enough, between his servant and his son.

So it was that, on that Friday morning, when Perry returned at dawn through the mist to report that there was no sign of his master at Charringworth, Edward, in spite of his angry dislike, had the mortification of being dependent on him for information as to whom else his father might have visited.

'And where the devil have you been all night?' asked Edward.

'Hereabouts,' said John.

'Then why didn't you come home? Wasn't it enough to have my mother crazy with fear about what might have happened to my father, without your disappearing too?'

'Got lost in the mist,' said Perry. 'Never known it so thick. The master's not at Charringworth.'

'You've tried everyone there?'

'All he called on. Ned Plaisterer—he paid him twenty-three pounds. Been a long time in arrears, he has; but he always promised to get up to date by mid-August. That's really why Mr. Harrison went.'

'Twenty-three pounds is a lot of money.'

'Ned Plaisterer rents a large farm.'

'I mean a lot of money for an old man like my father to be carrying about in times like these when God knows who may be about.'

'He's used to it.'

'Was that all he had or did he call anywhere else?'

'Seems as if that was all he had. He called on Will Curtis, but he was out. Gone over to Bourton-on-the-Hill, they say. His sister's sick.'

'No one else?'

'No.'

'You're certain?'

'As certain as can be. Those were the only two in Charringworth. Unless, of course, *you* know of anyone else.'

'You insolent blockhead!'

'Thank you, Mr. Edward.'

'Well, don't stand there like that. What do we do now?'

'You're the master, Mr. Edward,' observed Perry. 'I'll do whatever you say.'

Edward, swallowing hard, asked: 'Where else do you think my father might have gone?'

'Well, he might have gone over to Yabberton to see Daniels.'

'Then that's where we'll go.'

But at Ebrington (known locally as Yabberton) old Daniels could tell them only that William Harrison had called on him the previous evening about six o'clock, had stayed and chatted for about half an hour when he said he must be getting along as he still had a visit to make at Paxford and wanted to get home before dusk.

Enquiries at Paxford were even more abortive. No one in that village had seen Mr. Harrison at all.

By now it was nearly eleven o'clock, the heat was intense and both Edward and John, neither of whom had eaten that day, were feeling the strain of it. Perry, breaking a long silence, suggested: 'Perhaps if we go home, we shall find the master's come back by now.'

Edward grunted and turned off the road to take the short-cut across the fields to Campden House. It was not until they had almost reached it that they overtook a poor woman who was also making her way there. She was carrying a hat, a band with blood on it, and a comb, which both Edward and John immediately recognized as those which William Harrison had worn the previous day.

CHAPTER II

The Explanations of John Perry

THERE WAS NO DOUBT IN THE GENERAL MIND OF CAMPDEN THAT William Harrison had been murdered; but beyond that simple and obvious fact, there was no certainty and little agreement. No one could suggest either a motive or a murderer.

The woman who had found the hat, comb and band proved to be one of those wandering gleaners who, at harvest time, went from village to village and farm to farm offering her services in exchange for food and a bed and a penny or two to save towards the winter. She knew no one in Campden, but when she discovered what seemed to her to be evidence of a crime, such was her terror of the law that she decided to take them straight to the authorities—though it is possible that, had there been no blood on the band, she would have kept the comb. When Edward Harrison and John Perry overtook her, she recognized at once that Edward was a person of quality and explained her intention. She told him that she had found the articles by the great furze-brake where the Ebrington road became so narrow that it was hardly more than a footpath. She would lead him to the exact spot. As they went back to it, they were accompanied by almost the entire population of the place. The work of harvest and of home were alike forgotten; as men, women and children streamed over the fields to look for the body of the murdered man. But though they searched till sunset they did not find it.

At what particular point suspicion began to fasten itself to John Perry, it would be impossible to say. It was a matter of atmosphere and hints springing from dislike and disconnected details of behaviour and circumstance. In great part he brought it on himself by his contradictory suggestions. At one moment he gave it as his opinion that Mr. Harrison had not been killed but kidnapped. At another, he suggested that a murderer who left evidence of the crime in one place would at least take care to remove the body to another. Later he hinted that his master might have his own reasons for disappearing and that the hat, comb and band, whose absence would not seriously discommode him, were merely a blind. Certainly he talked too much, but the damning circumstance was the plain fact that from nine o'clock the previous night till dawn, he, like his master, was missing; that, as far as anyone knew, he had no alibi; and that he knew—and he alone—that in all probability Mr. Harrison would be carrying a substantial sum of money.

He was that evening made aware of the suspicion, savagely, by Edward Harrison. When he took his leave of the family for the night to go to his own rooms above the stables, Edward said: 'You're staying here to-night. I'm not letting you out of my sight.'

'Why, Mr. Edward?' he asked in surprise. 'What have I done?'

'You should know best; but when Sir Thomas Overbury comes over from Bourton in the morning, I shall let him decide whether or not you murdered my father.'

At this John started to laugh, at first quietly to himself, then rising to a note of hysteria, until old Mrs. Harrison came in to see what the noise was and Edward slapped him sharply on the face. The blow quietened him. He looked at them both for a moment in silence, then said gravely: 'Thank you, Mr. Edward,' and refused to speak again until the morning.

Sir Thomas Overbury, the local Justice of the Peace from Bourton-on-the-Hill, was early in Campden next day. Rumour had outdistanced the Harrisons' message to him the previous evening and by the time their request for his presence arrived he had been given most of the details of the case. As a friend of the family, he would in any case have visited them in a private capacity. The call on his professional services made him decide to conduct immediately a thorough examination of the circumstances in the privacy of the Harrisons' house. Unless the discovery of the body made a public sitting of the court a necessity, it was wiser at this stage, he thought, to keep the matter as private as possible.

'Young Tom Overbury' (as he was always called locally to distinguish him from his more famous uncle, that Sir Thomas Overbury who had been murdered in the Tower nearly fifty years before) came from generations of Gloucestershire stock, but had spent the greater part of his life in foreign travel, which had extended as far as India. Now, in his early fifties, prematurely old, grey with his adventures, his right arm almost crippled with rheumatism and his hearing failing so that occasionally on the Bench he had to use an ear-trumpet, he was taking his expected place in his native county. The Overburys had served the Crown in one capacity or other as long as men could remember. Sir Thomas's grandfather, the Squire of Bourton, had been Recorder of the City of Gloucester and a Judge in Wales; and now he, the favourite grandson and the family's heir, had foresworn his wanderings and come back to take up the family's duty. His knighthood, but seven weeks old, had set the seal on it. But his spirit was restless still and the East troubled his dreams. For this reason he enjoyed above most things a bout of talk with old William Harrison who, in his youth, had visited many of the places he knew, and who, in addition, could give him gossip about his ill-fated uncle whose death remained the *cause célèbre* of the century. It was natural therefore that he should approach the matter of his friend's mysterious disappearance with something more than the strict impartiality of an examining magistrate; though, in the circumstances he was a fairer judge than any that could have been found in Campden, since not only was he free from the local prejudice against John Perry, but so antipathetic was he to Edward Harrison that the attempt Edward made, immediately on his arrival to vilify Perry in every way produced the opposite of the intended effect.

When Perry was at last summoned to his presence, he looked at him searchingly for a moment or two before he spoke. Perry's glance never wavered. There was in it no hint of fear or servility. Indeed, of the two it might have been not the withered magistrate but the young manservant who was in charge of the situation. For Perry brought into the room a sense of immense vitality. His habitual coldness had vanished. He stood and moved with the natural grace of a young animal, with his skin bronzed with the sun and his great shock of wiry black hair ruffled as if the wind were still in it. His vivid red coat—once the property of a dead soldier—made all the other colours in the room seem dim.

It was Overbury who dropped his eyes as he asked: 'What have you to say to me?'

'Mr. Edward here thinks I murdered the master.'

'And I'm not the only one by any means,' Edward interposed. 'Why, the whole of Campden knows——'

'I can manage this alone, thank you, Edward,' said Overbury brusquely, 'and I am not interested in gossip.' Then, to Perry: 'Did you murder him?'

'No, Sir Thomas.'

'Then tell me what happened on Thursday night.'

'It would be about half-past eight when Mrs. Harrison told me to go to Charringworth to see what had delayed my master, so I went down the fields about a land's length when I met Will Reed.'

'Who is he and what was he doing there?'

'He works over at Pudlicote Mill. He was coming home. I asked him if he had seen Mr. Harrison, but he said "No"; then I told him where I was going and asked him to come with me.'

'Why?'

'It was getting dark and I didn't like going over the fields alone. So he said why didn't I ride down the road instead of walking across the fields; and I thought this was a good plan, so I came back with him to borrow Mr. Edward's horse.'

'That's a lie,' said Edward. 'You never asked to borrow my horse. Not that I should have let you if you had.'

'I shouldn't have asked you, Mr. Edward,' retorted Perry, 'but anyhow, I didn't take it. After Will Reed had left me, Jack Pearce came by and——'

'One moment,' said Overbury. 'Where was this?'

'By the courtyard gate—the one that goes into the town. It's nearest the stables.'

'And when?'

'A minute or two past nine.'

'How do you know?'

'I heard the clock strike.'

'And who is Pearce and what was he doing?'

'He'd been at *The Eight Bells* and was going home. He lives up beyond the church. Been working at the harvest all day, he had. When I saw him I thought perhaps he'd go with me, so I asked him to. At first he said he would, and we went off down the fields again; but then he said it was too dark and anyhow he must be getting home or his wife would nag his head off. So we came back to the lodge-gates.'

'How far had you gone together?'

'Only about a bow-shot into the fields.'

'I see. And then?'

'Then I came back and lay down in the hen-roost—it's by the wall near the courtyard-gate—and stayed there till I heard the church clock strike twelve. Then I got up and started to go to Charring-worth.'

'But if you were too frightened to go at nine o'clock, why were you not still frightened at midnight?'

'At nine o'clock it was as dark as pitch; at midnight, with the moon, it was almost as bright as day.'

'And you set off without asking whether, while you were still in the hen-roost, Mr. Harrison had returned?'

'I knew he wasn't at home by the two lights.'

'What two lights?'

'There was a lantern Mrs. Harrison had set on the balustrade of the little Banqueting House, and there was the light in his room.

It'd have never been there—the one in his room, I mean—as late as
that if he'd been at home. He goes to sleep early, the master
does.'

'But you knew he would have come in very late that night, so it
would be natural for the light to be there late on this occasion?'

'I suppose it would, but all I was thinking of was getting to
Charringworth.'

'It seems strange to me that you returned home twice after you'd
been sent out and then set out a third time in the middle of the night
without going into the house to find out whether Mr. Harrison had
come back in the meantime or not.'

'Well, they all thought I was at Charringworth and I didn't want
them to know I wasn't. Mr. Edward can be very violent when he
likes.'

'I've had cause enough,' said Edward.

'Did you go to Charringworth at midnight?' asked Overbury,
ignoring the aside.

'No.'

'Why?'

'There was a great mist, and although it was moonlight, I was as
lost as if I'd been in the dark.'

'What did you do?'

'I lay the rest of the night under a hedge and as soon as it was
light and I could find my way I went to Charringworth and
knocked up Mr. Plaisterer, who told me my master had collected
£23 from him the afternoon before. Then I went to Mr. Curtis who
said his daughter told him my master had called but he'd been away
all day and didn't see him. Then on my way back home I met Mr.
Edward and we went over to Yabberton together. But he'll have
told you that, no doubt.'

'Yes, I'm not concerned with that at the moment. What I'm
trying to find out is what you were doing between sunset and
dawn.'

'I've told you, Sir Thomas,' said Perry with a quiet, unexpected
gravity.

What verification the story could have, it had, on oath, from William Reed and John Pearce and Edward Plaisterer and William Curtis. All confirmed exactly John Perry's account in so far as it affected themselves. The two labourers, indeed, unwittingly strengthened it, for both revealed their own fear of venturing across the fields in the darkness. In daylight and in gregarious security, this particular timidity seemed so childish that the admission of it was a conspicuously weak spot in Perry's already weak story; but as Reed and Pearce answered Overbury's questions something of the terror of darkness invaded the matter-of-fact room— terror of things not tangible, the nightmare subjects of the Queen of the Night; terror of the transformation by which a familiar field became an uncharted waste, terror of wandering strangers who might be lurking there to trap the foolhardy or the unfortunate. By their stolid unawareness that there was anything unreasonable in such a fear, they made Perry's account of how he spent the night almost credible. And that he had, in fact, arrived at Charringworth with the dawn, Plaisterer and Curtis both bore witness.

The hard fact remained, however, that for the vital hours between half-past nine and four, there was nothing but Perry's unsupported word; and Overbury, whatever his personal opinion might have been, considered he had no alternative but to order his detention for a day or two, in the hope that in the meantime more evidence would come to light.

That night John Perry spent in the insanitary little cell beneath the old Court House, which stood behind the new Market Hall.

Few things are more irrational and less predictable than the changes in public opinion. No sooner had Perry been committed to prison than Campden gradually forgot its hostility and began to show if not partisanship at least a measure of sympathy. It was over his pint in *The Eight Bells* that Tom Barnes, hitching up the leather belt which just managed to enclose his not inconsiderable girth, gave it as his opinion that things were going too fast. His twinkling blue eyes were grave for the moment, his red cheeks a little redder

than usual, and his close-cropped grey hair bristled more challeng-
ingly than ever over his forehead. There might be no doubt, he
said, slowly and judicially, that Mr. Harrison was murdered. He
wasn't denying it for a moment. But equally there was no doubt
that, as his body had not been found, no one could prove it. As for
John Perry's story, it might be a farrago of falsehoods, but as he had
been sent out alone, how could 'that Mr. Edward' expect there
would be anyone with him to say whether he was telling the truth
or not? Tom was all for keeping an eye of him, but that was a long
way different from putting him in the dirty little cell that hadn't
been used for Lord knows how long and anyhow wasn't fit to
keep a pig in.

Campden, after debating it, agreed; and when Overbury rode
over again on the following Tuesday morning, the feeling was
strong enough for it to be reported to him. After he had again
questioned Perry, who obstinately repeated point for point his
original story, he gave orders that, though he still could not order
his complete release, he might return to the Harrisons' house.

But Edward said: 'Not even for you, Sir Thomas, will I have my
father's murderer under my roof again.' So Perry was lodged,
under what amounted to mere house-arrest, in *The George Inn*
opposite the prison.

He asked to see his mother and when she came the meeting was
hardly of the kind that Campden, knowing their mutual affection,
had expected. Joan Perry was composed, aloof, almost, it appeared,
angry. She and her son talked in low tones in a corner of the room,
so that none could overhear what they said. But, just before she
gave him a parting kiss, she said in a voice accidentally loud enough
to carry to the bystanders: 'I warned you, son John. Don't forget
I'm your mother and I shan't hold my peace for ever.'

After this meeting, John's manner changed. Hitherto he had been
a miracle of taciturnity, as of one long disciplined to silence; now
he became as loquacious as he had been on the previous Friday when
his tongue had drawn suspicion on himself. He talked to everyone
who would listen. To one he said that a tinker had murdered his

master; to another that a gentleman's servant in the neighbourhood had robbed and killed him. On being asked if he was referring to himself, he suggested that they could come to a conclusion on that by looking for the body in a bean-rick near Sheep Street. There were, in fact, three bean-ricks near Sheep Street, each of which they energetically searched, with no result. When they told Perry this, in no little anger, he laughed and said he hoped they had now arrived at the correct conclusion.

They had their revenge by keeping him short of water in the day and awake all night.

On Friday morning, he said that he was prepared to tell the whole truth of the matter to Overbury (who was in town visiting the Harrisons) but to no one else. So it was that on St. Bartholomew's Day, Friday, August 24th, Perry stood for the third time before the Justice of the Peace.

What passed between them in the five minutes before Overbury flung open the door and called in Edward Harrison, old Mistress Gilby, Ambrose Frewen and the Reverend William Bartholomew to witness the deposition will never be known. As Overbury published his account of the matter during his lifetime, his motive for silence is obvious enough and Perry's silence could, in any case, be taken for granted. Those who hold that Perry merely rehearsed quickly the circumstances which in public before the others he described in more detail, have strong support for their belief in Overbury's refusal to allow old Mrs. Harrison to be present at the hearing and only with reluctance permitting Mary Gilby, her close friend for forty years, to take her place. But though this effort to spare a wife's feelings was what might have been expected from Overbury's sympathy and courtesy—and incidentally showed Perry in a not altogether discreditable light—it is more probable, as may appear before this story is ended, that the two spoke of different matters. What was said openly is not in dispute and remains on record.

When the witnesses had taken their seats in the room and the clerk was ready with his quill, Overbury said: 'You say you wish to tell me what has become of your master.'

'I do,' answered Perry.

'We are ready.'

'Mr. Harrison was murdered.'

'You know this for a certainty?'

'Yes.'

'Was he murdered by you?'

'No.'

'But you know who.'

'Yes.'

'Then it is your duty to tell us.'

'It was my mother and my brother.'

'John Perry'—there was a new sternness in Overbury's voice—'before you say anything else, I must warn you. Blood will be had for blood. It may be that you will have to suffer. But do not bring more innocent blood on your head by accusing falsely her who gave you life.'

Perry met his eyes and again, as on their first meeting, mastered them. Quietly, but almost as one explaining to an inferior, he said: 'I have said it. If I were to die now, I would justify it. Mr. Harrison was murdered by my mother and my brother.'

CHAPTER III

The Accusation

'EVER SINCE I HAVE BEEN IN MR. HARRISON'S SERVICE,' PERRY continued, 'my mother and my brother have been at me to help them to get money. They are very poor, you know. And I should have liked to help them if I could, but I only just get enough for myself, above my keep. But they said I could help them all the same; and when I asked how my brother Richard said all I need do was to tell him when my master went collecting Lady Campden's rents, he'd do the rest. So last Thursday morning I went into the Street on an errand and met my brother and told him that Mr. Harrison was going to Charringworth in the afternoon and that he would have plenty of money on him when he came back, so that if he wanted to get it it would be quite easy.'

'But if Mr. Harrison had come home at the time he was expected,' Overbury interrupted, 'it would not have been dark. Your brother could not possibly have robbed him in broad daylight on the road without someone seeing it. It's harvest-time, remember, and there are plenty of people about.'

'My master wasn't going to be home till dark.'

'Is that true?' asked Overbury, turning to Edward.

'No,' said Edward. 'My father was always home in daylight. I never remember him being later than six. That's why my mother began to get anxious about seven o'clock.'

'What have you to say to that?'

'Nothing,' answered Perry, 'except what I've said. I knew he wasn't coming back till dark.'

Edward interjected: 'May I say something else, Sir Thomas?'

'Yes.'

'Daniels at Ebrington said definitely that my father didn't stay long with him because he wanted to get home in the light. Perry heard him say that.'

'Well?' said Overbury to Perry.

'I don't mind what old Daniels said or what Mr. Edward thought.' His voice suddenly assumed that hard arrogance which, in his present plight, sat more strangely on him than ever. 'Mr. Harrison did not mean to return till it was dark.'

'How do you know?'

'He told me.'

'He told you, but not his wife and his son?'

'He told me a great many things he'd never dream of telling them,' said Perry, glancing at Edward.

Unexpectedly Edward said: 'You can accept that, Sir Thomas,' and explained the admission: 'By some means the rogue had wormed his way into my father's secrets.'

'In that case, I will accept it. Go on with your tale. You told your brother in the morning that Mr. Harrison would be returning at nightfall, carrying a fair sum of money. Did you see your brother again?'

'Not till the evening.'

'What time in the evening?'

'It would be about quarter to nine, I suppose. It was after I'd left Will Reed. I went to the courtyard-gate and whistled for Richard.'

'Whistled? Where was he?'

'At home. Our house is only a stone's throw away. You can easily hear a whistle.'

'And your brother was expecting it?'

'Yes. Anyway, he came at once and we walked up to the lodge-gate together. Then we thought we'd better separate in case someone saw us, so I went down through the churchyard and out on the Yabberton road that way, and he came round the church by the road and met me.'

'Where?'

'By the gate into the Conygree.'

'Then what did you do?'

'I told him that I thought my master had just gone into the Conygree.'

'You thought? Why didn't you know?'

'It was too dark to see.'

'Then how did you know anyone had gone in?'

'I heard the gate creak, It always creaks badly.'

'That would explain why you thought somebody went in—or came out. But why should you suppose it was Mr. Harrison? Couldn't it have been someone else?'

'We should have heard if it had been anyone coming out and no one would go in that time of night except someone going to the House who had a key of the garden-gate. Then it's the quickest way to the House from the road. And anyhow,' said Perry, as if tired of the cross-examination, 'it *was* my master. I told Richard to follow him if he wanted to get the money and I'd take a turn in the field.'

'But why didn't you go with him?'

'I didn't want to have anything to do with it.'

'Did you "take a turn in the field"?'

'Yes. Then in a few minutes I came back to where they were—it was about the middle of the Conygree—and I found Mr. Harrison on the ground with my brother kneeling on him and my mother standing by.'

'Mr. Harrison was dead?'

'No, because as I came up I heard him say: "You rogues, are you going to kill me?" Then I asked Richard not to do it, but he just said: "Hold your tongue; you're a fool," and strangled my master. Then he searched his pocket and took out a bag of money and threw it into my mother's lap.'

'What did you do?'

'Nothing.'

'You did not lay a hand on your master?'

'Not till he was dead.'

'What do you mean?'

'I helped my brother to carry his body into the garden. I always carried the key of the gate, and——'

'This is into the garden of Campden House?'

'Yes, through the gate between the garden and the Conygree.'

'Then what did you do with the body?'

'We didn't know what to do with it at first. Then we decided to throw it into the great sink of Wallington's mill—that's just behind the garden. My mother and my brother said I'd better go up to the courtyard and listen to see if anyone was about. So I did; and then I went out by the gate into the road.'

'You mean you didn't go back to them?'

'No; I didn't see them again.'

'You didn't throw Mr. Harrison's body into Wallington's sink?'

'No.'

'Then where is the body?'

'I suppose it's in Wallington's sink.'

'But you said you didn't throw it there.'

'*I* didn't; but I suppose they did.'

'Why did you leave them?'

'I didn't want anything to do with it.'

'Then what did you do when you got into the road again?'

'That's when I met Jack Pearce, like I told you.'

'So the murder was committed between the time you left William Reed and the time that you met John Pearce?'

'Yes.'

'And you walked with Pearce in the very field where ten minutes before you'd seen your master murdered?'

'Yes.'

'You felt afraid?'

'I have told you so.'

'You have also told us that you spent the time till midnight in the hen-roost and that you then went towards Charringworth but got lost in the mist. Is that true?'

'Yes.'

'Then how did your master's hat, band and comb come to be found a mile away from anywhere you had been by the Ebrington furzes?' asked Overbury, suddenly.

Perry was quite unperturbed as he answered: 'I put them there on my way to Charringworth.'

'But if you didn't see your mother and brother or Mr. Harrison's body again, where did you get them?'

'I brought them with me, when I came up to the courtyard.'

'You mean you were carrying them when you were talking to John Pearce? Didn't he ask what they were?'

'No, I'd thrown them in the hen-roost on my way to the gate. Then, when I'd got rid of Jack Pearce, I went back there and hacked the comb with my knife and pricked my finger for blood to put on the band.'

'Why did you put them among the furzes?'

'I wanted it to look as if my master had been set on and murdered up there.'

'That was your idea? Not your mother or your brother's?'

'Yes, it was mine.'

'But you still say you don't know where the body is?'

'No; unless it's in Wallington's sink.'

'That we can see soon enough,' said Overbury.

'This means a formal hearing at Bourton to-morrow,' said Overbury, when Perry had been taken back to prison.

Mary Gilbey's timid old voice interrupted: 'If you will pardon me, Sir Thomas, I'll go and break the sad news to poor Susannah. Poor soul, she's always feared the worst, but I'm afraid she'll take it hardly now there's no doubt.' And without waiting for an answer, she hobbled away on her errand of sympathy.

Edward went out at the same time to give orders for the immediate dragging of Wallington's sink and to make certain that Overbury's warrant for the arrest of Joan and Richard Perry was carried out without delay.

Overbury, left with the Vicar and Ambrose Frewen, looked from one to the other and was undecided as to which he found the more intolerable, the Vicar's rubicund face, with its beady eyes contradicting, by their malice, the artificial smile which had become second nature, or Frewen's pinced, parchment hardness, the mean mouth, the thin, claw-like hands which were never still.

The Reverend William Bartholomew was a close approximation to his younger contemporary, the Vicar of Bray. His one principle, through all the recent changes in Church and State, was to keep his benefice. He had come to it at the age of thirty-two and, as Laud was Archbishop, he was an emphatic High Churchman; when the issue between Anglicanism and Presbyterianism seemed in doubt, no one could tell whether his services, shorn of their Laudian dignity and embellished with prayers pillaged from the new liturgies, were Anglican with a touch of Presbyterianism or Presbyterian with a touch of Anglicanism; when Cromwell, having won the war, made it clear that officially Independency was the preferred wear, the Reverend William Bartholomew tried to make himself indistinguishable from an Independent; now, the return of Charles II signalized the return to Campden Church of militant Anglicanism and the Reverend William Bartholomew at fifty-six was able to appear in the congenial role of a persecuting loyalist.

Ambrose Frewen was a retired wool-merchant who had made a fortune in the Civil Wars by selling inferior goods at exorbitant prices to both sides and had later been made one of the contractors to the standing army of the Commonwealth. Like the Vicar, he was not a native of the place, but he had elected to purchase the fine old house with its fluted mullions like pillars and its two fantastic gargoyles, still known as 'Grevel's House,' which had been built nearly three centuries earlier by William Grevel, 'the Flower of the Wool Merchants of all England' who had been to the Campden of his day all that Sir Baptist had been to his and who, like him, lay buried in the church. Frewen informed his friends that by retiring there he had, so to speak, consolidated the tradition of his calling. Campden, however, obstinately refused to see the connection, and, in spite of all his efforts, had never taken him to its heart. He remained a stranger.

'It'll be a good thing to see the Perrys out of the way,' said Frewen. 'A disgrace to the place, they are. I suppose there'll be time to send them to the autumn assizes at Gloucester, Sir Thomas? Not that it'll be anything but a formality, with that confession.'

'Praised be to God,' murmured the Vicar, 'that the truth has come to light at last. But there is nothing hid that shall not be made manifest.'

'That, I thought, was at the Last Judgment,' said Overbury.

'In a sense, Sir Thomas, and in strictness, I suppose you might say so. Yet you may also say that the earthly judgment of His representatives in Church and State—Church *and* State—is but an anticipation of the Almighty jurisdiction.'

'I should be happier if I had your—er—strong convictions, Vicar. But, you see, I do not think John Perry was telling the truth.'

'Come, come, Sir Thomas,' said Frewen, 'why should he lie? To save his own skin, I suppose you mean.'

'Many strange and horrid things may be said and done when a man is afraid,' said the Vicar.

'They may indeed,' returned Overbury drily. 'But in this case Perry has not saved his own skin. He has confessed himself a guilty accessory. If they hang, he hangs.'

'But the lout is too stupid to realize that,' said Frewen.

'I do not think so,' said Overbury curtly.

He was finding it increasingly difficult to mask his feelings. In his travels in foreign lands, he had more than once had to choose on instinct some one companion to be with him in possible danger and isolation. Such a one needs not only the qualities which make him dependable in a fight, but also those which make him tolerable in the long, unexciting periods when the most important knowledge is when and how to speak and when to keep silent. If Overbury had to make such a choice now, it would not have been Edward Harrison or William Bartholomew or Ambrose Frewen, with none of whom would he voluntarily have spent an afternoon. It would have been John Perry.

'It may be that, by the grace of God,' the Vicar was saying, 'I shall be able to persuade the guilty wretches to confess their crime. Indeed, I will address myself to it.'

'How?' asked Overbury.

'I will admonish them from the pulpit on Sunday in the presence of the godly. On so solemn an occasion, it may be that their hearts will be touched. "By the hands of the Apostles were many signs and wonders wrought among the people." The epistle for to-day. *My* epistle. St. Bartholomew, you know.' He chuckled at his clerical joke.

'But surely, Sir Thomas,' said Frewen. 'you'll keep them in gaol at Bourton? They won't come back here?'

'No, they can come back here when I've examined them.' His tone suggested that he would have been glad to wash his hands of the whole matter.

The formal examination of Joan and Richard Perry next day at Bourton-on-the-Hill was short and far from satisfactory. They merely denied everything and said that John was mad.

'I knew harm would come of giving him the name,' said Joan. This enigmatical remark, though it seemed for the moment to provide a new line of approach, led in fact nowhere. On being asked what it meant, Mrs. Perry explained that John was the name of her first child who lived for only five days and that when, twelve years later, this son was born to her, her husband had, despite her entreaties, insisted that he should be given the same name. 'No good could come of that,' she said. It seemed to weigh on her heavily, but the Court was not interested in such family matters.

'You say that everything your brother says is a lie?' Overbury asked Richard.

'That it is,' said Richard. His dull, patient face looked resentfully at his brother. 'And he knows it.'

'Then you didn't meet him in the Street that morning?'

'Yes, I did, but——'

'But what?'

'Well, we didn't talk about what he said.'

'What did you talk about?'

'Well, just—just things.'

'What things?'

'I can't really remember. He asked me how my little girls were and whether Mother's rheumatics were better and if I'd heard that Margaret Copley was going to have a baby and that it was a very good harvest this year, and—well—that kind of thing. I can't remember them all.'

'But he didn't mention Mr. Harrison at all?'

'No.'

'And you didn't see him at night?'

'No.'

Richard then explained that from eight o'clock onwards he was at home with his mother, but neither his statement nor his mother's confirmation of it was considered of any value as evidence. His wife had been spending the afternoon and evening of the day with her parents in Sheep Street. Her brother brought her back about half-past nine. She would bear witness that they were both indoors when she returned.

No doubt she would and no doubt they were, thought the Court.

'And where, your Honour,' asked old Joan suddenly, 'is the poor gentleman's body? Have you seen the marks of strangling on the throat?'

The question was a shrewd counter-thrust, for the dragging of Wallington's sink had yielded nothing; neither had an investigation of Campden fish-ponds which Edward had subsequently had carried out; nor had the searching of the ruins of Campden House. The body of Mr. Harrison was as far from being found as ever.

Before Overbury could answer, John Perry intervened.

'I have something else to say.'

'The only thing you can say that we want to hear is where the body is hidden.'

'I've told you I don't know. I never did know. It's no good asking me that. . . . Don't you want to hear what else I've got to say?'

'Has it any bearing on the case?'

'Yes.'

'Then you may tell us.'

To the obvious indignation and surprise of Richard, John explained that his brother was the chief actor in the February robbery and that his own subsequent outcry in the garden in May was an invention designed to make it appear that there were marauding strangers in the neighbourhood.

'What have you to say to that?' Overbury asked Richard.

'It's a lie, like everything else he's said. Why is he doing this to us all?'

'I told my brother,' insisted John, 'that there was money in that room. I showed him the window and where he could find a ladder to reach it, and told him it was quite safe as we should all be at church at the "lecture." We were going to share the money this Michaelmas. It's buried in the garden at the back of his cottage.'

Richard suddenly turned to his mother. 'Mother, why is he saying this?' The helplessness was unexpectedly poignant.

Joan, inflexible and with no comfort in her voice, said: 'I don't know, son. It is wrong of him. He will repent it.'

The proceedings over and the prisoners formally committed to the autumn assizes at Gloucester, the Perrys were taken back by their guards to Campden. The little procession straggled over the fields in the glare of the August afternoon, over the stubble where the hay had been, between the stooks of corn, through cattle meadows where the grass was parched and yellowing and only mud cracked with the drought showed where water once was, between dusty hedges where the white flowers of the bindweed matched the swarms of white butterflies. Joan and Richard found these familiar things a relief to their spirits after the strange, stifling Courtroom.

John walked on alone and ahead of the others. Behind him came his mother, in spite of her age, the distance and the heat, erect and apparently unwearied. Only Richard, far behind, seemed to find the way difficult, His large body, become flabby by indoor service, took the heat badly.

It was when they neared the edge of the quarry by Hangman's Hall (from which, coming the field-way from Bourton, the traveller can first see Campden down below in the distance) that Richard stopped and felt in his pocket for a rag to wipe away the streaming sweat. With the rag came out a ball of inkle which fell to the ground. One of the guard picked it up and though Richard held out his hand for it did not return it.

'It's only my wife's hair-lace,' said Richard.

The guard discovered a slip-knot at the end of it.

By now John, far ahead, was almost at the bottom of the slope and the guard decided that this circumstance offered an opportunity for a piece of private investigation. He overtook John and, showing him the ball of inkle, asked him if he had ever seen it before.

'Indeed I have,' said John. 'It's my brother's. That's the cord he strangled my master with.'

CHAPTER IV

The First Judgment

THE MEDIÆVAL BUILDERS OF CAMPDEN CHURCH HAD SET IT ON a hill. The great square limestone tower, with its twelve delicate pinnacles and arrow buttress, was a landmark in the district and the pride of it. Local lore claimed for it kinship with Gloucester Cathedral itself—

> A man by the name of Bower
> Built Gloucester Cathedral and Campden Tower.

The road, winding down from it, ran between the Almshouses and the courtyard wall of Campden House, then turned sharply to the right to join the incomparable High Street which made its way between the golden-grey houses and cottages, past the arches of Sir Baptist's Market, to the prison beneath the Town Hall. On an August Sunday, with drowsy gardens glimpsed through the arched entrances by the side of each house-door ablaze with the colours of rose and purple clematis, marigold and hollyhock and pansy, it was the most peaceful street of any town in England. But on that Sunday, August 26th, 1660, it was thronged and restless as if for a fair. Along the quarter of a mile from the prison to the church, men, women and children loitered to watch the Perrys being taken to their formal admonition from the pulpit before themselves crowding into the church behind them to listen to it.

It was outside the Perrys' cottage that the spectators were rewarded for their pains. By the door stood Anne, Richard's wife, with their two children. On seeing her father, the five-year-old Joan, ran to him and took his hand and asked why he had gone away and if he would take her a walk with him now he had come back.

'You can come as far as the church gate with me, darling,' said Richard, looking defiantly at his guards and the crowd as if fearing that someone would say him nay. No one did.

'I can walk further than that,' said Joan, slipping her small, dirty hand into his huge one. 'Can't I, Granny?'

'Yes, my pet,' said old Joan, 'you're a fine walker now. But we're only going as far as the church to-day. Your father'll take you a walk another day.'

Though she was speaking to her grand-daughter, she was looking at her younger son and the bystanders noticed that, for the first and last time, John seemed on the verge of breaking. The arrogance and inflexibility had vanished from his face; his mouth was working as if tears were not far away and he turned his head quickly to avoid his mother's eyes. So he did not see Richard hold out his arm to his wife who came timidly over to him to give him the other child, the nine-months-old Anne, to hold.

It was the outcry of the onlookers, first an incredulous undertone, then a shrill excitement, that made him look again at the others to discover the reason for it. It was plain enough. Blood was pouring from the noses of both children and as little Joan, frightened, clung the more tightly to her father, it was wet on his hand and sleeve. The gods had branded Richard a murderer.

The crowd grew gradually silent, as if awed by the omen. Anne took the children from Richard and hurried them into the cottage, while he fumbled for a rag to wipe away the blood. Suddenly the voice of Ambrose Frewen came piercingly through the silence. He had watched the Perrys coming up the High Street from the windows of his house, as being more appropriate to his dignity than mingling with the crowd; but as soon as they turned up Church Street he had hurried out and overtaken them just in time to witness the judgment of Heaven.

'Let him leave the blood on his hand,' he shouted. 'Let it be seen.' A low murmur from the people showed that his suggestion was approved and Richard's guard snatched the rag from his left hand before he could use it to cleanse his right.

Richard made no effort to prevent him. Dazed, inert, he stood as if already condemned, looking at the door of his home.

'Get along, now,' said the guard. 'You know the Vicar doesn't like late-comers.'

As they moved on, old Joan came to her son's side and put her hand in his, where little Joan's had been, so that her hand shared the stain. And so they went to church.

Inside the Church of St. James it was light and cool and spacious, without any sense of mystery or atmosphere of devotion. Since the Reformers had pillaged it a century ago, melting down the precious crucifixes, stealing the golden, jewelled chalice and the monstrance and the tabernacle where once the Blessed Sacrament was enthroned; despoiling the five chantries, looting the lead and rifling the tombs; smashing the rich-coloured glass of the windows which told the unlettered of the Passion of Christ and the Doom of God; cutting up the rare embroidered Mass vestments as finery to deck their women, the Church had become little more than a meeting-house. Only the dark oak pews, carved with the arms of individual wool-staplers had, since they had no intrinsic value, been left in their places; while the craft of builder and mason, living still in the structure and the proportions, in the pillars and the windows and the wide arches, gave a hint of the beauty that once was.

Sir Baptist, in his day, had done what he could to restore at least a sober dignity. He had given the church a new leaded roof and another window, built a gallery at the west end and restored one of the chantries (which was now occupied with his own tomb and monument) on the south; presented a mediæval lectern of the same age as the church—a 'brass falcon' which had cost him £26—and had a new pulpit and canopy * made by one of the best craftsmen of the age and district. The two silver communion cups, the cloth-

---

* The canopy disappeared during the second (Victorian) pillage when the 'restoring' Vicar had it made into a knick-knack table for his drawing-room. At the same time the screen and the mediæval pews were removed, other incidental damage done and the pulpit moved to its present position.

of-gold tissue which formed the cloth and covered the cushion of the pulpit, the hour-glass and the bell (which made the peal in the church tower up to eight) were his gift and—partly for his own convenience it must be admitted, since it adjoined his garden—he had had the churchyard walled.

But the new decency did not compensate for the old glory and it was not altogether to be regretted that the very name of the church had been changed. The founders had dedicated it to Our Lady Mary the Blessed Virgin, and though one of the altar-frontals depicting her Coronation had been overlooked in the pillage, the Reformers had removed her statue from the niche over the porch. Thus when, fifty-five years ago, King James had granted a new charter to Campden, there had been no difficulty in altering the dedication to St. James as a compliment to a monarch for whom no flattery was too fulsome.

The Perrys, with their guards, were placed on the front pew on the south side of the aisle. Level with them, on the north, and just under the pulpit, were the Harrisons. The Vicar had deemed this arrangement tactful since, had the Harrisons occupied their usual seats, they would have been under the necessity of having to see the murderers. As it was, any inspection of the guilty—and Edward turned his head in their direction continually—was voluntary.

Behind them crowded Campden. To some it was a disappointment that the Vicar and Ambrose Frewen had not had their way and made the occasion one of official pomp, so that the two bailiffs with their sergeants-at-mace, the other twelve capital burgesses in purple and the twelve inferior burgesses in red might have appeared in their robes of office. But the burgesses, led by the bailiffs, had demurred and the only uniforms in the church were the blue coats, decorated with the silver buck's head (Sir Baptist's crest), of the almshouse pensioners. The occasion, none the less, was considered the most important in living memory. In all his twenty-four years there, the Reverend William Bartholomew had certainly never had so large a congregation and for one unnerving moment he was almost tempted to preach the Gospel to them. The temptation passed and his shrill, nasal voice was steady as he gave out his text: 'Now art thou cursed from the earth, which hath opened her mouth to receive thy brother's blood from thy hand.' He coughed, adjusted the hour-glass and commenced slowly: 'O unhappy day for this fair town that we have among us those bearing the brand of Cain!' He paused, repeated 'The brand of Cain,' and looked fixedly in turn at the three Perrys.

Richard was unaware of the glance, as he was looking down at his hand to see how much of the dried blood had come off after being rubbed violently on his breeches. Joan sat staring at the altar in front of her, a hint of a smile playing round her lips, and apparently as unconcerned as if she were sitting alone in the church, absorbed in her thoughts. But John met the Vicar's gaze, narrowed his eyes in a message of unuttered scorn and deliberately turned his head away in the opposite direction.

He was then just able to see, from his place by the pillar, the emblazoned coat-of-arms which surmounted Sir Baptist's ornate marble tomb. The strong morning sunlight heightened the colours of the silver fleurs-de-lys on their blood-red ground. But it was on the two supporters of the arms that his gaze rested—the rampant bulls, with their heavy, menacing faces, their cruel forefeet raised rather to crush than to support, their erect sex on which painter and sculptor alike had bestowed such careful skill. It was as if they had been struck into the immobility of stone in a moment of ecstatic dance—two primal bulls, in insolent triumph, dancing their way back into a church, left empty by the expulsion of the Presence, for the return of the devils.

John Perry gained much comfort from them. The Vicar's voice ceased to reach him except in disconnected phrases . . . 'in a field was it, just such a field as we know, that Cain rose up and slew him and let his blood water the ground' . . . 'and he said "I know not," but he lied for he knew where he had hidden him nor was the Almighty God in ignorance' . . . 'the most abominable crime of witchcraft hand in hand with the most abhorrent sin of murder' . . . 'thou shalt not suffer a witch to live' . . .

At last, the hour-glass emptying, the exhortation drew to its close. The mention of his own name brought John Perry back from his strange prayers. 'John Perry, Richard Perry, Joan Perry,' the Vicar was saying, 'I solemnly charge you here in the name of Almighty God and before this congregation here assembled that you ease your guilty souls by a full confession of your crime. Think how short your time is! You are to be taken to your trial before your earthly judges and from there dispatched to your Heavenly Judge. If you do not fear them who will kill your body, fear Him Who, from His dread Judgment Seat, will cast you into the flames of Hell. Think how short the time is! It may be that no more than six Sundays will pass before this earth will know you no more. How, then, will you answer at the Judgment Seat of God——'

Joan rose slowly to her feet and held her hand up as if to stop him. The tense silence was broken and emphasized by the Vicar's voice, trembling with triumph: 'See, my brethren, the power of the Word of the Lord! Now is the hard heart turned, the stubborn spirit humbled! Look, she confesses.'

'No, Parson Bartlemew, I've nothing to confess.' Her rich deep tones reached to the corners of the church. 'But I thought it right to tell you that you will be cold in your grave before we shall.'

The trial of the Perrys at the Gloucester Assizes a month later had an unexpected issue. Two indictments were found against them, one for breaking into William Harrison's house in the February and robbing him of £140, the other for robbing and murdering the said William Harrison on the 16th day of August. But Sir Christopher Turnor, the Judge of Assize, refused to try them on the second count because the body had not been found; and on the first count they were persuaded to plead 'Guilty' in order to shorten the proceedings. It was explained to them that, if they did, they would be immediately pardoned under the gracious Act of Pardon and Oblivion which the King had granted to celebrate his happy Restoration.

They returned to Campden, free, at the beginning of October. It was unfortunate for them that, three days after their return, the Reverend William Bartholomew died.

CHAPTER V

★

Overbury Acts

THEY WERE RINGED ROUND BY HATRED, THE MORE DEADLY because it was born of fear. None now seriously doubted that Joan Perry was a witch and her sons murderers, if not worse. Campden suddenly remembered how, in the year John Perry was born, the town had suffered the worst outbreak of the plague within living memory. It had raged for two months with such intensity that death had claimed almost a hundred men, women and children, and, among the living, all work was stopped so that the very necessaries of life depended on the generosity of neighbouring towns.

In vain Tom Barnes reminded the self-constituted jury in *The Eight Bells* that the cause of the outbreak had been thoroughly investigated at the time and had been traced to the circumstance that a dead dog had been thrown among the growing hemp so that those who gathered the hemp a month later suffered infection from it.

Maybe, they said, that was what it seemed at the time. Now they knew better. And, anyhow, even if it was the dog, who threw it there? Who but Joan Perry? There was no actual proof, of course; but it was clear enough for any sensible man. Not that there was any need to rely on past memories, in any case, when the present was so palpable and damning. Whatever was the truth about the plague, there could be no doubt about the Parson's death. That everyone was a witness to. Or was Tom Barnes going to try to deny the old witch's threat?

'No,' said Tom. 'Curious that was, I grant you. But Parson

Bartlemew wasn't a well man, all the same for that. He'd had a turn or two in the heat, as it was, and with that flush on his face and that fat on his belly, he'd be the kind that's struck down sudden.'

Was Tom suggesting that Joan Perry had nothing to do with it? No, he wouldn't go as far as that, but it was only right to look at the facts all round. And he was quite prepared to admit that Parson might well have worried himself into his grave after a scene like that. Anyone might.

This was not felt to be sufficient. Would Tom give a straight answer to a straight question? Did he or did he not believe Joan Perry was a witch?

'How'm I to tell when, as far as I know, I've never met such a one? Mebbe some of you knows more'n I do about that kind. All I can say is, she may be. And then again she may not.'

The atmosphere was such that Tom thought it wiser in future to refrain from mentioning his views on the matter. He had no wish to make things worse for the Perrys than they already were. Especially after the impression created by the conduct of Ambrose Frewen's daughter, Marjorie.

Until now Miss Marjorie had held herself aloof from the entire matter. She had even been one of the very few absent from the church on the occasion of the sermon. When her father had pressed her to attend, she had answered with her quiet smile: 'I think it would be rather cruel, father—unless, of course, you feel you need me with you.'

Both her reproof and her filial submission revealed her character. An only child, her devotion to her widowed father was notable and universally noticed. She seemed to live only to supply his wants. Her missions of mercy, so regularly undertaken, might be postponed or delayed by one thing only—that Ambrose had a sudden need of her to accompany him on a walk or a ride or a visit or to act as hostess to an unlooked-for guest. For her father's sake, so it was rumoured, she had even renounced the possibility of marriage. Had she been a Papist, they said, she was of the kind of which nuns are made. This impression of her was enhanced by the serenity of her pale face and the black dress and simple head-covering she always affected and by her custom of spending some time each day on her knees in church. Though one skilled in such matters would have seen immediately that her simple face gave no hint, as a nun's might, of peace won by disciplining a strong character and a varied experience, of a will voluntarily surrendered, of the triumph of supernatural grace over natural desires, no one in Campden had such discrimination. To the town she was their Miss Marjorie, so sweet and good and simple and devoted. Not even her own sex could find a word to say against her and the general dislike of her father was even a little abated by reason of the respect which men and women alike felt for her.

So when, one afternoon, she returned from one of her walks in the countryside with her arms full of sprays of mountain ash and set about arranging them over 'the street doors and windows of the Frewen house, her action did more than anything else to foment feeling against the Perrys. For mountain ash, thus employed, is the most certain specific against the machinations of witches. Not only can they not pass it, but it wards off even the effects of their evil eye.

'Being on the safe side, I see, Miss Marjorie,' said John Kyte, passing her as she was securing a spray, heavy with red berries, over the lintel.

Marjorie gave her gentle smile. 'Yes. Mr. Kyte, that is the best way to put it. One dreads to be uncharitable even to those poor wretches and, for myself, I'm not afraid; but I've my father to think of.'

Joan Perry, who could see the decorations from her door, looked for a long time at them. She understood. Miss Marjorie had taken her revenge for the day, six years ago, when she had come across her unexpectedly in the dusk taking leave of her lover. Marjorie in a panic had overtaken her and offered her money, which she had contemptuously refused, poor as she was, with: 'You've no need to pay me to keep my mouth shut, girl. I'll take no tales to your father. Who'd have guessed you had the spirit?'

Marjorie spent much of her time these days with old Mrs. Harrison. 'The poor soul needs all the comfort we can give her,' she explained. As Mrs. Harrison had not been seen outside the grounds of Campden House, except on the occasion of the sermon, since the night of August 16th, no one in the town had a clue to her real feelings. Not that it mattered one way or the other. When private persons are thrust, for whatever reason, into the public eye, they lose, in that transition, their individual identity and become merely pegs on which every observer considers himself entitled to hang a placard proclaiming the set of emotions considered appropriate to the situation. If hitherto Campden had ever thought anything about Mrs. Harrison beyond the fact that she was observably a mean woman and reputedly a nagging wife, the favourable opinion had remained unvoiced. She had indeed rarely been mentioned except in the context that it was a pity that a decent man like Harrison should be tied to such a vixen; but then, there was no accounting for people's choices. But now, overnight, she had become a brave, deeply-wronged widow, sorrowing in silence, and traits which had previously earned another name were seen as courage and reticence.

On her last public appearance in the church that morning, she had sat by her son Edward's side as grimly quiet as was her custom. Her habitually hard face had given no hint that the proceedings in any way concerned her. She had remained unmoved even when the place was in an uproar after Joan Perry's interruption, and though she had turned to watch the prisoners taken out by their guards and had given a sour half-smile of approval when the young constable had hit Joan on the mouth, a sense of cold detachment remained.

Mr. Antony à Wood, of Oxford, noted impartially in his diary that she was 'a snotty, covetous, presbyterian woman.' Campden would never perhaps at any time have used those exact terms. At this time, it would not even have admitted the justice in them. Yet had it been generally known that her first action after Harrison's disappearance had been to write to the Lady Juliana, begging that Edward might be given the post of steward without delay in order to alleviate the dire poverty in which, by the brutal murder of her husband, her family was now compelled to live, the balance of sympathy would, widow or no widow, have tilted against her.

It was, of course, known that Mr. Edward was now away, though not that he was in Rutlandshire on a visit to Lady Juliana to give her a detailed account of events, to receive her official confirmation of him as her steward in his father's place and to persuade her to use her influence in official circles—which, since the Restoration, was considerable—to have the Perrys rearrested and retried. His absence had left his mother, who doted on him, lonely enough, for she was on indifferent terms with the rest of the family and frankly hated her daughter-in-law; and as her friend, Mary Gilbey, was too ill either to visit her or to suffer a visit from her, she welcomed Marjorie Frewen's company. Campden watched approvingly its Lady of Mercy daily making her way to console its Lady of Sorrow.

It is unusual for new friendships to take root in the aridity which follows the end of youth, but the two women, one sixty-five, the other forty, found themselves held together by a bond of hatred—a particular hatred of Joan Perry and a general hatred of men. The latter emotion sprang in the elder woman's case from disillusion and in the younger's from disappointment, but though the causes differed each recognized and embraced in the other a similar effect. Also each excepted one man only from the general loathing, Mrs. Harrison her eldest son, Marjorie Frewen her father. What overflow of twisted love they had to spare from these obsessions was, by some alchemy of the emotions, transformed into reserves of hatred which spilt over on to Joan.

'I hear the Perrys are starving,' said Mrs. Harrison one afternoon, as they sat together at their needlework. 'I'm not hypocrite enough to pretend that I wish them well, but they oughtn't to die like that. Edward wouldn't wish it.'

'I'm sure they're not starving,' said Marjorie. 'They've got their garden.'

'There won't be anything in that, since it was dug up to find the money they'd buried there.'

'I wonder where that money really is. It's never been found, has it?'

'No, and it's not likely that it will be. But when Edward gets home, he'll be Steward and have the right to turn them out. Then we can search properly everywhere.'

'Where will they go then?'

'Back to prison we may trust.'

'I've heard that both the boys go out poaching at night.'

'Edward'll stop that soon enough. Catch them red-handed, I hope. Of course, I always knew John was a thief, and Richard's so feeble-minded he'll do whatever the others tell him.'

'You've heard, I suppose, that his wife and children have left him? Gone back to live with her family in Sheep Street. I'm glad of that.'

'Why?' asked Mrs. Harrison, with a deft thrust of her needle. 'She's as bad as the rest.'

'But think of the poor, innocent children. No one would want to hurt them, surely.'

'No, I suppose not. But bad stock's bad stock all the same.'

'When you come to think of it,' said Marjorie smiling, 'there are just the three of them in the cottage now, so that if anything *did* happen, it would be only the guilty who'd suffer.'

'Is anything likely to happen?'

'Father tells me the town's very bitter about them. People say things to him, you know. Of course, everyone's afraid to do anything alone. The old witch would blast them if they tried. But if they all got together and went to the house . . . It *is* right that witches should be burnt, isn't it?'

'Certainly it is,' said Mrs. Harrison decisively, 'but we don't want the cottage set on fire. There's no knowing how far it would spread.'

'There is that, of course,' said Marjorie, and fell silent for a while. She was working a large cushion decorated with a profusion of autumn fruits, leaves and berries. With every shade of red and brown and gold silk she could procure, she had painted it with her

needle until the work itself seemed almost alive and glowing with
a sense of ripeness and fulfilment.

Presently she said: 'I suppose old Joan would have the witch's
teat?'

'Naturally.'

'They say that a witch gets great joy from giving suck to her
familiar. I've often wondered about it.'

'About the witch's teat? Such filth!'

'Not so much that, Mrs. Harrison as . . .' She paused. She found
difficulty in putting into words the thing she wanted to know but
had never had anyone to ask. 'It must have been beautiful for you
when Edward was a baby.'

'Things weren't too easy. Money was tight with us in those
days.'

'I meant actually . . . suckling him.'

'Yes,' said Mrs. Harrison, 'that was the best of it. He milked me
well did Edward. Dear lamb!' Her face was suddenly young and
gentle. 'Who'd have thought it was forty years ago?'

'Witches can have their familiars however old they are, can't
they?'

'So it's said. Don't talk of it, Miss Marjorie. It's not fit for decent
ears.'

Marjorie's opinion that it was only fear which gave the Perrys
what precarious safety they had was certainly the truth. None,
however high his words, cared to risk consequences of which the
new tombstone over the grave of the Reverend William Bartholomew was a reminder. But where each alone is timid, many, given
sufficient provocation, may be brave.

The riot in Church Street was—at least to all appearances—a
spontaneous demonstration. Late one afternoon, as the October
dusk was setting in, a stranger rode into the town. At the *George*
she inquired of the ostler who took her horse the way to the Perrys'
cottage. As she was undoubtedly a person of quality, as well as of a
commanding presence and imperious manner, he told her with as

little hesitation as he would have shown in answering a less surprising question; but no sooner had she set out up the Street than he rushed off to inform the landlord and anyone else he might meet. Within quarter of an hour, as might have been expected, a crowd whose curiosity had overcome their fear, had collected outside the cottage.

It so happened that, that same afternoon, Mrs. Harrison had been persuaded by Marjorie Frewen to pay her first visit outside the grounds of Campden House. Mary Gilbey had been pronounced out of danger and the doctor had given permission for her to see her friend for a short time if she cared to call.

'It would do you good,' said Marjorie. 'Take you out of yourself. And think of the joy it would give Mistress Gilbey.'

'Mary wouldn't wish me to go out to be gazed at,' said Mrs. Harrison.

'But it will be very quiet now, and it's almost dark. We're not likely to meet anyone; and even if we do, what does it matter? I shall be with you.'

But when they came through the courtyard-gate, they found themselves confronted with a street filled with people. Mrs. Harrison made at once as if to turn back; but it was too late. She was immediately recognized by the crowd who welcomed her with a quick murmur of sympathy.

A moment later the door of the Perrys' cottage opened and the visitor and Joan appeared on the threshold. The crowd, its attention diverted between two interests, ensured a meeting which it would have been difficult in any case to avoid. Still all might have been well had Joan immediately closed the door or her visitor gone straight back to the *George*. But the stranger, instead of hurrying down the street, paused to look round with such an air of haughty indifference that Marjorie Frewen was constrained to say: 'You are a stranger here, Madame, so I feel it is only right that I should tell you that you are in the toils of a witch.'

'Of that, my girl,' retorted the woman, 'I consider myself a better judge than you.'

Then Joan began to laugh. 'Do not mind the poor creatures, my Lady,' she said.

Mrs. Harrison gave a little cry. 'Poor creature,' she called to the crowd. 'You hear what she calls me—poor creature. She is right. A poor creature indeed I am—because of her and her sons.'

It was more than enough. Job Stiles, the carpenter, called out from the heart of the crowd: 'Let's burn the witch!' A stone narrowly missed Joan's head, the first of a hail of stones that clattered on the door hastily shut. They surged forward to break into the cottage; an axe was fetched from *The Eight Bells* opposite; and it was a matter of seconds before the hate-driven, indignant townsmen—no longer respectable Campdonians, but an indeterminate mob welded by evil excitement—would have had the Perrys at their mercy.

But suddenly, from the corner of the High Street, Sir Thomas Overbury appeared, riding hard, with a posse of officers and constables at his heels. The crowd paused to face this unexpected intrusion.

'The first man that moves,' rasped Overbury, 'will be arrested.'

'You shouldn't arrest them, Sir Thomas,' said Mrs. Harrison. 'You should arrest the Perrys.'

'That is exactly why I am here, Ma'am,' said Overbury. He flourished a warrant. 'They are to be lodged for safe-keeping in Bourton gaol. . . . Men, do your duty!'

At the sudden restoration of order, the mob resolved itself into individuals again, and with the change came a sense of surprise not altogether free from shame. They watched quietly enough as the constables entered the cottage and brought out the Perrys and led them away to their new imprisonment. They noticed that Richard was white with fear, that John was sullen, but that Joan was laughing quietly to herself.

'If Sir Thomas hadn't come just when he did,' said Marjorie Frewen, 'there's no knowing what would have happened.'

'That's true enough,' said Mrs. Harrison.

On the evening of his return, they were giving Edward an account of the affair.

'I'll go over to Bourton to-morrow,' said Edward, 'and see how matters stand. I'd like to know where he got the warrant from. The Lady Juliana said it was likely to take some months, even if we got it at all. I don't understand it.'

'You're Steward now and they're in prison again, and that's all that really matters, isn't it, dear?' replied his mother. 'What I can't get out of my head is that woman.'

'Which woman?'

'The stranger. Old Joan called her "My Lady".'

'What happened to her?' asked Edward.

'She went away at once,' said Marjorie. 'At least, that's what they told my father at the *George*. Out of Campden before Sir Thomas had made the arrest. And I don't think she'll come back.'

'Does it matter?' asked Edward.

'Not a bit,' said Mrs. Harrison, 'except that I'm sure I've met her somewhere before and I don't like to think my memory's going. I'm not as old as all that, you know.'

'What was she like, mother?'

Between them Mrs. Harrison and Marjorie managed to give him a description which was creditably exact.

'If you hadn't told me she was a person of quality,' said Edward, 'I should have said it was the gleaning-woman who found father's things by the furze-brake.'

'Of course,' Mrs. Harrison exclaimed. 'That's who it was. I'm sure that's who it was.'

CHAPTER VI

★

Schofield at Bolton

A<small>T THE TIME OF THESE HAPPENINGS IN GLOUCESTERSHIRE,</small>
Thomas Schofield was living, far from the traffic of the
world, in his cottage in the Valley of Desolation. Since the
day, twelve years ago, when he had thrown the reins on his horse's
neck and let it take him where it would, he had never willingly left
the place to which Chance had thus brought him; for he had, as his
mother had prophesied, found home. It was, certainly, a home far
different from his father's manor house where he had spent his
boyhood or the ruined castle by the Danube which had been his
mother's only tangible legacy to him; but in his heart it had come
to displace both. Gradually surrendering to its spell he had found
something of the peace which must have rewarded the first founders
of Bolton Priory when they placed their sanctuary among that
secluded loveliness.

Always he returned, as first he had come, to the Priory ruins
themselves on their low headland, round which the brown trans-
parency of the river ran suddenly quiet after its turmoil among the
rocky crags above. But though familiarity never dimmed the image
of that place which he had come upon in the mist of a late October
afternoon, there were now others which had become hardly less
dear. He loved the river itself in all its moods—in its swift turbulence
dashing itself against the purple-deck Scar and tall rocks whitened
with lichen, in the still reaches where the branches of sycamore and
alder dipped to it, in the shallow pools where the cattle stood and
the stepping-stones invited trust from men. At times he would lose
himself in the woods where the luxuriant foliage gave him the

exciting security of an impenetrable hiding-place; at others, he would seek the bare heights, so barren of cover that his progress could be seen, like a moving ant, by any who cared to look. In an hour's walk he could pass from the rich pastureland, through upland terraces of tree-studded grass, to the wild grandeur of ravines at the edge of the fells; and each in turn held its secrets for him.

His own cottage was at the lower end of the Valley of Desolation, within sound of the great waterfall cascading down a sheer fifty feet into the little beck which ran through the valley to meet the river. Behind, rising to the summit of the fell, stretched the boulder-littered heath where the red deer roamed, and the forked antlers of the herd, moving against the horizon, seemed to reiterate the immovable pattern of the stag-headed, weather-beaten oaks which broke the skyline.

Sometimes he would go further up the valley, with its gloomy ravines and chaotic trees, to the cottage by the upper waterfall where lived the old man and his daughter who had given him hospitality on his first coming to Bolton. Sometimes, but less often, he would visit other cottages and farmers who lived more humanely in the kindlier pastures of the river valley. Twice a year he called on the steward and his family who kept Bolton Hall in readiness for the unexpected and erratic visits of Lord Clifford. But for the greater part of the time, he was content with his own company. His soldier's training made him order his days as scrupulously as if he had been living in society—or in camp. In the winter he read considerably and on the rare occasions when he had to visit London or York or Cambridge, he brought back a new selection of books for his careful library.

The discovery, seven years ago, of Izaak Walton's newly-published book on angling had given him a new interest, and, taking heart from the author's dictum that 'as no man is born an artist, so no man is born an angler,' he had proceeded to make himself an expert. Also he rode much and walked more.

The result of this way of life was that, at thirty-seven, he appeared scarcely older than he had when, at twenty-five, he had first come

there—already a hardened soldier and a man tormented by intolerable inward conflicts. The stresses to which he had been subjected
had been on every plane, and, in retrospect, it was difficult to realize
that, in mere temporal reckoning, they had occupied so short a
space. The twelve years during which he had lived quietly at Bolton
had passed as quickly as if they had been so many weeks in comparison with that sixteen months between the Midsummer Eve in
1647, when in the shadow of the ruined castle by the Danube his
actions had been foretold, and the Hallowe'en of 1648 when his
horse led him to Deerstones, here at Bolton, finally to fulfil the
foretelling.

'In the Valley of Desolation, you will find at last the dear stones
of your home. But before you come to it, between Hallowe'en and
Hallowe'en, you will deny your faith and renounce your love,
unmake a King and betray your trust, kill what has saved you, and
save what would kill you'—that was how it had run. When it was
uttered, he had thought the speaker nothing but an old witch on
her way to an incredible and accepted death. Not till he returned
to England to find his father dead and his half-brother in possession
of the family estate had he learnt, from the letter his father had left
for him, that she was his mother and he himself a bastard. But
neither of these revelations, in spite of their immediate emotional
shock and their practical outcome, had had the paralysing effect of
the predetermined fatality given by the prophecy itself.

The sense in which he had fulfilled it was not, indeed, the sense
in which he had understood it. The faith he had renounced was no
metaphysical belief, but the creed which in fact had been the main-
spring of his actions—a desire for and love of property. The re-
nunciation of Margaret, whom he had loved, had been the voluntary
act of his own will. The King he had unmade was a masquerader,
Cornelius Evans, calling himself the Prince of Wales and deceiving
many. The trust he had betrayed, though it led to the assassination
of his Colonel, might, having regard to the circumstances, have
been extenuated. The man who had saved his life in a tavern brawl
was a Royalist commander whose execution after the siege of

Colchester was an official act over which Schofield, as a Parliamentarian, had to preside. The man who would have killed him and whose life he saved was his half-brother Richard.

When at last these things were over, he might have gained some kind of release by exclaiming with Macbeth—a play he had known from boyhood:

> And be these juggling fiends no more believed
> That palter to us in a double sense;
> That keep the word of promise to our ear
> And break it to our hope.

But the 'juggling fiend' was his mother. Nor for other reasons was there any solution that way. On the one hand it would have committed him to a superstitious belief that would have made life a prolonged nightmare; on the other, his mother had told him, during their brief meeting, enough of hidden matters for him to know that, whatever supernatural power the Craft of the Wise could command if necessity arose, it had little in common with the popular caricature of 'witchcraft.'

What, on the contrary, he suddenly realized on that Hallowe'en when he first came through the mist to Bolton was something simpler, though, in its final implications, hardly less disturbing. He remembered how, before his mother told him the future, she had said that 'at the doorway of death many things are revealed that are usually hidden,' and thereby made no claim for her pre-vision which the most sceptical might not have granted her. In that moment of love and exaltation she had seen, simply, what he would do. His actions, springing from character and circumstance, would be capable of many interpretations and could be combined into various patterns. To the notes of his life she, by her words to him, had given grouping, rhythm, accent. Without her, he would have made a different air.

Had he never seen her, he would still have chanced to meet Margaret and Cornelius, loved and deserted the one and unmade the plans of the other. He would, disinherited, have joined the

Levellers and urged the abolition of property, have served under Colonel Rainsborough and left him, on that last night, unguarded. He would, because of his training as a soldier, have commanded the firing-party which shot Lisle and, because of his nature and the ties of brotherhood which it would not allow him to deny, have released Richard when he had him in his power. But without the prophecy to guide him, he would have ascribed to these things a different value. He comprehended this the more clearly when he remembered that it had been many months before he had realized that his attack on the principle of property at the Leveller debates at Putney was, in fact, a denial of his deepest faith. When he had at length realized its import, he had become obsessed by his fear of Fate. But at last he had seen it truly for what it was—his mother's way of revealing to him that twist in himself which would lead to a discord in his life.

She had, indeed, explicitly in words told him of it. That meeting and what she said there remained indelible on his memory and phrases of it took suddenly their true meaning—'the fool wishes to possess; the wise man asks only to be possessed': 'you are one who hastes to proclaim "This place belongs to me," and will not understand that the only lawful word is "I belong to this place" ': 'you are of a divided nature and will find no peace by denying the one part to appease the other. It may be that your mother's blood contends with your father's for you.' He had, indeed, gone back to his father's house, but she had reached out through the future to bring him back to her. Though she could speak no longer to him in life, she had so moulded events in his mind that life itself became her ally.

He saw that the events in which he had taken part, the laws he had questioned or accepted, the morality by which he had tested his actions, belonged to an order which her nature—and his, in so far as he shared it—repudiated. It defiled the deepest loyalty and darkened the surest vision and denied the most certain knowledge of their hearts; and to make truce with it meant an eternal disharmony in their lives. It was the order of men who wish to appear great by reason of what they possess; not of those who desire to be great by virtue of what they are.

And, as he apprehended this, so he made the response which, he believed, she would have wished him to make. Here was the home she would have chosen for him and which he now chose for himself. And in it as the years passed, for him uneventfully, he had found peace. His strong black hair was now flecked with grey, but the creases on the straight forehead were no deeper and the drawn lines round the mouth had been smoothed away. The idiosyncrasies which long ago had earned him the nickname of 'The Cat' remained. He still walked with that stealthy sliding forward of the left foot. He still noticed things without apparently looking at them. Yet now his whole bearing had changed; there was in it a directness, an ease, a quiet assurance of power which contradicted the least suggestion of guile. Even his taciturnity had been corrected by his self-chosen loneliness. Now that he had ample time for silence, he could talk freely when he was in the company of others.

In the simple rhythm of his existence, there was one outstanding ritual. Every year, on Hallowe'en, he went down to the ruined Priory and stood by the great oak where, on that particular day in 1648, he had first glimpsed the meaning of the prophecy. Though he was never again to feel as intensely as he did then his mother's presence near him, he had, in the years between, by the mere process of living there and so isolating himself from the fever of a world where men strove only to gain possession or to keep inheritance, liberated her spirit within him. Her wisdom was now his own. No longer could she have said to him: 'You are one who hastes to proclaim, "This place belongs to me," and you will not understand that the only lawful word is, "I belong to this place." ' Thus, in a sense, he had no more need of her; nor could he have explained, even had he attempted to analyse, why he continued to perform that yearly rite. Yet it had become a habit not to be broken.

So it came about that, on the last day of October, 1660, he was musing by the Prior's Oak when suddenly he realized that he was not alone. Through the dusk and the rising mist, just as once he himself had come, a woman was making her way towards him.

For a moment he thought it must be his neighbour from the cottage in his valley and feared that she had come to find him because something was amiss with her father. But as soon as he could see her clearly he realized it was a stranger he did not know.

She, however, seemed to know him, for there was only the merest hint of interrogation in her voice as she said: 'Thomas Schofield.'

'Yes.'

'I was told I should find you here. I have come a long way to seek your help.'

'Mine?' He could not mask his surprise. 'May I know who you are?'

'If I told you my name it would mean nothing to you.'

'Then let me know at least who told you of me.'

'No one you know.'

'Then why——'

'Our bond is your mother,' she said.

'You knew her?' he asked eagerly.

'No, but I come from one who was her friend. It is she who asks you aid—for the sake of that friendship.'

'There could be no better claim,' said Schofield.

'That is what we believed you would say. I am glad that it is so. Now I can speak freely?'

'Of course. Shall we go to my cottage? It is over there in what they call the Valley of Desolation.'

'I know. That is where I went first. But an old man I met said I should find you here. So let us talk here. It is quiet enough.'

'As you wish—but, first, I must say one thing. I am not one of you.'

'That, of course, I know. But because of your blood you will not betray us.'

'No. I shall not betray you. All I doubt is my power to help you much, since there are things I cannot do.'

'That has been considered,' said the woman, 'and you have been approved—if you are willing.'

'As far as is in my power, yes,' said Schofield.

At any other time or in any other place, it is doubtful whether his assent would have been so quickly or uncompromisingly given. As it was, his reminder that he was not a member of the Craft of the Wise—the witch-cult—was as much to safeguard himself as to warn her. Because of his mother's adherence to it and death in it, he assumed that he might have some inherited strain; but he had turned away from its full implications and its practice. On two simple levels only had he come, almost insensibly, to understand it. By living close to the earth, he found that the ordinary 'country magics' were not only comprehensible but conventional; by renouncing the struggle for material power, he divined that the clue to Reality lay on another plane and in a different order. But these, he was sure, were the very outskirts of the matter, and he did not wish to be drawn nearer the centre.

In recent years in England the persecution of the cult had reached a new peak of horror, and though its victims were for the most part poor old women who knew no more about it than their accusers, some of the genuine believers had been enmeshed in the net of torture and death. Yet it was not this external danger which deterred him. The revolt came from that part of him which was not his mother—a distrust of secrecy and the existence of a strain of quiet Christian faith which was the legacy of generations on his father's side.

But at this moment, inevitably, it was his mother who claimed him. He could not refuse help to one who had been her friend. That was a debt.

'Who am I to help and how?'

'I cannot tell you how,' said the woman. 'That is for you to decide. But the person is Joan Perry, one of our faith, who is in danger of unjust death at Campden in Gloucestershire.' And she narrated the circumstances as far as she knew them.

'May I ask how you are concerned in all this?' he asked.

'I undertake certain duties for our leaders. Most of my time is taken in travelling secretly from one congregation to another. These are dangerous days.'

'I know that.'

'Sometimes I am given other work which I do not understand. As I have told you, at harvest time I was ordered to spend some days in the fields round Campden, so that the villagers there should be accustomed to seeing me—a poor gleaning-woman. Then, one morning, I had to take William Harrison's hat and band and comb to his family. I do not know why or what was afoot; and as you will understand, I do not question. A few days ago I was sent again to see Joan Perry to give her what comfort I could. She asked me to find you.'

'But she knows nothing of me.'

The woman smiled. 'We of the Craft know more than men think we know; but there was no mystery in her knowledge. You are your mother's son; you have been a soldier; you are well travelled—that any of us can learn. And that seems to be what she needs.'

'But you must have travellers and soldiers among your own people.'

'Certainly; but there are occasions when our own men would be useless because they would be marked. This, I think, must be such a case.'

'You *think?*'

'If I knew more, I would tell you.'

'But I must know more, if I am to be of any use. Surely you must see that?'

'You will learn it from her. What she can tell you, undoubtedly she will.'

After a moment's silence, Schofield said: 'I will go to Campden, but I cannot promise now to go further.'

'That will serve,' said the woman.

'And if I need more help, will you give it me?'

'It is unlikely that you will see me again, but our people will, of course, give you what help they can.'

'But how shall I know them?'

'Your neighbour will tell you.'

'My neighbour? What neighbour? I've no neighbour but old Joseph, and I'm sure he's not——'

The woman nodded. Schofield was completely taken aback. 'But surely,' he said, 'in all these years I should have had some hint, some suspicion!'

'Your surprise is the measure of his discretion,' she said. 'But he knows he may speak freely to you now and I think you see that you can trust him.'

She held out her hand to him. 'Even if you fail, we shall not forget you.'

He took it and was surprised to find that, though by her dress she looked a peasant, it was as smooth as damask. 'For my mother's sake,' he said.

Her nod was almost a dismissal; a renewed request that she should come to his cottage and discuss the matter with old Joseph died still-born on his lips. She had done what she had come to do and she had finished with him. By her air, indefinably, she checked the protest and persuasion of courtesy. He merely bowed, as he might have done to a queen, as she turned and went away into the mist.

'None of us is certain who she is,' said old Joseph as, that evening, he sat by Schofield's log-fire answering what questions he could. 'It's said she's of noble blood and we call her "My Lady," but I've never known her travel in her own character. A gleaning-woman, a pedlar, a poor farmer's wife—someone men don't notice; that's her usual way. It's safer like that—for us as well as for her.'

'And can you tell me anything of Joan Perry?'

'Nothing at all. How should I? I hardly ever move from here, as you know better than anyone.'

'But, if she's my mother's friend, you might have met her in the past years ago.'

'No. No more than I met your mother. I never had occasion to visit our people in Gloucestershire. Though I know, of course, where their meeting-place is, if that's any use to you.'

'Everything may be of use. Are you allowed to tell me?'

'There's no harm in that. "My lady" said I could treat you as one to be trusted. It's a tree-circle called Seven Wells, not far from Campden. The highest point round there and a lonely hill, they say. It was one of our famous holy places centuries before Julius Cæsar came; but now I think it's only used by the local coven, though it was once a centre for divination and sacrifice.'

'Am I likely to find anything there?'

'No, nothing you would understand. Certainly no people, if that's what you mean.'

'But you said the local people still meet there.'

'If you went by night when they were meeting, you would not reach it, my friend; and if you went by day it would be deserted.'

'Then there is nothing at all that you can tell me?'

'Until you have seen Joan Perry, neither of us knows what it is you want to know.'

There was silence between them as they gazed into the fire. Then suddenly the old man said: 'There is one thing perhaps you should know. The coven there is seven, not twelve. You understand me?'

'You mean seven without "the devil"?' Schofield thought that at least he might air his knowledge that the priest-leader of every witch-congregation was known as the 'devil' of that particular coven.

'Of course; counting "the devil," eight. But do you understand the difference between the sevens and the twelves—or the eights and the thirteens, if you think of them like that?'

'No,' said Schofield. 'Tell me.'

'You are not permitted to know the inwardness of it; but I can tell you that a seven is a higher grade than a twelve and its "devil" has a more absolute power.'

'Do you know who the Campden "devil" is?'

'No. No one knows that except members of the coven and the arch-priest.'

'It couldn't be Joan Perry?'

'Of course not. It must be a man.'

'But she will know who he is?'

'Naturally; but she, like every other member of the coven, is sworn to secrecy by the most sacred of oaths. Whatever she may tell you, she will not tell you that.'

'It seems she will be able to help me as little as you can or the woman you call "my lady." I think I have involved myself with a hopeless cause.'

'But all the same, you will go to Campden?'

'Of course,' said Schofield. 'That far I am pledged.'

Next morning, leaving his cottage in the care of Joseph, he rode southwards for Gloucestershire.

CHAPTER VII

Schofield in Gloucestershire

THERE ARE MANY DEGREES OF KNOWLEDGE IN THE UNDER-
standing of a place, but only two of capital importance. The
first is a savouring of its essence. This comes from long and
loving familiarity and sometimes can be achieved only by those
who are born in it. The second is a perception of its accidents. This
mode of knowing usually attends on first sight, if the stranger has
comprehending eyes and, in his heart, another place known in the
first way.

Thus, because Schofield knew Bolton he was able to see Campden
in a way which would have surprised most Campdonians. To them,
their home was the most familiar and unsurprising of English towns
where the past had grown unobtrusively into the present; to him,
what obliterated all other impressions was the intrusion of a fantastic
and foreign note.

The Street, the Market Hall, the inns, the houses old and new,
even the splendid Church—these were but particular variations on a
general and unexpected theme. Had he stayed long with them, he
would doubtless discover the secrets which made them unique to
their lovers, but now he dismissed them with hardly more than a
glance, for there was nothing in them arresting enough to dispel
that first impression.

As he had ridden in by the Ebrington road his attention had been
caught and held by the little Banqueting House at the edge of the
fields, with its three tall chimneys, with their curved finials, standing
like tiny minarets against the November sunset. Then, as he
followed the road round the church and into the town, the greater

73

Banqueting House, with its five chimneys of similar design, appearing so close to him over the wall of the garden, overwhelmingly reinforced the impression. He hardly noticed the solid ashlar almshouses on the other side of the road, he forgot the great church tower behind him, as he reined his horse and sat gazing at this alien Eastern gesture in native stone. Where Church Street meets the High Street, he turned back to look at it once more.

The almshouses have been built so that, from this point, they obliterate all sight of the church and the eye is directed inevitably to the greater Banqueting House, peering over the wall. Five chimneys here; three on the smaller one on the other side of the hill. Why not four and four? Because that would be an unnoticed regularity, whereas five and three dictate eight? . . . The inn up there on the left is the *Eight Bells*. . . . The Campden coven is eight, if you care to count it that way. . . .

This, he decided, was mere foolishness. He was constructing a fantasy on a coincidence. Forget the numbers. They might mean anything or nothing. But the Eastern touch in this Western town could not be gainsaid. Nor, he thought, its deliberateness.

He put up for the night at the *George* where, as an ignorant but interested stranger, he soon elicited the story of the Perrys, told with an accumulated wealth of detail, but adding to his knowledge in one particular only. He learnt that Joan Perry was no longer, as he had been led to suppose, in Campden, but in custody at Bourton-on-the-Hill. This was an undoubted obstacle, since he could think of no reason for asking to see her which would not arouse suspicion.

'Why have they taken them there?' he asked mine host. 'You've a prison here, haven't you?'

'That we have,' said the innkeeper. 'But small it is and dirty; but there, I could have 'em here again, as I had young John before. That room at the top of the stairs bars and bolts well and would keep the old witch tight enough—not that I want her kind here, mind you; but I'd not say "no" if 'twas my plain duty. And as for Dick, he could go in with John in the room he had before, down

the end of the yard over the stables. But that won't do for Sir
Thomas—no. He must have 'em under his hand at Bourton.'

'It was his doing, was it?'

'I've no proof of that, but I reckon it must have been. Very hot
against them, Sir Thomas is. Has been, all along. Wouldn't want
'em to escape. Not but what they'd have been safe enough here, as I
say. We don't want 'em loose again, either; that we don't.'

'Will they stay there the rest of their lives, then?'

'I've no law-learning so I can't say how they'll settle it; but I've
heard it said that Mr. Edward and Lady Juliana between 'em have
fixed up for 'em to be tried again in the spring by a new judge, and
he'll be the hanging sort, I'll warrant. And even if he isn't, well,
there's other ways of dealing with 'em, isn't there?'

'Certainly,' said Schofield, and casually turned the conversation
on to the topic of the scenery round Campden as compared with
Yorkshire, so that he could learn without asking the whereabouts
of Seven Wells.

Immediately after breakfast next morning he settled his reckoning
and set off for the tree-circle. It was not that he hoped to find anything tangible there—he had no reason to doubt old Joseph's word
in that matter—but at least its solitude might give him something
of the atmosphere to which he was accustomed and in which he
would find it more easy to put his thoughts in order. He was not
disappointed. A thousand feet up, it was as high and desolate as
Hammerthorn Gate on the fell behind his own valley. Under the
grey sky, the peopled plain lay stretching far in the distance below
him on every hand, but there was no human habitation within call
or any man to see him. The trees, oak and elm, ash and thorn,
beech and sycamore, which enclosed the open ground where the
wells were, brought him the smell of his Bolton woods again; the
startled call of a bird and the whirr of its wing, the sudden crack
of a small, dry branch and his own footfall on the fallen leaves
reassured him that he was safe in hiding once more.

He let his mind wander over the strange story in which he had
involved himself—a murdered man whose corpse could not be

found; a son who had accused his mother of the murder; a trial refused but an imprisonment continued; a vengeance determined on death, with or without the law; a village which the East had for a moment invaded and where, probably, there were more witches than one; and behind it all the glimpse of a more formidable mystery, in that the unknown lady had been sent by her masters to lay a trail which was presumably false.

Still occupied with his turning thoughts, he left the shelter of the trees for the nearest well and idly dropped a pebble into it. He was surprised how long it was before the sound told him that it had reached the water. The well must be considerably deeper than the one by his cottage. He threw in another stone and another; then repeated the process at each well, counting carefully to estimate the relative depths. At the last he discovered with a certain surprise that he was disappointed that the water always answered. Unconsciously, he supposed, he must have hoped to find one of them blocked up; that would at least have given him something practical to investigate.

He was about to toss the remaining pebbles down the last well when he noticed lying among them on his palm something not a pebble. He looked at it more carefully and found that it was a metal button with clay adhering to it. He scraped the soil off, polished it first with a handful of leaves, then on his sleeve and started to examine it closely. It was silver, embossed with a crest—three stars running diagonally across a shield. Since he was unversed in heraldic devices, he failed to read its exact message; and, after a momentary excitement, was forced to reflect that it afforded no basis for even a general deduction.

It might have been dropped by one of the coven; it might even lead him to the 'devil' himself. On the other hand, he had no clue as to how long it had lain there and he had to admit that it might equally well have fallen from the coat of some passing stranger like himself who had been driven by curiosity to examine the tree-circle.

He put it in his pocket. If all else failed, he could make an enquiry in the neighbourhood as to who, if anyone, bore as their coat-of-arms a bend of three stars; but first, before he did anything else, he must gain access to Joan Perry in her cell at Bourton.

Whistling, he rode off down the hill.

Long before he arrived in Bourton-on-the-Hill he had decided on his plan of action. It was simple and direct. He would make no attempt to gain an official entry into the prison by representing himself to the magistrate as a friend of the prisoners. Quite apart from the inevitable suspicion he would incur, the information he now had that Sir Thomas Overbury was 'very hot against them' made this foolish, if not impossible. He would bribe the gaoler.

In the event this proved to be of no great difficulty and Schofield suspected that though they were in close custody he was not the first to see the Perrys by this well-understood method. Only one condition the gaoler made as the money changed hands. He must leave immediately the word was given.

'You are a gentleman, sir; that, I can see. I won't enquire your business, but I must have your word.'

'You have it,' said Schofield. 'But you'll give me time to speak.'

'All I can, sir; your generosity can rely on that. But I'm not always my own master.'

It was unfortunate that Sir Thomas Overbury decided to visit the gaol that afternoon on his way over to Campden. For the last week his rheumatism had been such agony to him that he had kept his room; he still felt unable to sit a horse and as his wife was using the carriage for a visit to Weston Subedge, he determined to ride with her as far as Campden, where she could call for him on her return. There were certain legal matters he wished to discuss with Edward Harrison and he thought that it would be as well to satisfy himself on the way as to the condition of the Perrys.

The result of his resolve was that Schofield had no time to hold the conversation he had planned with Joan Perry. When he entered her cell, she came up to him, took him by the arm and looked into his eyes. He had no need to introduce himself. She said: 'You are your mother's son; I was not mistaken in you.'

He answered her as directly: 'How can I serve you?'

' "My lady" told you how things are?'

'As far as she could, yes; but it is only you who——.

There was no time for more. The gaoler rushed in: 'You must go at once, quickly.'

'But I——'

'You gave your word. Quickly. Sir Thomas is here. His coach has just stopped at the door.'

There was nothing for it but to go. As the gaoler pulled at his coat, he reassured Joan: 'I'll come back.'

But to his surprise, she shook her head; came close to him and whispered what sounded to him like: 'Smyrna—silver bowl'; then ran back to huddle on her stool in the furthest corner of the cell, as the gaoler dragged him away.

As Overbury had to be helped out of the coach slowly by his body-servant, Schofield was just able to leave the prison before the magistrate got to the door. Overbury, indeed, who was speaking to his wife, did not notice him; nor had Schofield eyes for anything but the armorial bearings on the coach which matched those on the silver button in his pocket.

CHAPTER VIII

★

The Beginning of the Quest

BACK AGAIN IN HIS COTTAGE, SCHOFIELD PUT THE PROBLEM TO Joseph.

'The Silver Bowl?' the old man repeated incredulously.

'Yes, I tell you, that is what I think she said. It means something to you?'

'Indeed it does. It means that this matter's too dangerous for you to meddle with.' This, with a snap of decisiveness.

'Let me be the judge of that when I know what it is.'

'I can't tell you.'

'I thought I was to be trusted.'

'I said "can't" not "won't." I'm too far on the outside for that secret. And very few have certain knowledge.'

'But something surely you can tell me. I'll swear secrecy by my mother's soul——'

The old man gazed into the fire, as if seeking a vision. Speaking to the flames rather than to Schofield, he continued in a low level voice: 'The Silver Bowl is the most powerful and dangerous of the Greater Hallows. It belongs to the heart of the Mysteries and may not be touched for profane matters. To use it for carnal enchantments means death—and, it may be, worse. We are told that it lies guarded in the East.'

'In Smyrna?'

'That I do not know. I tell you, such knowledge is only with the most secret initiates and for others speculation is idle. But, like all of us, I know it is whispered that the great Simon used it in London fifty years ago—and paid the price of using.'

79

'The great Simon?'

'Simon Magus, our Arch-Priest. To the world, Dr. Simon Forman, who lived in Lambeth, cured diseases and did much good
to the poor. To us, he was our Father Simon.' Joseph sighed. 'Since
he died—it will be fifty years ago next year—we have been sheep
without a shepherd here in England.' He fell silent for a little; then
murmured: 'It was strange, certainly; and lends colour to it.'

'What was strange?'

'His death.'

'Can you tell me?'

'Again, only what is known to all. But you will see, it lends
colour to the belief that great matters were at stake. . . . He was in
perfect health and wanted a year of sixty, yet on a Sunday night
while he was sitting with his wife in his garden-house, he told her
that he would die on Thursday. Monday came—all was well.
Tuesday—Wednesday—still he was not the least ailing. His wife
laughed and blamed him for teasing her, but he assured her he could
not escape. On Thursday after dinner he was as well as he had ever
been in his life and went down to the waterside and took oars to go
to some building he had in hand in Puddle Dock. In the middle of
the Thames he suddenly stood up and cried: "An impost! An impost!"
and so died. Immediately a great gale of wind sprang up. That's the
outward mask of it that all the world knows. It's printed in history.
But what no man knows is what he meant by his last cry. The
vulgar—and those in the boats near by who heard it—took it to
mean an imposthume and thought he came to his death by the
bursting of an abscess; but no such thing was discovered when
they examined his body, which was clear of all disease or cause of
death. But we interpret it differently as meaning that by his death
he paid an impost levied on him for some action. It may well be
that it was for the using of the Silver Bowl.'

'But I thought you said that Bowl lies guarded in the East. Did
your Simon travel there?'

'As far as anyone knew, he was never out of England those
years.'

'Then how could he have used it?'

'It might have been brought.'

'By whom?'

'I do not know.'

'And why?'

'I tell you, I know nothing. There is no certainty in matters like these. . . . Thomas, it is better not to meddle with them. Let it be.'

But Schofield could not let it be. It was not the memory of Joan Perry merely, though that momentary glimpse of her—an old woman, betrayed by her son, helpless in the hands of her enemies—continued to challenge his chivalry. It was not simply the stirring of his old zest for adventure, the call to the excitement of action after so long a spell of contemplation, the prospect of pitting his brain and will against the brains and wills of his fellows. Undoubtedly both these motives aided a resolve which was itself hardened by Joseph's warning of some secret and metaphysical danger. But the decisive factor in his resolve to continue the quest was that precisely which had made him take the first step in it—his mother.

In life he had met her only for the bare half of an hour as she was on her way to death. Had he known then who she was, he would, in spite of herself, have rescued her from it. Now for her sake and to redress vicariously that ignorance and inaction, he would save her friend at the cost, if need be, of his own life.

When Joseph realized that nothing would turn him from his purpose, he withdrew not indeed his opposition but the voicing of it, and gave him what help he could. Together they discussed the implications of what they knew and debated possible courses of action. In the first place, it was obviously foolish to return to Gloucestershire. Joan had, by her fierce head-shake, shown that she did not wish it; the discovery that Overbury seemed to have been at Seven Wells suggested that he knew with whom he was dealing and explained the bitterness which had been noticed in his attitude; it also made it unlikely that Schofield would be able again to see Joan even if he revisited Bourton. And, reinforcing these reasons, was the virtual certainty that Joan was safe for at least five months—until the Spring Assizes. If, then, the Perrys were again acquitted, she would certainly be in danger. 'Other ways of dealing with 'em' would be found. But, having gained a new trial, Overbury and the Harrisons would see to it that the prisoners survived to stand it; they would not starve or poison them in gaol while there was the prospect of a legal hanging. And this gave Schofield twenty weeks at the very minimum.

But what use was he to make of them? What suggestion lay behind that 'Smyrna—Silver Bowl'? Certainly there was time for him to go to Smyrna and back. The ships of the Levant Company made regular voyages, and letters could be written and answers received within four months. The mere accomplishment of the journey presented little difficulty, if that was what she intended. But for what purpose? To find the Silver Bowl and make use of its enchantment to liberate her?

Joseph was vehement in denying that this was a possibility. No member of the Craft, even in danger of death, would think of such a thing. If they did, then it were better for them to die.

'I think it is easy to talk like that,' said Schofield, 'but when death is at the door, things may look different.'

'For us, not even then,' said Joseph, 'but no argument could convince you. You must take my word.'

Past this point, argument or understanding refused to go. Only one thing seemed to both of them to emerge with tolerable clarity. Schofield was intended to go to Smyrna, the city of the Silver Bowl. And that he might be aided both by learning all that was possible to be told and by gaining introductions of practical value, Joseph gave him a letter to deliver to one of his co-religionists in London.

'You will find him a very wise old man. In his youth, he had much to do with the Court and will tell you more than I can of the affairs in which Father Simon was concerned. Now he lives a life as lonely as you or I in his little house outside London. It is in Marylebone Fields on the way to the deer-park. But he's near to the heart of things and knows many people, so that if you've any difficulty in getting a passage to Smyrna, he'll put you in the way of that too.'

'And the Silver Bowl?'

'I doubt if he knows more of that than I do. But I've told him he can trust you with what he does know.'

On his visits to London Schofield was accustomed to leave himself time to spend a day or two wandering idly among his old haunts. Both the city and his own past in it demanded this ritual to allay the nostalgia that came upon him once he was actually among its streets and buildings and gardens. For if in memory the outlines had dimmed and, with the dimming, deadened the pain or softened the excitement of the events played among them, the actuality of them—the fragrance of the gardens, the smell of the river, the shape of the buildings on the skyline, the noise of the taverns—restored them in all their vitality. In Spring Garden, with its abundance of sweetbriar and woodbine, jessamine and musk-rose, lavender and rosemary, its formal groves and less formal thickets, Margaret would be waiting where he first met her. At the 'Bell' Tavern in King Street, five minutes away, Cornelius must surely be provoking another brawl by his insolent bragadoccio. In Southwark, by the Bridge, there would still be the plots hatched against the Government into which he might be drawn. Further afield, there was Rainsborough's house at Wapping, by the river thick with the masts of ships as if a wood grew on the water, which held so many memories, but above all that of the night he had last seen Margaret there and ridden off with Rainsborough to Doncaster and—for Rainsborough through his fault—death.

And everywhere—by Temple Bar and eastward into the City, by Charing Cross down to the Houses of Parliament, by the Tower of London, which he had once known as a Captain in the Tower Guards—there were reminders of those events which men call history, the plots and constitutional plans and debates and riots, into which he had thrown his energies in that crowded, tangled year before they killed the King on a scaffold in Whitehall. As he paced the streets or visited once more the taverns, he surrendered to the past, acknowledged its power and, by that courtesy, gained quittance to continue in his present peace. But on this occasion he denied himself the ritual, for there was no time to spare. He contented himself with the merest savouring of the curious atmosphere of the capital which made those weeks at the end of October and the beginning of November uniquely memorable to Londoners. It was an atmosphere of accomplished vengeance, of the stench of death, of rejoicing and expectant hopes, of the beginning of questioning and disillusion.

Less than four weeks earlier, the grand jury had met at Hicks's Hall—the Hall in Clerkenwell which Sir Baptist Hicks had built and presented to the City of London—and indicted those who had sat in judgment on King Charles I. Within a few days, ten of the 'regicides' who had not managed to escape abroad were publicly executed with every circumstance of cruelty that the law allowed and the hangman could devise. At a great gallows, specially erected for the purpose at Charing Cross, one by one the first eight had died in a carnival of blood extended for four days and their hacked and tortured limbs now decorated the Bridge and the Gates of London. But the courage with which they met death so impressed the crowds that the King's advisers deemed it politic to stay their hands and have no further scenes at Charing Cross. The two last were hanged at the common gallows at Tyburn in an atmosphere incipiently dangerous. The crowd would allow no incivilities or reproaches towards them; their words were received with tears, and the man whose cart had brought them to the gallows refused to drive it away or to participate further in their death.

The executions over, the scene changed to a different and more acceptable demonstration of loyalty. The King went to meet his mother and conduct her back from her long exile in France to the London she had fled from eighteen years before. The entry into the capital of the ageing Henrietta Maria, the 'widow of the Martyr,' had taken place but two days before Schofield's arrival and the city was only just recovering from its orgy of sentiment and enthusiasm.

He was aware of it as he rode through the streets to Tyburn where
the bodies of the two Cromwellian Colonels whom he had once
known in life still hung; but he paused only for a moment before
he struck off on the country path which led to the little Church of
St. Marylebone, isolated in the fields, not far from which was the
house he sought.

In those last few minutes of his journey, the full impact of the
world to which he had returned struck him with an accumulated
force. The remote country tragedy in which he had become implicated was suddenly seen as a microcosm of the vast, seething disorder
and struggle and hatred and blood displayed here on a gigantic scale
at the heart of the kingdom. It was from just such a world that he
had once escaped. For one moment of cowardice he was even
tempted to return to his cottage in the wilds, which seemed now
more desirable than ever. The temptation passed before it had taken
root, but it was with a sense of relief that he gave to the door that
curious knock in which Joseph had instructed him—a knock which,
in his own mind at least, sealed the irrevocability of his resolve.

The door was opened immediately by an old man whose manner
and bearing would have told Schofield, had he not already known,
that the lowly condition in which he had chosen to live was not his
natural element.

'Come in, my friend,' said the old courtier. 'I was expecting you.'

'You were expecting me?'

Schofield repeated the question for the second time—since at first
it had gone unanswered—as they were sitting at ease after a meal
which he had eaten with avidity.

'That is, perhaps, putting it too precisely,' said his host. 'But
"my Lady" warned me the day before yesterday that I might have
a visitor who would need speedy help to get to Smyrna.'

'So she knew?'

'Knew what?'

'That I was going to Smyrna.'

'No. Only that you might. She was not sure exactly what poor

Joan Perry would expect you to do—or what you would consent to do.'

'It seems that you all know more than I do.'

'No, I fear not. In this letter Joseph has told me the circumstances, and I know no more than he does the clue to events.'

'Or about the Silver Bowl?'

'No, nor that either—though I can tell you something more of Father Simon's supposed using of it than he could. But that's not much. It's more practical help I can give you. You start for Smyrna to-morrow, by packet for Lisbon. There you'll join the *Plymouth*, which is taking Lord Winchilsea to Constantinople. He's just been appointed our new Ambassador there. If you'd have arrived a few days ago, you could have gone aboard here in London, but she's already on her way.'

'But can a packet overtake her?'

'She'll be in Lisbon some days, after the storms she'll run into in the Bay of Biscay. And she'll take her time weathering them. You'll have a day or two to spare before she's refitted at Lisbon. And Captain Allen will take you aboard immediately. He's an old friend of mine.'

'You mean he's——?'

'One of the Craft? No, no. No more than you are—and knows much less about it than you do. No, he comes to chat with me here sometimes because I was a friend of Walter Ralegh's and his father was one of Ralegh's men. . . . That reminds me. I'm getting forgetful in my old age. Will you take a pipe with me? I've some of the weed here which I'll warrant is finer than any you've smoked; or will smoke.

When they were settled with their pipes, he continued: 'You'll have to leave early in the morning to catch the packet with the tide as it is now, so I'd better tell you now all I can of Father Simon and his great enchantment. It all started in Dominic's house, fifty years ago. . . .'

CHAPTER IX

Fifty Years Ago

I

IT ALL STARTED IN DOMINIC'S HOUSE, FIFTY YEARS AGO. THE SCOTTISH James, grandfather to our returned King Charles, had reigned for eight years in England. Reigned, mark you, not ruled. The ruling was still done by little hunch-backed Cecil, who'd managed it well enough for the great Elizabeth and saw no reason to let it out of his hands under a poor thing like James. But now Cecil was dying; it was clear he couldn't last more than a few months and Dominic wanted to make sure of the future. What there was of it. Dominic was seventy-one himself.

Henry Howard, Earl of Northampton, Knight of the Garter, Lord Privy Seal, Lord Warden of the Cinque Ports—to give him his name and title. But he was Dominic to me and all the Court. It was his nickname in the family. No one knew why. He was a bachelor, but no saint—a lean, cunning spider, with his long fingers always picking at his sleeve. I wish I could make you see the man, but words can't catch the true air of him. Like all the Howards, he was divided against himself—half ruler, half rebel; the miser in him for ever fighting the prodigal, as courtesy and contempt fought for the mastery of his face. The Howard face, with the high forehead, the long nose and the straight mouth, with the ugly lower lip protruding as if thrust out at you under his beard and the clever, searching eyes that never laughed.

That he was a Howard—the greatest noble house in England—meant something. His own place in it meant more. You won't understand that now. We've seen too much change in these fifty years for you young ones to know or care what we knew and allowed for in his blood. But his father was the poet Surrey, who'd been killed at the block by King Harry, because he stood too near the throne and cast his eyes at it. And his elder brother, Norfolk, would have married the Queen of Scots if Elizabeth hadn't discovered the plot and sent him to the block too. So, you see, Dominic came of dangerous stock. The passion for power was in his nature, but it was curbed by a liking for life. That explained him, partly. He would flatter where he despised and charm where he meant to kill.

He was born a Papist, but, for convenience, changed his religion openly five times; but his real beliefs were neither Papist nor Protestant. When he was a child, an Italian astrologer told his father that in middle life the boy would be so poor that he would lack even a meal. Surrey laughed at the impossibility. So did Dominic when he was old enough to understand it. But it happened. When Norfolk was executed, the Queen took all the Howard estates and Dominic found himself a pauper. You could often see him in those days, I've been told, lounging on Paul's Walk among the booksellers, rubbing shoulders with poor scholars and poorer rogues, filling his mind as though he hoped it would mend an empty belly. He learnt much in those years—they were his thirties; about your age, I judge—and not only from books.

He got his patrimony back in the end; and the first thing he did was to write a pamphlet against what he called 'the Poison of Supposed Prophecies,' denouncing astrology. He, of all men. But when Cecil looked into it, he found so much treason there, whatever the title might pretend, that he persuaded the Queen to clap Dominic in prison. Not for long; but long enough to teach him more discretion. He never meddled again openly, though he held his own way in secret.

He was over sixty and still plain Lord Henry Howard when Elizabeth died. He knew he'd nothing to hope from her; but with James he thought his stars propitious at last. James was Mary of

Scotland's son; Dominic's brother had been her martyr. James paid
the debt with an Earldom, the Garter and the Privy Seal. But not
with the power Dominic wanted. That remained with Cecil.

He made the best of his honours and his new wealth and built
himself the great palace by Charing Cross. Northumberland House
it is now, though we older ones still think of it as Northampton
House. He packed it with treasures—pictures and statues from Italy,
rare tapestries from France, silks and curios from the Levant and
further East. But these, though they pleased his taste, were more
for show to others than for enjoyment for himself. His own love
was his library, with many strange books beyond price and dangerous to keep. You can see the great window of it from the river. In
that window Dominic sat, pulling his beard, spinning his webs.

You understand his problem—how to master James when Cecil
died so that he and his house might rule England at last. There was
no direct way to it. The King would never give him Cecil's place.
Nor, I think, by this time did he want it. His nature was inured to
indirections. Though even here, one way had failed. The Howards
had already exercised themselves enough trying to hook James with
his favourite bait of boys. They schooled what poor relations with
pretty faces they could muster—gave them a wardrobe, washed
their faces in buttermilk, perfumed their breaths, did what they
could with their minds and then threw them in James's way. But
they had no success. James ignored them. When their failures
became a court jest and a matter for wagers, Dominic thought it
time to change his tactics. If the King would not choose at Dominic's
taste, Dominic must snare the boy James had chosen for himself.

That boy was Robert Ker. He'd been one of James's pages in
Scotland. Son of a knight of one of the Border families. Poor, but
not ill-born, as the Scots go. When James came to England, Ker
went soldiering in France for a time. Then he came back to court,
a well-set, strong-shouldered young man with golden hair and red
cheeks, just ripe for the King's eye. He caught it at a tilting-match,
where he was unhorsed and broke his leg. They took him to
Dominic's house at Charing Cross, and when the King came to

visit him every day to see how his leg was mending, Dominic saw the way the wind was blowing. But he thought it a passing gust which would change quickly—as was James's way. That time he was wrong. It increased to a gale. In a couple of years, Ker was absolute king of the King. Was made Lord Rochester and given more wealth than Dominic.

If he never meddled with Cecil, it was because he didn't at that point understand that kind of power; or want it. But, with Cecil gone, it was probable that he'd rule England through James. Or so Dominic calculated and saw his way was to entrap Ker. But how? Ker was too rich to bribe, too simple to blackmail, too powerful to care one way or the other for Dominic's friendship. One day Dominic hit on the answer by accident. It was his great-niece, Frances.

She was eighteen and had been four years married to the Earl of Essex, a dullard of twenty. The son of Elizabeth's Essex, whom, by the way, Dominic had played Judas to. The marriage, of course, was political—to heal the breach between the Essex and the Howard families—but young Essex was, in his way, in love with her. Anyhow, he wanted her as a wife and insisted on his rights. She couldn't bear the touch of him and was burning with lust for Ker. When she confided this to Dominic, he suddenly saw his way clear. She should have Ker, and, by her having, the Howards would hold the King.

There were obstacles, of course. One was Ker, who showed no interest in her whatever. Another was Essex, who showed too much. A third was Ker's bosom friend and confidant, Sir Thomas Overbury—uncle to the one you've told me about in Gloucestershire—who hated Frances even more than he loved Ker. He understood what she was at. So the affair, you see, needed skill enough, but Dominic decided the prize was worth it and sent for Anne Turner.

She was a doctor's widow who lived in a little house in Paternoster Row. She was known by the world for setting a new fashion in yellow starched cuffs and by most of the Court for arranging opportunities for adultery and dabbling in love-philtres. But to the

inner circle she was known as the devoted intimate of the Master—
Father Simon—Dr. Simon Forman of Lambeth—whatever you like
to call him. That was why Dominic wanted her. Whether or not
he knew Father Simon—and I think he did from the old days—he
dared not take the risk of showing it now, with King James crazy
against necromancy. So Mistress Turner had to act as go-between.

For a time Dominic paid handsomely for the usual love-philtres
and spells, but, as nothing happened, he insisted on seeing Father
Simon. Anne Turner brought him to Northampton House one
night, disguised as her servant and he told Dominic bluntly that, as
matters stood, the thing was impossible. Dominic stormed and
called him a charlatan. Father Simon weakened and admitted that
there was one way. He could accomplish everything if he could use
the Silver Bowl. That's why the Bowl was brought to England, if
it *was* brought. I've no more proof of that than you. I only know
that it was sent for.

2

The person Dominic decided to use was little Baptist Hicks, a silk
mercer with an itching palm, no conscience but reasonable discretion. He'd supplied Dominic with most of his silks and stuff from
the East for Northampton House. What he knew about other
matters, I don't know. Probably nothing. But he'd do anything for
money and in particular was anxious to put Dominic under an
obligation. Unpleasant little creature, Hicks. At least, I could never
stomach him and his kind.

He'd started quietly enough, in his house in Old Jewry and his
shop at the sign of the White Bear in Cheapside. Built up quite a
good business with the City fathers, when the chance came to jump
into Court circles. That was when his brother Michael was made
secretary to Cecil. As long as Elizabeth was Queen, he used his
entrée with decency and confined himself to selling silks to the
courtiers his brother sent to his shop. But when James and all his
rag-tag-and-bobtail Scots came in, he jumped in with both feet.

They were all poor and dressed like scarecrows, including the King. So he started by giving James the best silks he had, lending him £16,000—and accepting a Knighthood. Then he proceeded to dress practically the whole court. They couldn't pay, so he let them have credit, doubled his prices, then lent them the money at a stiff interest. Meanwhile brother Michael let him know when the King made grants to them, so that he could put the screw on at once and get it all back. He was known as Shylock, but they were too afraid of him to do more than mutter it behind his back. Except Dominic, who could have bought him up, and a few others of us who weren't in his debt. Dominic once said it to his face—but he took it with that humble, tradesman's smile of his. Although, mind you, he admired Dominic, in his way, in spite of it.

After he'd been knighted, we waited for him to give up his shop. But not Hicks. He knew it was against the law for a knight to keep a shop in London, but he decided he had enough friends—if you call them that—to see that he won a case if he appealed. He brought the case and won it and the White Bear in Cheapside went on. But it had shaken him. He knew what people were saying, so he thought he'd better become a country gentleman. He searched round till he found a good estate he could get for a song because the owner was in difficulties and became Lord of the Manor of Chipping Campden in Gloucestershire. They say he loved the place and behaved well to it—lorded it among the country yokels with a certain air of generosity. He could afford it and they didn't know his reputation. But in London he was worse than ever. Even the King hardened, and, although he offered double the usual price for a baronetcy, James wouldn't grant it—then. Later, it was a different story.

That, anyhow, was the Baptist Hicks who went to see Dominic that day in 1610 to be asked to get one more treasure from Smyrna. Whether he got it and, if he did, how he got it, I can't tell you. That's part of the mystery of the Bowl. But I can tell you what happened to Hicks and you can make your own guess. Within eighteen months he had more than trebled his fortune and started to build in a way that Dominic might have envied. In Clerkenwell, at the very gates of the Northampton estate, he built a Sessions House, called it Hicks's Hall, and gave it to the City to show how generous he was at heart; and further to win the vulgar he had an inn near it called *The Baptist's Head*. Then he bought an estate on a hill in Kensington and built a great house on it, planted an avenue of elms up to it from the village and named it Campden House on Campden Hill, after his property in Gloucestershire. I've never been inside it, but those who have tell me it's an elaborate affair in the modern style—thirty rooms or more, a private chapel, Eastern cupolas on the turrets; and in the gardens some wild olives and a caper-tree. They may have come from Smryma, too.

When he'd spent a fortune on that house, he started another in Chipping Campden which must have cost him even more. At any rate, it was bigger and more elaborate; but you'll have seen what was left of it after the fire, so you can probably judge better than I can.

He'd established himself by now. He got his baronetcy at last; became a Member of Parliament—not that that meant anything—and in the end was given a peerage. The motto he chose was 'Nondum metam'—'Not yet the goal.' Everyone wondered what his goal was.

As I say, there's no proof that it all sprang from that interview with Dominic; but, on the other hand, there's no doubt that it happened after it. And, if you want another circumstance, there's this. When Dominic's scheme was successful and Frances got free of her husband and married Ker, Hicks lent them his new house at Kensington to use as their home.

3

Yes, the enchantment was successful in the end—that's another reason to suppose the Bowl was used—though it wasn't till Father Simon was dead that it began to work. After he'd seen Hicks he did what he could with the ordinary magics. Anne Turner took

Frances to him secretly; and she took the oaths and gave him what help she could. Including a piece of her husband's skin. It must have been his, from the way in which it was used. You may or may not understand that.

Father Simon seems to have made one mistake. When he put his things in order before his death, there was one box which he left for Anne Turner to keep. Not the important things, of course. They went to Gresham, who succeeded him as our Arch-Priest, and were safe enough. But in this box were certain letters and some of the things he'd used for Frances. I suppose Anne Turner knew enough to be able to use them herself if Gresham didn't want to be drawn into it. And there was a list of all the adulteries at Court which would let Anne Turner live like a Queen on blackmail for the rest of her life. The mistake Father Simon made was not to give her the box before he died. He left it in his room for her to take. When she came for it, his widow wouldn't let her have it. So it was opened, and the whole thing made public when Ker and Frances were on trial for the murder of Overbury.

What was in it? The usual things, as I said. The list of all the names of God mentioned in the Scriptures; another of the names of devils conjured to torment Essex and seduce Ker; the chart with 'Corpus' in the centre and a small piece of skin attached—that, as I say, must have been Essex's. If you don't understand the use of it, it's not for me to explain it to you. And, of course, there was the $+B+C+D+E$ parchment. There was the black scarf with white crosses; the brass mould for casting the wax figures of Frances and Ker joined together in the manner of nature; and the picture of Frances sitting naked, with her hair loose, looking in a looking-glass.

It is amusing that people are so credulous. When these simple things were shown in court, there was as much of an uproar as if the real mysteries had been exhibited. There was a crack in one of the scaffolds where the spectators were sitting and the whole place was in a panic for a quarter of an hour. They said it was the Devil who was angry at having his workmanship shown to those who were not his own scholars. If they only knew! But that's no part of the story. It didn't happen till some years afterwards. I'm telling it to you, because it shows what Father Simon was doing at the beginning of the matter. No wonder he couldn't get any further. You can even sympathize with Dominic for calling him a charlatan.

He hadn't Frances to help him, either. Essex suddenly decided to enforce his rights and took her away with him to his house at Chartley in Staffordshire. She was nearly mad with lust and fear. Wrote wild letters to Father Simon—'Sweet Father,' she called him—saying that nothing was of any avail. She put the powders he sent her in her husband's food; she saw that no linen came near his body that hadn't been rinsed in the wasting liquid that Simon had given her. But Essex continued to be quite well and anything but impotent. And Ker, who was a hundred miles away, never, as far as anyone knew, gave her a thought.

Then, quite suddenly, everything was changed. A few days before he died Father Simon sent her some paper which he had soaked in a new preparation he had made. He told her she was to use it to write a letter to Ker and was to send with it a nutmeg, which he had also infused with some new and powerful enchantment. She sent it. Father Simon was dead before it got to Ker; but from the moment Ker received it he was her slave—as hot for her as she for him. And, at the same time, Essex lost the ability to be her husband. You can make what you like of it. The facts, after the trial, became public enough.

After that there was no further need for magic. The rest could be left to Nature—and Dominic.

Dominic wasted no time. As soon as he heard from Frances how things were, he arranged for her to come back to London and bought her a house out at Hounslow where she and Ker could meet secretly and safely. Then he started, in that subtle, certain way of his, to work on the King. I was in attendance at Court at the time and watched it. The perfection of it made it a delight, in its way. It was the master-work of an artist in courtiership.

Dominic played on three strings—James's passion for Ker, his pity for Frances and his vanity. I can't give you a true picture of the subtlety and delicacy of his touch, but you can see something of the tune. Here was Ker, loving James, of course, above every creature yet wishing, in propriety, to marry—as was seemly. It was the King's wish that he should, in any case. Would James, who was so ineffably generous to Ker in everything else, deny him the one woman he wanted to marry? . . . And Frances, an innocent child, forced to marry for reasons of policy a boor she disliked—and who was impotent into the bargain. Poor innocent little Frances, who was so gay and affectionate in spite of the frustration of her womanhood! Dominic painted it so well that James started to cry. He believed it, of course, He was a fool without parallel, though he liked to be known as the 'English Solomon' and prided himself on his shrewdness. . . . It would mean a divorce, certainly; and that was contrary to the law of the Church. Of course. But, in England, was not James Head of the Church, and, moreover, a greater theologian than the entire bench of bishops? The King admitted it. Then, as theologian, he would doubtless be able to inform the bishops that nullity has at all times been allowed by the Church as grounds for the dissolution of the marriage bond, since there has been no true marriage where no consummation is possible. Yes, there was no doubt of that. Frances would give evidence of it and if Essex were examined . . .

The upshot of it was that James became as set on the marriage as Frances herself. He instructed the Bishops with a marvellous show of learning. It didn't impress the Archbishop of Canterbury, who was an honest man; but most of the rest of them were venal enough —including Lancelot Andrewes who had the reputation for being a saint. Frances should get the divorce without much difficulty. Success was almost in Dominic's grasp when, suddenly, Sir Thomas Overbury kicked.

4

I heard the beginning of it. It was in the gallery at Whitehall at one o'clock in the morning. One or two of us were about, as our duty was, but none of any consequence—court servants who heard, forgot and did not speak. Ker came out of the King's bedchamber and met Overbury who was passing through. Possibly he had been waiting for him. I don't know. Ker seemed surprised to see him, and said: 'How now, are you still up?' Then they started quarrelling and though we couldn't hear everything they said, the end was loud enough!

'Well, my lord,' shouts Overbury, 'if you marry that filthy, base woman, you will utterly ruin your honour and yourself. You shall never do it by my advice or consent; and if you do, you had best look to stand fast."

'I can stand well enough on my own legs,' returns Ker, 'but in faith I will be even with you for this.'

So they parted in rage enough. None of us could know it at the time, but, as events turned out, Overbury signed his own death-warrant that night.

You must know something of Overbury and his part in that matter, since his nephew's in this affair of yours. He was thirty-one, Ker twenty-five. They'd met first in Scotland, eleven years before. For nine years they'd been inseparable. They were the David and Jonathan of the Court. The Queen, who hated both of them for comprehensible enough reasons, dubbed Overbury 'the keeper of the King's keeper.' Not that Overbury lacked a reputation of his own. Ben Jonson himself had praised his poetry. Everyone of taste had read his prose 'Characters' which had an engaging wit. He had travelled in France and the Low Countries and written a book on each of them, which showed him a skilled observer in politics. Cecil himself had been his patron—and Cecil was no fool in choosing men, whatever you might think of his purposes. Overbury could have made what career he chose. Unfortunately for himself he chose Ker. But whatever they may say and have said and however he came to hate him in the end, he chose that way because he loved him. If when Ker ruled England he had the very power that Dominic coveted, that was the way things fell out. Overbury had chosen Ker when Ker was nothing but a poor page in disgrace—

when neither of them could have guessed the future. You can envy him the power which came to him because of that, but it's false to say he schemed for it.

But when it came to the point of Frances's divorce and Ker's marriage to her, it was sufficient that he knew what he knew. He could have told enough to stop it. Enough, perhaps, to have sent them all to the Tower. A word to the bishops, a hint to the King. . . . Not, I think, that he would have done. But he did more than enough by writing a new poem, called *The Wife*, which a good many more people than Frances herself saw was intended for her. Ker agreed that he must be silenced.

The question was how it was to be done. And here Dominic stepped in again to give Ker the benefit of his more-than-fifty-years experience of how these things are handled. He suggested that Overbury should be appointed Ambassador to Russia.

When Ker suggested this to James, the King was delighted. He had always been jealous—and with reason—of Overbury's friendship with his minion. Overbury in Russia was as pleasant a prospect to him as it was to Dominic, Frances and Ker. But when Overbury was called before the Privy Council and told of the new honour the King had bestowed on him, he refused it. Said he had no desire to leave his country for any preferment in the world. The Lord Chancellor and the others, who had no idea of what was really going on, were quite naturally shocked and went to consult James about it.

James who, as usual, was drunk, fell into a rage and said it was pitiable that it should be published abroad that he could not obtain so much of a gentleman, and one that he had always thought was one of his friends, as to accept an honourable employment from him, and ordered Overbury to the Tower where he would have leisure to change his mind.

That was at the end of April. By the middle of September, Overbury was dead.

5

That Dominic and Frances arranged the poisoning of him, there is no possible doubt. That Ker was privy to it, I do not believe, even though, afterwards, he was found guilty of it at his trial. Nor, you will understand, was it anything to do with magic. It was a straight-forward matter of murder. This I can assure you. It is important that you remember it, for since Father Simon's enchantments and Anne Turner's love-philtres were made public at the same trial, the vulgar do not discriminate. But the supernatural ended when Simon laid the enchantment on Ker with the letter dipped in precious liquid and the nutmeg. All that followed was human enough. But there is still one person I must tell you of, because he's involved in both sides of the affair—Richard Weston.

Weston had been apothecary's assistant to Anne Turner's husband. He was now completely her servant. He'd been used to carry letters between Ker and Frances and to get in touch with Franklin, the poisoner. He'd known Gresham, too; but, as far as I know, he wasn't of the Craft. It's this that makes what Gresham did the more difficult to understand and may explain what happened to the Bowl. *If* the Bowl was there. There's always that 'if.' That's why I repeat it.

Gresham didn't live a year after Father Simon died, and, for some reason that none of us can understand, he made no preparations for handing on his things to his successor—our present Arch-Priest. They got to him, of course, but all that Gresham did was to gather together the lesser things—such as Father Simon had left in his box for Anne Turner—wrap them up in a scarf and give them to Weston, with instructions that they were to be buried securely in the earth. Assuming the Bowl was there, that's what may have happened to it. It certainly never found its way to our Arch-Priest. Some of our people think that Gresham had been against Father Simon meddling with the Bowl in the first place. But, of course, he was sworn to obedience, could do nothing and reveal nothing. He could not even refuse the custody of it, when it came to him from Simon. The only power he had was not to use it himself and to dispose of it as he thought proper. As he saw that it brought death to both Simon and himself, he may have thought it proper to send it back to Smyrna. Or he may have given it to Weston to bury.

Could he do that? Certainly, if he wished and thought it right. There was no one to question him. . . . But to go back to Weston. What I've just said explains the part he played in the secret matters. But he also had a part in the poisoning and that was public enough. Weston would do whatever Anne Turner ordered, and Anne Turner would do whatever Frances asked. Obviously, he was the man to carry the matter to its conclusion. So Frances got the Lieutenant of the Tower to appoint Weston as Overbury's keeper. After that, the way was easy.

At first Overbury seems to have had no suspicion. He even thought that Ker was still his friend and would plead to James for his release. He accepted Weston, of whom he knew nothing, with a good grace. When first he became ill, he thought it partly his confinement, partly the result of the stress of his life—which, indeed, had somewhat pulled down his health. Also the first poisons were mild and not successful.

No sooner was Overbury safe in the Tower than the divorce suit began. Dominic presented Frances's plea to a committee of Bishops and Privy Counsellors. They thought it would not take long, with the King pressing for it and everything arranged. But they were wrong. The case was without precedent in the history of England and men began to ask themselves what was behind it. Archbishop Abbott continued stubborn in his honesty and, as long as he stood firm, there were certain of the bishops who would stand with him. As it happened, he stood firm to the end and was disgraced because of it—though they gave other reasons. So they had to bring pressure on the others and pack the bench. But it all took time and the smell was reaching further and further. And there was Overbury in the Tower, still alive, and beginning to be aware of what was being plotted against him. When Dominic heard from Weston that he was spending all the time he was well enough to do it in writing an account of what passed between him and Ker, he saw that the matter must be brought to an instant conclusion. He must have stronger and certain poison. And at once.

So they found a boy who worked for an apothecary—not Franklin, whom they'd lost faith in, and who had been managing it up to now—who could lay his hands on his master's most deadly drugs. They bribed him to make a clyster * compounded full of the strongest poison and sent him to Weston with it. Weston forced it in Overbury's guts and that was the end of him, with some agony.

Dominic, in joy, went to see the body and wrote Ker an account of it. None of us who were at the trial when that letter was read— and it was read three times—will ever forget it. Dominic was dead by then and beyond the reach of justice, but it was as if he'd come back and stood there, smiling, for all men to see him as he was.

'Sweet Lord,' it ran—I think I can give it you fairly as it was— 'Sweet Lord, Overbury being viewed, there was found on his arm an issue and on his stomach twelve kernels, each as big as three-pence; one issue on his back with a tawney plaster on it. This was strange and ugly. He stunk intolerably, as he was cast in a coffin with a loose sheet over it. God is gracious in cutting off ill instruments. Thus, sweet Lord, wishing you all increase of happiness and honour, I end. Your lordship's more than any man, Henry Northampton.'

But it wasn't Dominic who was Ker's' more than any man! From that moment it was Ker who was Dominic's, body and soul.

6

About ten days after the murder, the divorce went through, and, from then till Christmas, nothing was spoken of but the new wedding. You've never seen and never will see such magnificence. Little Hicks, of course, was in ecstasies. He must have got a small

* An enema.

fortune out of the clothes he supplied, even if he didn't get paid in full for all of them. And by lending his new house on 'Campden Hill' to the bride and bridegroom, he knew that the favourable wind would continue. As for Dominic, he'd done what he set out to do. The Howards were masters of England. The King was Ker's slave, Ker Frances's, and Frances—because of his knowledge, not her affection—his. He had little more than six months of life left to him, but for those six months he ruled the country, as he had determined to do.

It was Dominic who was 'brideman' to Frances—led her to the Chapel Royal for the ceremony. She chose to go in white, with her hair down, to show her virginity and innocence. She wore the £10,000 worth of jewels the King had given her. We poor courtiers disliked that more than her audacity. James, you see, had bankrupted himself and the country. He couldn't even afford to pay his personal guard or his post-rider. The navy had been left to rot away—you'll understand that was one of the things I had against him!—but he'd have put the whole land in pawn to get money to pour out on the Howards at Ker's nod. Ker himself he made an Earl—Earl of Somerset—and was given £90,000 to squander. What James spent on the wedding festivities alone (he paid for the whole of it and they lasted a week) would have sufficed for him to rule England well for a couple of years.

I tell you this because it's the measure of Dominic's triumph. And that day, dressed for once not in black but in red and gold, he savoured every moment of it.

But three months later we heard that he was taken ill at Greenwich, where he was staying for the spring. He was seventy-five and knew that the sickness was mortal. But he determined to die in his house at Charing Cross. There were things there he wanted to destroy. And, as he drove through London for the last time, it should be as the king he was. James himself had never moved in such state and the whole city turned out to watch Dominic as his procession with a retinue of more than sixty horse took its way from Greenwich over London Bridge to Northampton House.

Dominic, ill as he was, roused himself to acknowledge the cheers. A London crowd, as no doubt you have observed, will cheer anyone.

The last thing he did was to write a letter to Ker to ensure that those about the court whom he had opposed in his life should not benefit by his death. Then, they say, having nothing more to hope for but a sufficiency to fear he made his peace with his Church and died a Papist. Of what really happened in those last hours, there is no certainty—of what he confessed, what he renounced or what comfort was given him. Only the outward show could be seen. As Warden of the Cinque Ports, he had ordered that his body should be buried in Dover Castle. So there he went on his last journey, the coffin resting at Kentish inns on the way, with two tapers burning on it by night and six of his gentlemen watching by turns. And there's an end of Henry, Earl of Northampton, the fine flower of English nobility—and the end of my story. . . .

What is the rest of it? It's nothing to your purpose, but if you're curious here it is.

Just over a year after Dominic died, there was another death. The apothecary's boy lay mortally ill in Brussels. He, too, wanted to ease his soul and confessed his part in the poisoning to the English agent in Brussels. The agent, who thought it too dangerous a secret to keep, crossed to England and told the King's Secretary, Winwood. Winwood told the King, who laughed at the whole matter, and said it was one of the fables that always appeared when anyone of importance died. And there it would all have ended, but for one circumstance. James was getting tired of Ker and was eyeing a new boy, Villiers. But Ker refused to give way—insulted Villiers, swore to spoil his beauty, and raged at the King.

So James, after pondering the matter, decided to allow the charges to be probed. If they were true and led to Ker, then at one stroke he was rid of Ker, had gained a reputation for stern juctice and could enjoy Villiers. Which is how it turned out—though his reputation, after all, stood a little lower than he thought it did.

Weston was tried first, condemned and hanged. Then Anne

Turner, Franklin, and the Lieutenant of the Tower. With them out of the way, the stage was set for the great trial of Ker and Frances—the Earl and Countess of Somerset—in Westminster Hall. They were both found guilty by their peers. She undoubtedly was. He, as undoubtedly, was not. That is how they pleaded it. But they were not hanged. The King pardoned them both, kept them in the Tower for five years—during which time they learnt to hate each other far more than they had once loved—and then allowed them to go into the country.

And Essex? Essex, when the time came, took the field as Commander of the Parliamentary Army against the King in the late Civil Wars. If I'd have been Ker—and he was alive at the time—I think I'd have joined him; for King Charles rubbed salt into the wounds of his disgrace.

A sorry story? You're still young. I'm old enough to have at least the wisdom not to moralize. Do you blame the wind for blowing a tempest or a tiger for killing its prey? Things act after their natures; and the nature of all politics at all times is greed, lust, fear and ambition. Nothing else. But, as a rule, there is secrecy, too. The people never know what their rulers are doing. Only what the rulers of their great-grandparents did. But here the secrecy was shattered and they knew the truth at the time. That is one reason why we had a civil war and men loathed the house of Stuart—and will, I do not doubt, loathe it again. There's too much knowledge about for any stability. Belief in the innocence of rulers depends on the ignorance of the ruled.

I do not say that these doings were not evil. I only say they were natural and therefore not to be blamed excessively. What was not to be forgiven, I think, was that the Silver Bowl may have been used for such purposes. If you should stumble on it, remember that . . .

CHAPTER X

Smyrna

EARLY IN THE MORNING, WHILE IT WAS STILL DARK, SCHOFIELD took leave of his host. Everything to facilitate his journey had been provided for him. Since it was impossible for a traveller to leave the country or to take abroad any sum of money exceeding £20, the old courtier had procured a pass made out in his name (which, as the forgery of them had under the recent restrictive rule of the revolutionary government become a minor industry, was not difficult) and had given him an introduction to Edmund Pentlow, one of the merchants of the Levant Company in Smyrna, requesting him to lay all necessary credit at the visitor's disposal and to give him any other help he might require, however long his stay. Armed with these, as well as a letter to Captain Allen of the *Plymouth*, Schofield rode off on the second stage of his quest.

The story told him the night before had given him a glimmer of hope. However obscure certain matters remained, it had become obvious that the remote tragedy in Gloucestershire to-day was in some way connected with the drama, involving great and famous players, of fifty years ago. And though the one was too humble to be easily traced, the other might provide a clue. No one in Smyrna was likely to have heard of Joan Perry, but it should not be difficult to learn something of the one-time movements of Sir Baptist Hicks —and even, perhaps, of his servant and steward, William Harrison. Schofield became impatient to reach Smyrna.

The old man's predictions about the speed and easy journey of the packet compared with the storms and hindrances which attended the passage of the *Plymouth* were amply fulfilled, as he found on his arrival at Lisbon. The *Plymouth* was still refitting and taking in stores when he arrived and presented his credentials to Captain Allen. Never, said Allen, had he know the Bay worse. His ship had arrived in Lisbon with her mainmast gone and most of her pumps out of action. Fortunately, since he had the Ambassador on board, repairs were seen to speedily: Winchilsea was invited to court and Captain Allen was allowed to choose from the royal stores all he needed.

When they put out to sea again, however, their ill-luck dogged them, and more than once Schofield feared he had embarked on his last journey. The passage between Lisbon and Algiers took eleven days of storms. At Algiers a new complication arose. There was an altercation about passage money with a Turkish merchant, who offered a sum quite ridiculously small to be taken to Constantinople. He was an unprepossessing man of about sixty, very lean and with cheeks hanging like Spanish leather, while continuous spasms gave him a jerking motion, as if he were afflicted by strong hiccoughs. Captain Allen, who knew the East, recognized immediately the marks of an Ophiunjé—a confirmed opium-eater—and his insular prejudice against the habit reinforced his professional dislike of being swindled.

On the other hand, it was certain that if the Turk returned with complaints to the authorities in Algiers, vengeance would be taken on the English captives and ships which, by diplomatic arrangement, had just been released but which were still in fact in the Turkish power. It was not even certain that, were offence given, the *Plymouth* would not find herself mysteriously attacked by pirates in mid-Mediterranean. In the circumstances, Winchilsea himself intervened, gave the Captain £50 of money provided for his official expenditure to cover the deficit and wrote home to his Most Gracious Majesty King Charles the Second earnestly hoping that he would approve the apparent extravagance.

The danger of attack thus averted, they left Algiers with a lighter heart. But they had no specific against sickness and the elements. On the way to Messina, there were six days of continuous storms, equalling in violence anything they had yet encountered; and when they arrived there, they were not allowed ashore for want of a bill of health.

It was thus with a sense of more than ordinary relief that Schofield greeted the first sight of Smyrna as, eight days before Christmas, the *Plymouth* entered the peaceful arm of the Gulf, with the gentle landward wind that the Greeks had called Zephyrus but which the new masters of Smyrna has named Imbat, freshening her sails. But his relief was quickly followed by another emotion which he did not attempt to analyse—a wonder and admiration that took him by the throat. In all his travels he had seen no city so lovely. Smyrna, the 'first of Asia in beauty,' held her ancient pre-eminence.

It was as if the city rose out of the sea and started to climb the Hill, Pagos, but half-way up had grown weary of the ascent and stopped abruptly so that the summit was left to wear her lonely crown—the ruins of those magnificent buildings which had once been indeed the 'Crown of Smyrna' above grass and trees. On the water-front itself, behind the landing-stage and the customs-house, was the imposing new Chancellery of Mohammed Kipruili, greatest of Grand Viziers, now on his death-bed. A single minaret separated it from the old Castle-by-the-Mole, with its strong bastions and square, castellated towers, where the Templars had made their last stand against the Turks and which still, by its very presence, was a reminder of Christendom. Opposite it, across the vivid blue waters of the tiny bay which was the Inner Harbour, the burnished domes of a mosque, with its minarets and palm-trees, mocked it, as if the two civilizations were still facing each other in defiance.

Behind the buildings on the water-front, the square, two-storied houses of the city marched up the lower slopes of the hill, closely packed yet with their density broken by innumerable cypresses and twenty minarets. Between the summit and the uppermost houses were the uncovered slopes, studded with trees and the ruins of Smyrna's ancient past. The fabulous 'street of gold' which once was 'Smyrna's necklace' had indeed gone; but the ruined Greek amphitheatre was there and, to the right of it, the strange square building known as Polycarp's Tomb. As a background to the Hill towered the distant mountains and, twelve miles away, the peak of Mount Olympus. Here every civilization and creed, East and West, the past of immemorial legend and the present of bustling gaiety, the buildings of man and the savage magnificence of nature were fused into a unity of beauty, hanging between the twin blues of sky and water, and lying, in the sunlight, in a haze of gold.

'It is something to see?'

Schofield turned to find the Turkish merchant at his elbow.

'Indeed. I've never seen its equal.'

'You will stay here for a time?'

'For a time.' Schofield was immediately on his guard against inquisitiveness; but the Turk's face was friendly. He was obviously pleased at having been transformed from a somewhat unwelcome guest into a proud host, showing a stranger the treasures of his inheritance. That he had spoken to Schofield at all was due to the look of admiration he had glimpsed in passing on the young man's face. Everyone else was too busy with the more mundane matters connected with landing to pay much attention to the place where they landed.

'Then if you are only staying for a time, you will beware of the Lotus Tree.'

'The lotus tree? You have one here?'

'Many,' said the Turk. 'But I meant the one up there by the summit of Pagos.' He pointed up to the Hill where, just below its crown of buildings, Schofield could distinguish a single tree, alone and isolated. 'That is *the* Lotus Tree.'

'But the lotus legend is surely only—a legend?'

'I could not say. I have often eaten the lotus-berry and my memory has not suffered. No, indeed'—his spasms merged into a chuckle—'you need a stronger potion for dreams than the lotus. Here, you know, we plant the lotus-tree for shade. It is like your English elm. But they say in Smyrna that he who seeks the shade of the Lotus on Pagos never leaves the city again. . . . Foolish, is it not?'

'I can imagine that it would need no enchantment to keep one

here.' Already he had half-surrendered to the city where an
incredible mission seemed less fantastic. Then suddenly he remembered Joan Perry's face and felt an autumn wind from the
Gloucestershire wolds. He added, in a hard, matter-of-fact voice:
'But I must get back as soon as I can.'

'You will no doubt find friends among the merchants of your
nation?'

'Yes.'

'They live, you know, very much to themselves in Frank Street.
It is the quarter over there.' He pointed to the extremity of the
shore, beyond the town proper, where landing-places and ware-
houses and little quays of wood and stone jutting into the water
indicated the houses and factories of the Europeans. Each nation
was distinguished by its flag, first the white and gold *fleurs-de-lys* of
France, then the blue, crossed with red and white, of Great Britain,
and, further on, the Dutch and the Genoese. 'But should you ever
tire of their company, young sir, you should visit my old friend
Ibrahim Paschazadé, the physician. He welcomes especially the
English, since he visited your country many years ago when our
Sultan sent an embassy to your King James. He is very old now, but
he likes to talk to the English and he speaks your tongue better
than I do.'

'How shall I find him?'

'Your merchants will know him; but his house is easy to find.'
He pointed again to the Hill. 'It is the top one on that side of the
slope—the nearest to the Lotus Tree.'

'I thank you,' said Schofield. 'If time serves I will certainly
visit him. If I might mention that you told me of him? Your
name . . .?'

'Achmed. That will be sufficient. He will know. But do not sit
under the Lotus Tree.' Another of his spasms seized the old man;
his head nodded furiously, though whether voluntatily or involuntarily, Schofield was at a loss to know. Then, with another soft
chuckle he glided away, leaving Schofield to wonder what might
lie behind the unexpected conversation till the shrill bustle of

preparations for landing dragged his thoughts to the practical matters of the moment.

'The Quarter,' Schofield soon discovered, was a town within a town, a civilization within a civilization, and, from its cosmopolitan and convivial air, was known as 'Petit Paris.' Among the merchants the French claimed—and were conceded—unquestioned precedence and, though English and Dutch were both spoken, French was the prevalent tongue as Italian was the *lingua franca* in the city itself. In another way, too, the French were distinguished from the other Europeans. Although everyone, when going abroad in the city or dealing with the Turkish authorities, wore the robes and pelisses of the Turks—more for safety than convenience—it was impossible to mistake a Frenchman. The English and the Dutch who, in addition to the clothes, cultivated the long mustachios of the natives, were usually to the eye indistinguishable from the Turks. But however Eastern his clothes, however exotic his mustachio, the Frenchman, by his gait, his gestures, his vivacity, betrayed his nationality.

In general magnificence, however, the palm went to the English. Their clothing, furniture, horses and houses were the finest in the Quarter—which meant 'in Smyrna'—and their feasts and hospitality had become legendary. Even the French admitted so much, and one of them had recently reported to his countrymen at home that 'one can add nothing to the magnificence of the feast nor to the quantity of wine drunk. They smash and break everything to do honour to those to whom they drink and the debauch is sometimes carried so far that, finding nothing more to break, they light a great fire and fling on it hats, wigs, coats, even shirts, after which these gentlemen are forced to remain in bed until other garments have been made for them.'

The feast with which the English travellers were welcomed on their arrival, however, though abundant and prolonged far into the morning, ran to no such extremities. It was even characterized by a certain sobriety, for there were too many questions to ask, greetings to deliver, gossip to exchange for any to wish to lose command of his wits.

He felt, in spite of Pentlow's courtesy and attention, somewhat isolated. The isolation went deeper than the mere circumstance of being a visitor to what, in effect, was a club. It was not only that he was unable to understand the references or, now and then, to translate the jargon. The cleavage was one of temperament and training: he was a soldier among merchants, a recluse among men who made a fetish of the gregarious virtues and to whom solitude was abhorrent. At a profounder level, they represented by their profession and outlook, the philosophy of life that he had repudiated.

On their part, they were aware that their guest, despite their efforts at courtesy, was aloof from any communication. He answered questions, but in such a way that his words were not a link in the conversation but an end of it. On so simple a matter as, for instance, the merits of Colchester oysters, he responded as if the topic were an insult to him. Schofield himself, indeed, was surprised at the impact which the very name of the town made on him, for here, sitting among wealthy young epicures, the unforgettable episodes at Colchester which had darkened his own youth suddenly intruded —the long, grim siege of Englishmen by Englishmen; the skirmishes and that attempted sortie when it was sword for sword and, on horseback, he had followed his brother into mid-stream where neither could fight except with words; the final storm and the vengeance of the victors. It was this past—the danger and action of his soldier's life—even more than the mission on which he had come and which was, by its nature, conducive to silence that made him increasingly uncomfortable. He was inordinately relieved when Pentlow suggested they should leave at the comparatively early hour of two in the morning.

Pentlow, as one of the few married men among the merchants, was allowed to go without more than a formal protest. He had, in fact, established this right within a week of his wedding, when his young wife, a Greek, defied tradition, European and masculine, and came to fetch him. Pentlow, it was said, had beaten her soundly afterwards, and a similar intrusion had never occurred since; but it was tacitly understood that when he left a gathering, he was not pressed too vehemently to stay nor was his going regarded as a signal for a general dispersal. It was, in fact, known to those who remained as 'taking Greek leave.'

Pentlow's house was built round the three sides of a courtyard. The ground floor, after the manner of a merchant's residence was used as a warehouse and, as they entered, Schofield was almost overpowered by the atmosphere, intoxicatingly heavy with the scent of rare perfumes and spices. But upstairs, in the living quarters, were spacious rooms opening out on to long galleries, which formed the balustraded roofs of terraces below, and were, like them, open to the cool night air.

Pentlow took Schofield immediately to his room, wished him rest and comfort, and left him abruptly with: 'We will talk of your errand to-morrow; but I promise you that all that can be done will be, if that will aid your sleep.'

Yet in spite of his tiredness and the wine he had drunk, he did not sleep well. He was troubled by a recurring dream of Joan Perry hanged on a lotus tree.

CHAPTER XI

Father Gabriel

P ENTLOW WAS AS GOOD AS HIS WORD. NOT ONLY DID HE OFFER Schofield the hospitality of his house for as long as he should require it and put at his disposal what credit he needed, but he introduced him to those he knew who might be of use.

'I see from our friend's letter,' he said, 'that you are interested in the past of our Company and the antiquities of Smyrna. I fear I can tell you little of either. But old Nicholas Leate knows as much as anyone about one and young Richard Staper about the other. Though before you ask questions I think it would be well if you gained the good-will of all of us by answering some.'

'I am afraid the matter is private——'

'Not about your matter,' interrupted Pentlow. 'No one will be curious about that, I assure you. We shall respect your privacy in it absolutely.'

'What then?'

'The way things go in England. Some of us fear it may be a matter of life and death for us here.'

In answer to Schofield's frankly puzzled expression, Pentlow told him in brief outline the events which were now the chief, if not the only topic, of discussion among the English merchants in Smyrna.

During the Commonwealth, the exiled Charles II had appointed Sir Henry Hyde as his Ambassador to the Sultan, but when he arrived Sir Thomas Bendish, who had held the post for some years, refused to recognize him. The Vizier supported Bendish and Hyde was ordered to leave Constantinople. He retired to Smyrna, placed himself under the protection of the French (whose King was giving aid and hospitality to the unfortunate Stuarts) and from the comparative safety of a French ship sent a missive to the English in Smyrna ordering them to render him obedience as the King's rightful representative.

The Smyrna merchants replied in a letter which had been composed with some care after a prolonged but cheerful meeting at the house of the Consul: 'Whereas your impudency is such as to make the port of Smyrna the stage to shout more of your mountebank delusions further to deceive our nation to summon us to your obedience and to belch out lies and Rabshakeh * language against our Ambassador the Rt. Hon. Sir Thomas Bendish and ourselves so much to the dishonour of the King and nation. Know this: that we scorn you and your summons and advise you speedily to depart with your lies (as you ought) else we shall by justice of the Porte put you aboard an English ship by which means, if you be carried whither you desire not, thank your foul mouth; and take this for a warning and answer to your scurrilous paper or what else you call it.'

They then proceeded to carry out their threats. Hyde was seized and sent back to England where, on the sole evidence of papers from Smyrna accusing him of 'mischievous and traitrous proceedings by which much damage was sustained to the Turkey trade and the Commonwealth,' he was tried, condemned and beheaded.

Now that King Charles had come into his own again and sent Winchilsea out to supersede Bendish would he take vengeance on Smyrna for its treatment of Hyde? To make matters worse they had heard that, six months after Hyde's execution, his widow had hidden safely for many days in their house near Salisbury, the young King when, a fugitive after the battle of Worcester, he was making his way to the coast and France.

Schofield would understand the apprehension at present rife among the merchants. What did he think? Had he seen Winchilsea on the voyage and had any conversation with him which might

* See 2 Kings xviii.

throw light on his attitude? Above all, what was the temper of the new government in England?

Schofield protested that, as far as his knowledge of politics was concerned, he was considerably more ignorant in Yorkshire than they seemed to be in Smyrna. As for Hyde, he had not even heard his name. He had spoken to Winchilsea only once on the voyage on an occasion of formality. He had thought him an affable enough man and—if they could extract any comfort from the diplomatic remark—he had then said that his one desire was to benefit all his countrymen of whatever quality.

None of the merchants believed that Schofield was as ignorant of affairs in England as he pretended, though they applauded his caution.

'But you can speak quite freely, sir. You are among friends here. We shall not remember anything you say, should the wheel of fortune turn once more and render it inconvenient.'

'If I could tell you anything, I assure you that I would.'

'Surely,' objected Pentlow, 'as you came through London, you must have gleaned something of what was afoot?'

'I was there for less than a full day. It would be foolish to form a judgment on so short an impression.'

'You could tell us, nevertheless.'

So Schofield told them of the vengeance that had been taken on the 'regicides.' The impression was considerable. For the next day or two everybody was disclaiming having had any hand in the proceedings against Sir Henry Hyde or protesting that any aid they might have given in the composition of the unfortunate letter was prompted by excess of wine. Nicholas Leate reassured them. 'We've nothing to fear,' he said, speaking from the accumulated wisdom of fifty years experience, 'so long as we see that the King gets his dues from us, with, perhaps, a little excess for a year or two. James, Charles, Noll or young Charles—it's all one to us. Politics—that's a different matter. But trade's trade.'

Eventually they decided to put up a larger flag on a higher flagpole on the official landing-stage, even though this would certainly irritate the French, who were peculiarly sensitive to such details of precedence.

As for Schofield, he reflected on the vast ignorances which separated each little world from the others. The ingenuous surprise of the merchants that he should never have heard of Sir Henry Hyde was a measure of their self-centred engrossment in theirs; at least he would have not made the mistake of supposing that they would ever have heard of Joan Perry who dominated his. To find a clue, he admitted, he would have to desert his circle for theirs—to come to the lowly by means of the great. The curiosity of such interactions added a savour to the mere observance of human relationships; and at least these two were linked by a unifying fear of death. . . .

His reflections might have taken even a fantastic turn had he known that, at that moment, he was pitted against Sir Henry Hyde's younger brother. In the house near Salisbury, where King Charles had been hidden in the 'priest's chamber,' Sir Robert Hyde, whose home it now was, had just received intimation that he was to preside at the Spring Assizes at Gloucester and that it was hoped that he would find it possible to re-try a case which had escaped the net of justice in the autumn—the case of some murderous peasants, John, Richard and Joan Perry.

But he did not know that till long after, when things were past mending. At the moment, his only possible clue was Sir Baptist Hicks.

Nicholas Leate was the 'father' of the English factors in Smyrna. Instead of following the usual course of making a fortune while young and returning to England to live on it, he had so fallen under the spell of the city that he could not bring himself to leave. Though he had long retired from active work, he remained in the 'Quarter,' himself an oracle among the merchants of all nationalities and his opulent house by the gate of Frank Street a Mecca for hospitality, advice and reminiscence.

Yes, he remembered little Baptist Hicks very well, though he couldn't put a date to the year. Not that he'd had much to do with him; for one thing, his own line had been currants, chiefly, while Hicks was a mercer and only interested in silks; for another, he didn't care much for Hicks's sort. He'd always tried to keep clear of that kind of dishonesty. Not that he was giving himself airs and not that many merchants didn't consider it merely a legitimate part of trade, but he preferred to call it by its right name—dishonesty. What was it? The way certain merchants in England had of purchasing direct from individual factors instead of through the Company, so that the Company was robbed of its dues and the factor pocketed whatever commission the merchant cared to give him. Not that Hicks gave much—or so he'd heard. He was mean, as well. But why rake up the past? Hicks was dead now and gone to judgment. And, to be just, he hadn't been the worst offender, by any means. Was there anything else that Schofield would like to know about those early days? The great controversy about the levy for fighting pirates, for example? There were some interesting points about that, which he believed that no one but himself now knew.

Schofield listened as politely as his complete lack of interest allowed and then led the conversation firmly back to Baptist Hicks. Was there anyone else who would remember him? Nicholas Leate thought not. The silk merchants were now all very young men— mere boys in their twenties. Which reminded him that he had played the leading part in sending the famous manifesto to the Company asking them to send no more factors till they were of the age of twenty-two or upwards or at least had attained some settledness in judgment and manners. Actually he himself had been only twenty when he came out, but now he looked back on it he was surprised how staid and conscientious he had been even at that wild age. But the modern young man . . .

Schofield sympathized, but persisted. Had Hicks ever sent out any servants or stewards? Did the name of Harrison strike any chord of memory? Might he have been in Smyrna with Hicks? Or for him?

Nicholas Leate was extremely sorry, but he was afraid he knew nothing of that. There was, certainly, a Harrison, but he had nothing to do with Hicks. His name was Robert and he dealt in gums, spices and herbs—rather like Pentlow to-day. Maces and mastick, storax and scamony, turmerick and turbith—these were his wares. A curious young man, rather foppish, who used to insist that he chose that particular line because he liked the names. Certainly he had nothing to do with Hicks. Could Schofield see him? Alas, no! He had died of the plague twenty years ago or more, and was buried in the European cemetery at the other end of Smyrna. In a way his death was his own fault, since he had been too careless about sprinkling his letters with vinegar and smoking them with sulphur before opening them. A most important precaution, always. Sulphur *and* vinegar—both. One wasn't enough for real safety. Nicholas Leate hoped that Schofield would remember that and not impetuously think that vinegar was enough, like poor Bob Harrison. Incidentally, if he happened to visit the cemetery, he'd see his grave. The merchants had erected an elaborately carved stone and chosen a text they thought he would have liked: 'Let my prayer be set forth in Thy sight like the incense.' Of course, there were some amusing stories about Harrison, but they were only scandal; and it was hardly fair now he was dead—*de mortuis nil nisi bonum*—and, anyhow, he certainly had no connection whatever with little Hicks. . . . Old Nicholas was so disappointed that he could give no help. . . . He would have liked to be of service to any Englishman, especially so charming and courteous a young man as Schofield. . . . If there was any other matter? In any case, he must call again whenever he wished and treat the house as his own. . . .

Richard Staper was a studious young merchant of twenty-seven with a passion, fostered during his Oxford days, for classical antiquities. Though he was on excellent terms with his fellow-merchants, could drink his own generation of them under the table and was seldom absent from the major convivial gatherings, he did not share the other amusements of their leisure. He neither gambled at cards in the evenings nor, at the week-ends, hawked and hunted in the surrounding country—the English pack of hounds at Smyrna was a prodigious mystery to the Turks—but spent his time in exploring most of the precious remains of the ancient civilization of the place and recording his discoveries in a journal conspicuous for its exquisite calligraphy.

A Silver Bowl? No, he had not heard of one in any particular connection with Smyrna, though he was quite willing to believe that such a talisman existed. Possibly to do with the Nemeseis and their worship. He had not yet gone into that thoroughly. At the moment he was interested mainly in what evidence there was that Smyrna was the birthplace of Homer. Personally he believed that it was. Pindar, of course, as Schofield would know, described him as a Smyrnæan; and Critias, in describing his father as a river, meant, of course, the Sacred Meles, the river of Smyrna. Aristotle had elucidated that by his story that Homer's mother gave birth to him on the banks of the Meles and immediately died. Staper himself was trying to solve the matter by tracing internal references in the Homeric epics to the countryside round the Gulf of Smyrna. Yes, there were quite a number of them—'swirling Hermos' and 'fish-stored Hyllos,' 'snowy Tmolos' and 'lovely Meionia,' the 'rock domain of Hyde' and the 'Gygaian Lake,' and many others. He had managed to visit them all and reconstruct Homer's vision. He had little doubt—though, of course. he could not actually prove it—that Smyrna was justified in her claim to the greatest of poets. . . . But he feared he was wearying Schofield with his hobby. . . . It was a silver bowl he wanted, after all, not a dissertation on Homer. . . . If he ever came across anything that seemed to lead to the track of it, he would let him know at once. The most fascinating thing about his study was its unexpectedness. You never knew what you would find or where it would lead you. . . .

Schofield asked if there were anyone else in the Quarter with similar interests.

'None of our countrymen I fear; but there is a French Capuchin, Père Gabriel, who has much curious knowledge. In fact, it was he who suggested to me the first thing I did here—to find where the famous Golden Street once ran. Aristides and Philostratos, you know, both mention it. It was known as 'the necklace of Smyrna.' But I hadn't much success with that. It would have meant working in the city itself and that's too dangerous, even if the Turks allowed it.'

'This Père Gabriel—do you think it would be possible for me to meet him?'

'Certainly. I'm sure he would be delighted. . . . You are not, by the way, a Papist?'

'No,' said Schofield. 'Would that make any difference?'

'Not the least,' laughed Staper. 'I am, incidentally; which is how I got to know him. We have no English priest here, you see; only the Protestant chaplain; so we Catholics have to use the French for our duties. But I assure you you need have no fear of your welcome. Why not let me take you with me when I go to visit him on Thursday?'

Immediately, on their first meeting, Schofield was drawn to Father Gabriel, a rotund little friar with, after the manner of his Order, an enormous, untrimmed beard; and he was grateful for the Capuchin's invitation to visit him, with or without Staper, when-ever he felt inclined. Taking him at his word, he went back on the following day and discovered to his surprise that Father Gabriel was expecting him.

'I thought you would come, my son, about this Silver Bowl of yours.'

'I will not trouble you with that again, Father, since you said yesterday that you knew nothing of it.'

'Yesterday we were not alone and what I said was that I could tell you nothing of it. There is a difference. I could not speak before that excellent young Staper. He has the simple mind of a careful scholar and it would not be right to disturb him by suggesting that there are other more important orders of knowledge. The Silver Bowl, I judge, belongs to such an order.'

'Then you do know about it?'

'I know that it is reputed to belong to one line of the Quest for the Mysteries and that it is said to have been stolen from Smyrna.'

'The quest for the mysteries? What should you know of these things, Father? Surely you, of all men, do not dabble in this—devil's knowledge?' Schofield was surprised at his own vehemence. It was as if he had been suddenly betrayed and the smiling little priest before him, with his glowing red cheeks and strangely innocent eyes, was indeed one of those sinister villainous Papists against whom he had been warned in his Protestant youth. To speak of these things or to assume them in conversation with Joseph, with 'My lady,' with the old courtier; to smell the air of them at Seven Wells; to feel them, in some measure, in his mother's blood in him—these he accepted; but it was only at this moment when he faced them in what might be called a representative of the 'other side' that he realised how strong his revulsion had become. And, though this he did not admit, his fear.

'Devil's work?' said the Capuchin. 'Sit down, my son. There is no need to run away so hastily. You do not escape the devil that way. No, I would not have anything to do with devil's work.' He crossed himself. 'May God keep me ever from the black gulf and bring me to salvation.'

'But surely,' said Schofield, a little reassured and more than a little curious, 'you would say that anything to do with such quests and mysteries is the work of the Devil.'

'How could I say anything so absurd? God Who is Wisdom has given man a mind to use for His glory—and how better can you be led to adore the Creator than by contemplating the marvel of His Creation? There are some who are content to find that wonder in the ways of men and in the secrets of the hearts and the working of God in them; but there are others who have natures which drive them to undertake the Great Work.'

'What great work?'

'The quest for the secret of the Philosopher's Stone—the secret of alchemy.'

'But that is a mere crazy quest for gold.'

'I see you lack understanding, my son, and where you do not understand you should not speak. It is true that everywhere there are those who play Judas and sell God for coin. We know their condemnation. But there are the faithful also.'

'I accept your reproof, Father. I am, as you say, in ignorance of this matter. But I assure you that I spoke in honesty. I did not think that your Church could countenance such things.'

'I am surprised you did not know that one of the most famous adepts was a Friar of my Order—and an Englishman: Roger Bacon. And the greatest of all, Father Basilius, was a Benedictine. All their work—and the work of countless others—was done in the Name of the Most Holy Trinity.'

And, in reply to Schofield's request for further enlightenment, Father Gabriel explained the underlying assumptions of the Great Work—the doctrine of the Unity of All Things, so that all bodies possess a common basis in the *prima materia;* the doctrine of the Two Contraries which, by their union, produce new life through a manner of death, so that, as male and female are in the animal creation, sulphur and mercury are held to be in the mineral; the existence of the Great Pattern, so that the interaction of elements in any one sphere had their correspondences in the others and their relation to the whole and the microcosm reflected the macrocosm—planets, metals, colours, beasts, parts of the human body and other more secret series being thus connected in a way not understood by the casual observer but clear enough to the initiate; the bearing of all pagan knowledge and all ancient lore on the meaning and elucidation of the central matter, so that the myths of India and China, of the Jews and the Greeks and the Romans were but as a manner of speech which, like the parables of Christ, conveyed one thing to the crowds and another to the disciples ;* then, crowning this natural knowledge to which all peoples and creeds were heirs if they took the trouble to examine their inheritance, was added an interpretative knowledge in the light of that supernaturally revealed Truth of which the Church was the guardian.

* Luke viii. 10.

'I am myself no alchemist and so cannot tell you of the way in which the one mode of truth illumines the other, but you should remember that our Christian adepts are wont to start their work with the prayer: 'O Unity in the Substance and Trinity in the Godhead, as Thou didst make all things out of the one chaos, so let me be skilled to evolve our microcosm out of one substance in its three aspects.' And they see the Stone as the earthly antitype of Christ, the Heavenly Corner-Stone.'

'Then you would say this magic quest is a thing to be commended?'

'I did not say that, my son. As I have already twice observed, your mind lacks exactitude. In itself the Quest is neither good nor evil. It is the purpose for which the knowledge is used which justifies or condemns it. What I said was that the Church does not forbid the Quest to her sons, since it can be and has been undertaken for the glory of God. On the other hand, it may be undertaken for quite other purposes. As you yourself said, it can be used by men to get power and wealth for themselves—or for the Devil's ends. But you should not call it magic.'

'I will not expose the inexactitude of my mind again, Father; but I should like to know how, if this can be a matter of religion, religion differs from magic.'

'As Heaven differs from Hell. Magic is not the means used, but the end for which they are used. The process is the same—the search for knowledge of the secrets which God has left for us to find in the world. In religion, you use that knowledge so that you may better conform yourself to God's purpose. In magic, you use it to try to make yourself a god and impose your own will and purpose on your fellows. That, as I said, is the difference between Heaven and Hell.'

'But suppose this knowledge—this power—were discovered by infidels?'

'I would not be so bold as to predict the outcome, but it is my opinion that the world would be destroyed by it. Sometimes I have fancied that that is how the world will be destroyed before the Last

Judgment. You see, my son, if the Stone, with its perfect power of transmutation, fell into the hands of those of a devilish complexion, it would be used not to regenerate but to destroy mankind. For destruction is the nature of devils.'

'Now, Father, may I challenge your exactitude? What meaning do you assign to "devilish"?'

'The meaning, my son, Saint Augustine gave to it—for it includes those in the spirit-world and those who have their natures on earth—men who have knowledge but lack a love of God. Knowledge without Charity. A cold, heretic, power-loving mind. They are the real allies on earth of the diabolic order, not the poor mistaken visionaries who, in their own way are humble before their distorted image of the Creator.' Father Gabriel smiled, half apologetically. 'You see, before I came to Smyrna, my Order sent me to Africa for some years of missions. I hope I saved some souls. I know that I learnt much for the good of mine.'

'I think I begin to understand a little, Father.'

'Do you, my son?'

'A discrimination of categories, at least.'

'That is, perhaps, the beginning of earthly wisdom.'

'Though I do not quite see the place of the Silver Bowl.'

'It belongs to the order of pagan knowledge only. As such, it is neutral—neither good nor evil. But I believe it has been so used for evil purposes through so many centuries, that evil clings to it as if it were embedded in the silver. Do not touch it, my son.'

'Before I do that, I should have to find it. And I do not know where to look.'

'You should thank God for that ignorance.'

'But Father, you said that it was the purpose which justified or condemned a quest. And my purpose is, I think, good. It is—or it may be—to save an old woman's life.'

'Yes?' The quiet tone invited his confidence.

'May I put the case to you?'

'Of course. And I shall treat anything you say as *sub sigillo*.'

With this assurance that his story would be treated with the inviolable secrecy of the confessional, Schofield threw his usual discretion to the winds and told Father Gabriel, in brief outline, the circumstances as far as he knew them.

For some moments the little priest did not speak. Then, as if every word had been weighed beforehand in his mind, he said: 'My son, your journey was permissible, since your motives were honest and not devoid of charity; but I think you can do no good by your interference in such a matter, even if you are able to interfere. If by chance you should stumble on the secret, you would yourself be in danger, since you have neither knowledge of their ways nor the strength of our Faith.'

'But I do not care about myself.'

'Perhaps not. But you will understand that I do. I cannot be asked to judge people or legislate for circumstances I do not know. What duty I have in this matter is to you.'

'Then what do you advise me to do?'

'Take the next boat home to England.'

CHAPTER XII

Ibrahim Paschazadé

SCHOFIELD COULD NOT BRING HIMSELF TO FOLLOW FATHER Gabriel's advice. He had that peculiarly English trait of being afraid of appearing afraid. The matter, as it presented itself to him on reflection was, without any nice discrimination of categories, merely one of courage or cowardice. So he stayed. But by that action he conceived himself cut off from further visits to the Capuchin—though, in fact, Father Gabriel would have welcomed him—and found himself increasingly restless in the narrowness of the Quarter. As is the way in a small English colony in a foreign land, the merchants were engrossed in their own affairs. Though the Hyde case still made incursions into their conversation, it was confined mainly to technical aspects of their business and to topics of scandalous interest. They talked interminably about the fluctuating prices of their wares and the incompetence of the Consul in protecting their interests; about the menace of 'interlopers' who undercut prices and evaded the Company's dues; about Arnold White, who continued unconcernedly to export potash in spite of Bendish's repeated prohibitions and whether or not Winchilsea would try to stop him or be successful if he tried; about the latest move in the long campaign of reciprocal slander between Broadgate, the puritanical chaplain, and Pickering, the notoriously dissolute doctor.

Schofield's boredom with this little world was only one strand of his dissatisfaction. Reinforcing it was the reflection that, for all the good he was doing, he might just as well have gone home. His almost superstitious expectation that he would stumble on some clue, discover in conversation some lead, was daily disappointed. At last he determined that he must investigate the city itself. How or for what he did not know.

When he told Pentlow of his purpose, the merchant was aghast. 'The only thing you will discover, my friend, is St. Veneranda.'

'And who is she?'

'It's the Christian burial-ground,' said Pentlow and proceeded to draw a gloomy, though accurate, picture of the perils which awaited Christians who ventured into the city.

Not only was it essential to be accompanied everywhere by a Janissary, but—since, by definition, a Janissary was a European who in childhood had been surrendered as tribute and brought up a Turk—they were not always to be trusted to defend a Christian. There was no predictability in renegade blood, even though the apostasy had been made involuntarily and in infancy.

On the other hand, though there were certain merchants whose popularity and long residence made them reasonably secure on business journeys, for anyone like Schofield to go into Smyrna without a guard was to risk being insulted, if not actually pelted and beaten, in the streets. He might even be kidnapped and sold as a slave. The Turks had a species of press-gangs for this purpose which made the English press-gangs for the navy a nursery-game by comparison.

'And if you disappeared,' said Pentlow, 'I assure you that we should not be able to find you again.'

'But surely they would respect an English gentleman?'

Pentlow burst out laughing. 'Respect? My dear Schofield, the Turks call all of us "hogs"; the Janissaries who go about with us are known as "swineherds"; and the meanest and dirtiest Mohammedan beggar considers himself superior to an English lord.'

'But cannot our Ambassador protect us? When I spoke to Lord Winchilsea on the voyage, he said he would do everything in his power for the English.'

'The poor man is now probably finding out exactly what his power is. When Bendish visited us once—you know his daughter's married to one of our merchants; they're away at the moment visiting him in Constantinople—he told us what an audience with the Sultan was like. It was one long insult which started by being left for two hours on a bench in the courtyard of the Seraglio till it should please the Grand Vizier to deign to notice him and it ended by his being introduced to the Grand Turk as 'the naked and hungry barbarian who had ventured to rub his brow upon the Sublime Porte.' If that's how they treat an Ambassador, you can imagine what chance you or I would have.'

'But I understood there were law courts here.'

Pentlow patiently explained that they had no protection whatever from the courts, since Christian evidence was not allowed against a Moslem and few Moslems had any compunction about bearing false witness against an 'infidel' Christian. Even if a Christian was killed, there was no redress since the murderers invariably protested that he had blasphemed against the Prophet, so that the dead man's relatives actually had to pay a fine on that account.

'You have no idea how dangerous it is. There was a case not long ago when a visitor from England like yourself was watching a rope-dance. He took out his watch to time it. Unfortunately the rope broke and the crowd accused him of causing it by enchantment because they saw him muttering over his watch. Luckily for him, it was only just outside the gate of our Street, so he was able to save his life with his heels.'

'I find it hard to believe,' said Schofield, 'that any people can be so intolerant, even infidel Turks. There must be men of learning and courtesy among them.'

'Of course,' said Pentlow, 'but you will not find them in the streets here—any more than you would in London. And as for justice, what justice would a Turk get in our law-courts at home? Of course, I admit that here they're superstitious as well. When they have one of their great festivals, especially the Bairam—that's their parody of our Easter after the fast of Lent, which they call Ramadan—it's absolutely forbidden for anyone to leave the Quarter. They'd never get back alive.'

'You're really telling me I'm a prisoner in the Quarter?'

'By no means. You have complete freedom to come and go as you wish. I'm only warning you that it is safer not to go alone and wiser not to go at all, unless you have to.'

'But there would be no danger in visiting a Turk?' Schofield had suddenly remembered his conversation with the Ophiunjé and the existence of the English-loving physician, Ibrahim.

'But you don't know any Turks, surely?' Pentlow asked in surprise.

'No. But a passenger on the *Plymouth* told me of an old Turkish doctor, Ibrahim—Paschazadé, I think the name was, or something like that—who welcomes visitors from England.'

'Old Ibrahim! So you've heard of him. Yes, of course. I don't know him myself, but many of our people do. Paul Bayning's a friend of his. Ibrahim, incidentally, does a good deal of cotton growing on a plantation he owns about six miles away and Bayning takes most of his supplies. That's their link with each other. You haven't met Bayning yet, have you?'

'Not except for a word or two during those first days when you introduced me to them all; but I think I know which he is. Tall, dark, with a slight scar on his cheek?'

'Yes, that's Paul. We'll call on him to-night and ask him to take you up to Ibrahim on his next visit. You'll be safe enough that way, and you can get into Smyrna without getting on my conscience.'

So it was that two days later Schofield found himself sitting at table as the guest of Ibrahim Paschazadé in his house high on the Hill. He felt strained and awkward in his Turkish clothes which, in spite of their magnificence, were less than a perfect fit. Pentlow and Bayning had decided that he must make a suitable impression on his host. There was no time for clothes to be made; Pentlow's formal Turkish dress was far too small and Bayning needed his own to wear himself, so they had asked Nicholas Leate to lend one of the outfits he kept for such a purpose. Unfortunately the one which fitted Schofield best had been used by a previous guest about six months earlier. There was no doubt that Ibrahim would have recognized it—which would have been most unseemly—and Schofield had to be content with one slightly too large for him.

The trousers, vivid scarlet interwoven with blue stripes and gathered into pleats at the calf with a golden cord, were manageable; but his upper garments hung loosely on him and the *usth-kurbi*—the superbly embroidered gala-coat, with a formalized palm-pattern worked in gold on the red velvet trimmed with sable—seemed to him ridiculously large. Its long empty sleeves, hanging from the shoulders, kept flapping in his way.

'What am I supposed to do with these?' he asked.

'If you felt so disposed, you could fill them with delicacies from your dinner and bring them back to my wife,' said Pentlow.

Schofield decided that his uxoriousness had overstepped the bounds of permitted absurdity and winked at Bayning.

'It has been done,' said Bayning solemnly. 'There's a famous occasion when a *hoja*—a schoolmaster—filled his sleeve for his family but found on leaving that what he thought was his sleeve was his neighbour's. On the whole, I don't advise you to try it.'

'You need have no fear,' said Schofield. 'All I hope is that I get through dinner without disgracing you.'

They coached him as far as they could and made him practice sitting cross-legged on the floor, eating a variety of dishes with the aid of a single long-handled spoon; but in spite of the rehearsal he felt both ridiculous and uncomfortable when seated thus, at Ibrahim's right hand, at the leather tablecloth in the middle of the exquisite carpet, at the dinner itself.

Ibrahim was himself a sufficiently disconcerting figure. He was eighty-five, just over six feet, with snow-white moustache and long pointed beard. His eyes, deep-sunk in cavernous sockets, fixed with a penetrating stare whoever he talked to, yet the dominant impression of the lined face was one of grave courtesy. He spoke English well enough to dispense with the presence of an interpreter; and listened with an attentiveness which never interrupted. He continually smiled, but no one had ever seen him laugh. His dress of green and yellow was simpler than either Schofield's or Bayning's yet it seemed—and not only on account of the air with which he wore it—to make theirs appear cheap, even a little tawdry, by comparison.

The conversation at first was desultory and addressed mainly to Bayning; but he made every effort to put Schofield completely at his ease. When he saw him looking at the enormous silver salver on a pedestal in the centre of the 'table,' on which his servants laid the dishes one by one, surrounding them with a circle of little platters of spices and condiments, he referred to 'our strange Eastern way of eating' in a tone which was almost depreciatory. He explained that the greenish hue of the rough porcelain of which the dishes were made was chosen because it was reputed to have the property of neutralizing any poison which might inadvertently have affected the food; but added that it was a foolish superstition at which the English would no doubt with justice laugh. 'Green,' he said, 'is most highly esteemed with us. You must pardon it.'

Schofield was charmed, not least by the reflection that here was the courteous, affable, intelligent Turk who, he was sure, in spite of Pentlow's earnest pessimism, was the truer mirror of this Eastern civilization. As the dinner proceeded, with its dishes of fish and game and meat, its risottos and pilaffs so subtly flavoured, its savouries, sweets and ices, washed down with draughts of sweet sherbet of many varieties, he forgot his awkwardness and his insularity and his undercurrent of apprehension and mellowed into a guest worthy of his host.

When Ibrahim was satisfied that he was at his ease, he led the conversation to England and Schofield found himself describing, with a facility which surprised himself, the countryside near Bolton.

'I never went so far to the North when I was in England,' said Ibrahim, 'and now you make me sorry for it.'

Prompted by Bayning, he then proceeded to tell Schofield of his travels in England when he was a young man of thirty-two and had accompanied Mustapha, the first Turkish envoy to the Court of King James.

'We could not stay all the time in London and your King was on his travels round the country. It was three months before we could see him. So we, too, went on travels round the country.'

'What did you like best?'

'A little island in the marshes with a great church called Crowland. I see by your face you think it a strange place to go.'

'I fear I've never visited it myself.'

'And to yourself you ask why a Turk should visit it.'

He proceeded to explain that they had all been interested when they had heard that the greatness of Crowland began under the Abbot Turketyl. It was so strange a name that they thought he must have some connection with their own race. No one could tell them anything about him, except that he was reputed to be a Dane, who was a convert to Christianity, and a relation of other great churchmen of his day.

'We found nothing out but Crowland itself. If I ever went back to England, it is to Crowland I should go.'

'If you speak so highly of it, I will visit it as soon as I get back,' said Schofield.

'There are perhaps other places you could tell me of, like your Bolton, so that I could see them through your eyes?'

This gave Schofield the opening he wanted. He described in detail Chipping Campden, laying particular stress on the Eastern note in Hicks's building which had made so deep a first impression on him.

'It may be, he hazarded, that you have met Sir Baptist Hicks. I understand that many years ago he was in Smyrna and one of our merchants remembers him.'

Ibrahim wrinkled his brows in thought, as if trying to conjure Hicks out of the past. But he shook his head. 'No. I did not meet him. Baptist Hicks! It is a strange name, Baptist. I should not forget it if I had known it.'

He went on to assure Schofield of his interest in and affection for the English—an attitude which he already made clear enough to admit of no doubt—and explained how he made it a rule to buy

English slaves in the slave-market whenever he could, so that they might be sure of kindly treatment and eventual liberation. 'Some of my countrymen are not very good to them,' he smiled.

Since the lot of Christian slaves in Turkey—of which there were tens of thousands—was the horror and scandal of Christendom, both Bayning and Schofield allowed this remark to pass in silence. 'I do not ask much of them,' Ibrahim continued, 'except that they talk to me in their language. That is why I can talk to you. As a rule they like to help me in the laboratory where I make my medicines.'

'Have you any now?'

'No. No Englishmen but Boll, who is standing over there in charge of our repast. Do not fear. He cannot hear. Poor Boll is deaf and dumb, but he has been here so long that he will not leave me, and I think he would not be happy anywhere else.'

And, as Schofield threw a covert glance at the impassive figure of the slave, whom he had assumed was a Turk in spite of his complexion, Ibrahim told him how, years ago, he had been kidnapped in England, sold to a Turkish slave-trader for seven pounds and eventually offered for sale in the market at Smyrna.

'He wrote down that he had some skill in physic, so I decided it would be as good for me as for him if I bought him. That is thirty years ago or more. He must be about seventy now.'

'Why do you call him Boll?' asked Bayning. 'Is that his English name?'

'I trust him to keep a precious bowl I use in some of my experiments in my laboratory. It is like that one he is holding now—only it is of a more rare quality.'

This time Schofield made no attempt to disguise his glance. As he looked intently at the slave, he noticed his fingers close tightly round a silver bowl.

CHAPTER XIII

★

The Lotus Tree

IT WAS ABSURD, OF COURSE. THE MATTER WAS BECOMING AN obsession. There must be hundreds, if not thousands, of silver bowls in Smyrna like the one the slave was holding. This coincidence had nothing to do with his quest, and that he allowed himself to imagine that it had was due merely to his long disappointment. Or was the sherbet less innocuous than it had seemed, so that he was imagining things which belonged to the world of dreams and fantasy? So part of his practical mind argued. But the other part insisted that there were at least two factors which lessened the absurdity of his suspicion—Ibrahim's connection with England and his reference to a precious silver bowl which he used in his laboratory. What were the 'experiments' of the old physician? Alchemy? And had he been telling the truth when he denied any knowledge of Hicks?

Schofield was not sorry that, at this point, Bayning turned the conversation back to more general topics. Bayning could never trust himself to speak for long, even with Ibrahim who was so kindly and enlightened, on the subject of the Turkish enslavement of Christians. He feared that his affable merchant's mask would be shattered and his own face—that of one who had been a soldier and was only half-heartedly a trader, of one who had gained the reputation of extreme friendliness to the Turks but in his heart hated them—would be seen plainly. Those who knew him best would have seen and recognized the stress under which he was labouring. The scar on his cheek showed white against the rising flush of involuntary anger. But neither Ibrahim nor Schofield knew or noticed it. The Turk politely followed his direction of the conversation and discussed the prospects of his next cotton crop, and Schofield fell silent, grateful for this permission to withdraw from the talk so that he might be able to think of some way of learning more of what he wanted to know.

The discourtesy—and even, possibly, the danger—of a direct lead was out of the question. He dismissed the idea of mentioning Father Gabriel, lest this should savour too much of that approach. The two men might have in common a territory of knowledge of which it was better to assume ignorance. Eventually he decided on Achmed, to whom he had so far needed to make no reference, since the introduction to Ibrahim had been otherwise effected.

Ibrahim showed an immediate, if detached, interest. 'A strange man! I once knew him well, but since he became an opium-taker I see him very little.' He embarked on a disquisition on the curious properties of the drug and told them that he himself had a patient who was an addict. He was about sixty years old, and when he woke in the morning he had not even the strength to raise himself in his bed, but after he had taken a little dose—about half a nut or more— he had enough vigour to do anything. It was for this effect, rather than for its property of inducing dreams, that the poppy was, possibly, to be recommended to some natures.

'Achmed said one thing which interested me,' said Schofield. 'He said that I was to beware of sitting under the lotus tree on Pagos or I should never leave Smyrna. Have you heard of that story?'

'Not I,' said Bayning, 'but then I am not the man who would think of sitting under a lotus tree.'

'I have not heard of the saying either,' said Ibrahim, smiling. 'I think it must have been one of poor Achmed's fancies.'

'The lotus is said to have magic properties, though, is it not?' asked Schofield.

The physician allowed himself the ghost of a frown. 'We Turks do not believe in that kind of magic,' he said. 'It is too like witchcraft—and that is an abomination to us. If we find any who practice it, we sew them in a sack and throw them into the sea. But,' he continued, charmingly, 'there is certainly a famous lotus on Pagos. It is very old and you can see it from my garden. We will look at it when we have finished our meal if it pleases you.'

From the garden, under the shade of the cypresses, they looked up the hill towards its crown of ruined buildings. A worn pathway ran almost from the house to the old castle and to the right of it, directly under the central archway, stood the great lotus, easily distinguishable from the other trees and shrubs—short, stunted oaks and *agnus castus*—which, here and there, broke the uneven expanse of grass and red-grey rock.

Bayning, who had spent many hours in the Turk's garden and was accustomed to the view, murmured politely that it was 'very interesting,' but Schofield's suggestion that they should actually climb to the tree prompted him to remember that he had much work connected with his business awaiting him and that it was time they returned to Frank Street.

'You might ask Staper to take you up to it one Saturday'—no one n the Quarter ever thought of working on Saturday—'and he could explain the ruins as well.'

Ibrahim intervened. Since it was so near and Schofield, unlike Bayning, had no business to attend to, why did he not stay and make use of this opportunity to visit the tree, if he wished to?

'There's the question of his getting back to the Quarter,' said Bayning.

'I could hardly lose my way,' protested Schofield. 'The street merely runs straight down the hill, doesn't it?'

'I wasn't only thinking of your knowing the way,' said Bayning. 'But stay, if you wish, of course. I can send a Janissary up to fetch you in an hour or two.'

'Allow me to assure you that that will not be at all necessary,' said Ibrahim. 'I will send one of my own servants with him, if he fears any danger.'

'I don't,' said Schofield, 'but they tell me that sometimes it is better for an Englishman not to be alone.' He was apologetic. The subject, he felt, was almost a slight on the princely hospitality they had received. But Ibrahim was charming in his comprehension.

'There have,' he said, 'been certain unfortunate happenings because of the foolish and ignorant in the bazaar quarter, but I like to hope that it is not as bad as you merchants think. And I will see that we take every care of our friend.'

When Bayning had left, Ibrahim continued the topic. There was no need, of course, to be alarmed; the hostility of the vulgar to the 'infidel' Christians had been much exaggerated; and it was virtually impossible for anything to happen to Schofield in the short distance between the house and the lotus tree. Yet, as he felt a responsibility for him, Ibrahim would suggest that he changed his magnificent gala-coat for a small jacket of Ibrahim's, which by its colour and design would assure him of protection.

Schofield, who had found the *usth-kurbi* incommoding enough merely for sitting and moving in the house, accepted with alacrity this opportunity of dispensing with it. It would have been, anyhow, an intolerable nuisance in climbing the rocky hill, accustomed as he was to ascents more steep and ground more uneven at home. He would have preferred not to replace it with even the light green coat which the physician offered him. There could be no possible danger from mobs in the short walk he was about to take in what seemed open and practically deserted country. Yet he felt it would be churlish to refuse, and allowed Ibrahim to put it over his shoulders.

He had, in fact, no particular desire to see the lotus tree at close quarters, but he welcomed the excuse to be alone for a short time, so that he might disentangle his thoughts, since on his return he wanted more conversation with Ibrahim. He wondered if any good purpose would be served if he asked permission, as an Englishman, to hold a conversation in writing with the deaf-mute Boll. Or would that be a breach of etiquette of an unpardonable nature?

In the distance, he heard the muezzin's call to prayer from the minaret of the mosque just below Ibrahim's house. He turned for a

moment to look at it. The tall tower seemed very near and he could
see the muezzin quite clearly. He speculated whether he ought to
stop in his ascent and, if not to prostrate himself (which could not
be expected) at least to stand still. *When in Rome* . . . But these were
infidels. No one could expect that of him. He continued on his
way. . . .

He was not certain, on thinking the matter over afterwards, at
what point he had the feeling that he was being followed; but by
the time he was half-way to the lotus tree that sixth sense, the
instinct which in early days his soldiering had given him and which
his country life at Bolton had immeasurably sharpened, warned him
that there was danger in the air. Turning round, with a leisurely air
as if to admire the view over the bay, he saw a chattering, angry
mob of Turks, brandishing sticks, coming towards him up the Hill.

He supposed that he must have given them some offence by his
ignoring of the call to prayer. If he could see the muezzin, he
reflected, the muezzin could equally clearly have seen him. To
attempt to explain to them was impossible. No mob can be reasoned
with, even if you can speak to them in their own language. He must
trust to the protective quality of Ibrahim's green coat. He shouted
to them and pointed to it. The only result was an increase of fury—a
howl of anger, during which some stones were thrown. Fortunately,
they were still too far off for any to fall even remotely within range.
Thinking they might not have seen the gesture, he took the jacket
off and waved it at them and then put it slowly and ostentatiously
back on his shoulders. But the effect was another surge of anger.

He did not know that it was the green coat which was the cause
of the tumult. No one, in Mohammedan countries, may wear green
unless they are descendants of the Prophet himself. For anyone else
to wear anything of that colour, even a cord or a shoelace, is an
insult. For an 'infidel' Christian to wear it was near enough blas-
phemy to merit death. Yet it was of this one obvious and elementary
thing which no one in the 'Quarter' had warned him. The oversight
was probably due to the fact that it was so obvious and elementary
that he was presumed to know it. It was a commonplace even in

plays introducing the Turks which he might have seen on the London stage. Yet he in his innocence had imagined the very contrary. When at dinner Ibrahim had spoken about the reverence for the colour, he had assumed that it had some protective merit—an assumption confirmed by the giving of the jacket.

It was now, however, quite clear to him that the physician's benevolent intention had failed. He also saw there was not a moment to be lost. He could not go on up the Hill and make use of the start which he still had of his pursuers, since that would cut him off from his base and ensure his eventual capture. His one chance was to run as fast as he could to the safety of Ibrahim's house, from which—as it lay over to the right—he was hardly further than the mob.

He reached it, thanks to his familiarity with the foot-feel of the fells at home, just in time to escape manhandling by the crowd, though not in time to avoid their stones. Several struck him; one badly bruised his jaw; another caught him on the back of his head.

It was by a great effort, and with a sense of failing consciousness, that he rushed into the safety of the open door. There he found Boll waiting and, towering behind him, Ibrahim, with a strange look of menace and amusement in his eyes. Schofield thought that the stone must have done some injury to his brain that he should see his kindly host as a sinister enemy. It was fantastic, too, that Ibrahim should speak quietly to Boll, who was deaf and dumb. Yet Schofield heard him say quite clearly as he pushed past him into the garden: 'Look after him Boll, till I have sent this crowd away.' And, as he sagged forward into Boll's arms, he heard too, in the last second before everything went black, the old slave whisper: 'I am William Harrison.'

CHAPTER XIV

Trial at Gloucester

SIR ROBERT HYDE, JUDGE OF COMMON PLEAS, RECORDER OF Salisbury, took his place on the Bench at the Gloucester Assizes to try, among other less interesting cases, Joan, Richard and John Perry of Campden for the murder of William Harrison, Gent.

The case offered two particular points of interest. The first was that, though one of the prisoners had confessed and given a circumstantial account on the murder, the body of the murdered man had not been found, so that, since the *corpus delicti* was not established, Sir Christopher Turnor at the previous assize had refused to try them. The second was that it had been asserted that Joan Perry was a witch. There was a third circumstance, which he endeavoured to dismiss from his mind. He knew, both from private conversations and from the mere fact that the case was being re-heard, that a conviction was expected.

It was not that this shocked him. At sixty-six and with the experience he had had, he was cynical enough. He had been deprived of his Recordership by the Parliament, because of his protest, by voting against Strafford's attainder, that the law should be above and apart from political feuds. His brother Henry had been condemned and executed under the law of the Commonwealth merely for his adherence to the House of Stuart—though the ostensible judicial reasons were certain ridiculous charges made but not proved against him by the Levant Company. He himself at the Restoration, reinstated in his Recordership, had been made one of the Commissioners for the trial of the 'Regicides'; but that he considered this as much

an act of political vengeance as any of the others of the time he
showed by his refusal to take any part in the proceedings other than
offering his advice on some technical legal points in drawing up the
indictment.

His friend, Sir Matthew Hale, had been more accommodating,
and though he professed the same principle of keeping the law apart
from politics, had expressed his understanding of it differently. He
changed sides whenever policy dictated it so that he might keep his
place in the law. Thus he had managed to retain his judgeship in
the common pleas under Cromwell and was made chief baron of
the exchequer when Charles returned. Hyde regarded him without
envy and with some amusement. He wished that Hale instead of
himself had been sent to try this case. It would have been worth
watching. For on the one hand Hale, out of his monumental knowledge, was never tired of insisting that he would never convict any
person of murder or manslaughter, unless the fact were proved to
be done, or at least the body found dead. (It was, in fact, as a disciple
of Hale that Turnor had refused to try the Perrys.) On the other
hand, Hale had such a horror of witchcraft that at the mere suggestion of it he threw any pretence of judicial impartiality to the
winds and would connive at any expedient—as when he had insisted
on an execution being hurried on because he knew that a pardon
was on the way—to secure a conviction. In this case, he would have
been subject to contrary stresses. It would have been interesting to
observe his conduct.

But, as it was, Hyde had to try the case. Not being a Puritan, as
Hale was, his attitude to witchcraft was less emotional and
vehement; being both a man of the world and one born in a legal
family—his uncle had been Lord Chief Justice; his father Attorney-
General to the Queen, who had led for the Crown in the prosecution
of Somerset—he was less of a legal purist. If the verdict of murder
or manslaughter was to be inadmissible unless the body was produced, the land could easily be a paradise for successful murderers.
To dispose of a body, with the vast, unvisited expanses of countryside at his door and the small inadequate number of mediocre

constables as his opponents, would be the least of the murderer's problems. Thus Hyde had no compunction about trying a case which Hale would have refused nor—on general principles—of acquitting a witch whom Hale would certainly not have allowed to escape. What irritated him was not the legal problems but the fact that someone was sufficiently interested in such poor people as the Perrys as to want them out of the way; and he did not know who or why. He wondered if it was the local Justice of the Peace, Sir Thomas Overbury, who might have considered his dignity somewhat damaged by the first acquittal.

He did not altogether like the way Overbury gave his evidence. On the one hand, he was competent, assured, keeping to the point, as a magistrate versed in the ways of law; on the other, there was almost a hesitancy, an evasiveness, in his attitude, as of one determined to say nothing beyond what was already on record.

The Perrys had all pleaded 'Not Guilty,' and the prosecuting counsel's first point was to prove the original confession made by John. This, through Overbury's testimony, presented no difficulty. Nor did John deny it. He merely said that at the time he made it he must have been mad and not known what he was doing.

It was when Overbury was examined with a view to ascertaining John's state of mind at the time that Hyde became most conscious that he seemed to be uncomfortable.

Overbury protested that, as far as the legal aspect of the matter went, he did not see that his opinion was either relevant or admissable.

Hyde intervened with: 'You are not on the bench now, Sir Thomas; but giving evidence in my court. Counsel is endeavouring to establish the prisoner's state of mind at the time he made the deposition before you. Your opinion as to whether he was mad or sane is therefore relevant to the case.'

'I had not seen the prisoner before that day; therefore I was in no position to form a correct estimate of his usual state of mind.'

'But you would recognize a madman if you saw one?' asked the counsel.

'Since to the best of my knowledge I have never seen one, except when I once paid a visit to Bedlam, I could not swear on oath that I should recognize one.'

'Come, come, Sir Thomas,' said Hyde. 'Do you mean me to assume that you arrested the other two prisoners on the confession of one you took to be mad?'

'With all deference, Sir Robert, I did not say that, nor could anything I have done imply it.'

'In that case, your arrest of Joan and Richard Perry may, *ipso facto*, be taken to imply that you regarded the confession of John Perry as that of a sane man?'

'At his trial in this court in the previous assizes, John Perry did not retract his confession.'

'That is to say, if the plea of madness be sound, the prisoner was mad between August and October, but recovered his wits when he understood that he was to stand trial again?'

'It would seem so.'

'That is your opinion?' asked the counsel.

'I have not any personal grounds on which to base an opinion.'

And beyond that Overbury was not to be shaken.

Hyde, however, had not done with him. Before he was released from giving evidence, the Judge asked: 'What were the exact circumstances in which you gave the order for the arrest of the prisoners for the second time?'

'I arrested them on my own responsibility as magistrate to prevent a breach of the peace.'

'You mean you had no warrant from a superior authority?'

'Not at the time, no.'

'What exactly do you mean by "not at the time"?'

'Instructions from London reached me three days later.'

'Did you know that these instructions were on the way?'

'No.'

'Then, Sir Thomas, did you not exceed your authority?'

'With deference, Sir Robert, no. I had reason to suppose that a riot would be provoked, which it was my duty, as local magistrate, to prevent.'

'Was there such a riot?'

'It had started just as I arrived with the constables.'

'Was it provoked by the prisoners?'

'It was directed against them.'

'But did Joan, Richard and John Perry actually provoke the riot?'

'I could not say.'

'Surely, Sir Thomas, you must know whether the prisoners were the instigators of the riot or the victims of it?'

'As I have said, it was directed against them. I was not there to see whether they gave provocation.'

'But you say, Sir Thomas, that you had reason to suppose that a breach of the peace was contemplated?'

'Yes.'

'Was it contemplated by the prisoners?'

'As far as I know, no.'

'Then surely your duty was to arrest those who contemplated it, if you felt you must arrest anyone at all?'

'In practice, circumstances made that impossible.'

'What circumstances?'

'I should have had to arrest practically everyone in Campden.'

'But were there no ringleaders?'

'I had no means of finding out who they were.'

'So what it amounts to is that you knew that a breach of the peace was likely to occur and to prevent it arrested on your own authority not the guilty but the innocent?'

Overbury was silent.

'Do you agree or not?' persisted Hyde.

'I agree that if I had not arrested them there would have been bloodshed.'

'Theirs?'

'In a riot one cannot tell who will be hurt.'

'I think, Sir Thomas, that your conception of your duty in

carrying out the law in that sphere in which you are empowered to administer it is open to severe criticism.'

'I shall be happy, Sir Robert, to answer for my administration to any court appointed with competence to enquire into it.'

Hyde made no further comment and Overbury was permitted to retire.

Of the four present when John Perry made the original confession to Overbury, only two were still alive. Mary Gilbey had died during the hard winter; and the occasion of the Reverend William Bartholomew's death was in everyone's mind. Edward Harrison and Ambrose Frewen offered formal evidence, confirming Overbury's account, and did as much incidental damage as they could to the Perrys until Hyde intervened to inform them and the jury that their observations could not be regarded as evidence.

It was thus established that John had made the confession, had adhered to it at the former assizes but now retracted it and agreed with what Joan and Richard had maintained from the beginning— that it was a lie and that none of them had seen Mr. Harrison on the night of his disappearance.

It was also established, by the examination of other Campdonians, that the Perrys were a family to whom witchcraft, murder, lying and thieving were easily credited.

In the end, it was the matter of the theft which turned the scales against them. The more the atmosphere of hatred invaded the court, the more suspicious Hyde became of the whole case. Carefully observing Mrs. Harrison and listening without interruption to her display of venom and self-righteousness, he decided that, had he had the misfortune to be married to her, he would have disappeared long before he was seventy and began to see Turnor's wisdom in refusing to assume Harrison's death until the corpse was produced. The death of the Reverend William Bartholomew, which all the witnesses regarded as proof of Joan's supernatural powers, he dismissed as coincidence. Edward's obvious hatred of John Perry told, he thought, in John's favour. In humble homes no less than in

F

palaces the heir is apt to dislike servants in proportion to their
fidelity to the reigning monarch. The evidence of those who had
met John on the night of August 16th was of no account one way
or the other, since, by John's confession, the time of the murder was
not covered by them. Even the confession itself might have been an
invention. In the course of his varied experience, Hyde had met
people on the borderline of sanity who were prepared to confess
the most incredible and absurd doings if thereby they could obtain
notoriety. And it had to be taken into account that, from beginning
to end of the business, Joan and Richard Perry had stubbornly
insisted that John was lying.

Amid all this conjecture, one thing stood with a rock-like certainty. John's story supplied a comprehensible motive where
otherwise there was none. The Perrys were desperately poor and
they knew that Harrison was carrying a sum of money. Moreover,
at the last assizes, they had pleaded Guilty to the earlier robbery.
This, Hyde decided, was the line of enquiry which must be pursued,
and as the counsel was wandering into what he considered the
irrelevancies of witchcraft, he intervened once more.

'At their last trial in this court, the prisoners admitted the theft
of £140 from the house of Mr. William Harrison. This admission
is also contained in the confession of John Perry. As this part of his
confession is true, does the prisoner expect the court to believe that
the rest of it is false?'

'It is false,' said John. 'We know nothing of the money.'

'But it is on record that you pleaded guilty to it.'

'May I explain, sir . . . my lord?'

'If you think you can, the court will hear you.'

'They told us that the King had given orders that everything
would be pardoned at those trials in honour of his coming back to
England and being King again; so it would be safe for us to say
"Guilty" because we should not be condemned; and it would save
the time of all of us if we said "Guilty," because if we said "Not
Guilty" we should have to be tried, but we should be pardoned just
the same. So we did as we were asked and said "Guilty." '

'You deliberately told a lie after you had taken an oath to tell the truth?'

'We were asked to do it.'

'No one in a court of law could possibly ask you to tell a lie on oath. What you were told was that even though you had admitted your guilt in your confession you would, by His Majesty's gracious Act of Pardon and Oblivion, be pardoned.'

'If we pleaded "Guilty."'

'Your guilt had already been assented to in your confession, which you did not retract.'

'But I tell you now that I was mad when I made the confession. It is not true. I don't know any more about the £140 than I do about where Mr. Harrison's body is.'

'After you have admitted that you lied on oath, you can hardly expect any jury to believe anything you say.'

'But that's not true of us, your Honour,' Richard suddenly shouted. 'We never——'

He was cut short by the cry of: 'Silence in the Court.' He was too frightened to say any more, but looked at Hyde in mute, pitiful protest.

'You have my permission to speak,' said Hyde. 'What have you to say?'

'Well, your Honour, mother and I never said we did it. It was only John there, and he was lying all the time.'

'But you and your mother pleaded "Guilty" just as your brother did at the last Assizes.'

'John's just said why we did that.'

'And I have just explained that he has made a mistake.'

'John's told you the truth about that.'

'He's not a liar, then?'

'Not about that, he isn't. Leastways, that's how we understood it.'

'It seems that you all make truth and lies suit your own convenience.'

'I've no learning like you have, your Honour,' said Richard. 'But this I do know——'

Joan interrupted him: 'Best keep quiet, son. They'll do what they want to do.'

'That is a most improper observation,' said Hyde. He looked at the jury: 'You will understand that you are here for one thing only—to sift the truth from the evidence.'

'Yes, my lord,' said the foreman of the jury. 'We understand that.'

'And now,' said Hyde to Richard, 'have you anything else that you want to say?'

'If I may speak, your Honour——' said Richard, avoiding his mother's eye.

'That is what I am giving you the opportunity to do.'

'I'd like to say that my brother John has accused others of the murder as well as me.'

'Who?'

'Well, he said it was a tinker and then he said it was a gentleman's servant near Campden. And there were others, I think.'

'Have you any evidence of this?'

'Some people here heard him.'

'Which people? Mr. Harrison? Mr. Frewen? Sir Thomas Overbury?'

'No, I don't think he said it to them.'

'Then who did he say it to?'

'Some of those who gave evidence against me.'

'Name them or point them out, and they shall be questioned.'

Richard looked round the court. There were several who had heard John's indiscriminate hints and accusations before he volunteered his confession to Overbury. There was the landlord of the *George;* there were the constables, including the one who had given the damning evidence about the slip-knot in the ball of inkle; there was Job Stiles, the carpenter, who had certainly been among those to whom John had suggested that the body was hidden in a bean-rick. There might have been more, but these Richard knew for a certainty. What he did not know was whether any of them would admit it. If they denied it, he would be branded an even bigger liar and he felt sure that Hyde would make the most of the circumstance.

In this he was wrong. Hyde would have welcomed such evidence because it would offer the first concrete suggestion that John was of an unstable nature and had made a series of wild charges not incompatible with the plea of temporary 'madness.'

'I am waiting for you to point them out to me,' he said.

Richard continued to look round, weighing in his mind if there were any whom he could trust. He wished Tom Barnes had been there. He was sure that Tom would have told the truth. He was equally sure that the constables would not. Neither, probably, would Job Stiles. He would risk the landlord.

As he was about to point him out, John suddenly gave a fierce whisper: 'Dick.' Richard turned instinctively to look at his brother and found his eyes caught in a relentless, commanding gaze.

'Please do not keep the Court waiting any longer,' said Hyde. 'Point out the person or persons whose evidence you wish to be taken.'

'There is no one, your Honour. I—I made a mistake.'

The Perrys' fate was sealed. Hyde had no option, as he had now no inclination, but to sum up against them. He did, indeed, instruct the jury that they were to pay no attention to the accusations of witchcraft, which were both irrelevant and unproved, and, in passing, let it be understood that he deplored that the town of Campden should be such an easy prey to superstition. The case was a simple one of murder with robbery as the motive. That the Perrys had already committed and confessed to one theft from Mr. Harrison's house had been established. The fact that they had been pardoned and not punished had no bearing on the commission of the deed. Nor should it be wiped out from the minds of the jury, since it was relevant to the question of motive. The prisoners' present denial of it was of a piece with the prisoner John Perry's attempt to discredit his own confession.

That confession, which had been sworn before a magistrate and admitted at the previous trial, was to be regarded as valid. The jury would probably see no reason to distrust it, whereas they would see only too clearly why the prisoner John Perry sought now to overthrow it and why the prisoners Joan and Richard Perry had maintained that it was false. They were to remember that the case against Richard Perry as being the actual murderer did not rest solely on the confession. The matter of the slip-knot in the ball of inkle provided independent evidence; or at the very least incontrovertible evidence that the material accusations in the confession were true.

As for the failure of the prosecution to produce the dead body of William Harrison, Hyde admitted that it would have been more satisfactory if it could have been found. He understood and sympathized with the decision made by his brother-judge, Sir Christopher Turnor, at the previous Assizes. But against this, the jury must consider whether it was not possible for two strong ablebodied men like the prisoners, with eight hours of darkness at their disposal, horses should they need them and such a wide extent of open, wooded or marshy countryside within easy reach, so to hide the body of their victim that it would never be found. Since the murder had been confessed to, articles of the missing man's clothing with blood on them had been found, and the man himself, after eight months, still missing, there was an overwhelming presumption in favour of murder. To allow the murderers to escape on the technicality that the *corpus delicti* had not been established would be tantamount to a grave miscarriage of justice.

The jury brought in a verdict of 'Guilty' without leaving the box.

CHAPTER XV

★

The End of the Perrys

THE PLACE OF EXECUTION HAD BEEN CHOSEN WITH CARE. BY custom, sheep-stealers and footpads suffered at the Cross Hands gibbet, a little beyond Broad Campden by the hilly track to Hangman's Hall; but both public interest and the enormity of their crime demanded that the Perrys should be hanged higher than that.

The first suggestion was Broadway Hill itself, but as Chipping Campden was not actually visible from the summit, Edward Harrison insisted that it did not comply with the terms of the warrant. He had, through the Lady Juliana's influence with the Lord Chief Justice, ensured that the sentence should be carried out not, as ordinarily it would have been, in Gloucester, but within sight of the scene of the crime. The last thing that the Perrys should see, as they slowly choked to death, was their home.

Eventually it was decided that a place just off the road which runs along the ridge of the hill would meet all requirements. In the valley below, the church tower stood out easily visible as a landmark of the countryside; and, at that height and in that position, the gibbet would be a warning to all travellers on the highway from Oxford to Worcester and from Gloucester to Coventry. Also it was within easy reach of the surrounding towns and villages whose inhabitants would wish to make holiday for the hanging.

The gibbet itself was the work of Job Stiles, the Campden carpenter, who had seen to it that, though the uprights were of oak, elm was used for the cross-beam. 'If we be hanging a witch,' he said, 'let's hang her safe and proper.' No one questioned his wisdom in that particular though some, including Tom Barnes, thought the gallows should have been wider.

'Waste o' good wood, that 'd be,' said Job. 'They be cutting old Joan and Dick down at night, so they say, and there's plenty room for young John to swing there alone till he rots. An' if they jostle each other a bit in their last dance—well, as Mr. Edward says, who'll it hurt?' There was saliva on his lips as he contemplated the possibility.

Tom Barnes turned away and spat. 'There are others I could better bear to see hung,' he said.

The decision that the body of John Perry alone was to swing in irons was made clear to the crowds that surged round and followed the two carts carrying the Perrys to their death as they went slowly up the long hill from Campden. In the first were Joan and Richard with their two cheap coffins for which Job Stiles had measured them, not without relish, when they came back to Campden gaol two nights before. But in the second cart John had no company but the iron harness in which his body, after death, was to be encased. Propped up in front of him, it swayed and jerked like a grotesque skeleton as the cart creaked over the ruts and stones of the uneven road.

Riding alongside on his pad-nag, the new Vicar of Campden unceasingly exhorted the prisoners to consider their approaching end, to repent and to manifest their repentance by openly confessing their crime. He even suggested that if John would, even at this late hour, reveal where Mr. Harrison's body lay so that it could be given Christian burial, he himself might be spared the ignominy of having his own body left for crows to peck at.

Pressing round the carts, which moved at walking-pace, the crowds were naturally thickest. No one wished to miss anything that the Perrys might say. But their attention was poorly rewarded. John did not speak, and Joan only said: 'Yes, son,' as she smiled and nodded in reply to Richard's one remark. He made it as they were passing the little wood near the top of the hill and the end of their journey: 'This is where I took those fat partridges you like so, mother. You remember?'

At the gibbet a larger crowd was already waiting. It had come from Aston and Weston and Broadway, from Saintbury and Willersey, Snowshill and Buckland, from Donnington and Evenlode and Longborough and Bourton-on-the-Hill. There were some even from Stow-on-the-Wold and Moreton-in-the-Marsh and Evesham, as well as a party which had come over with the officials in charge of the execution from Gloucester itself. But Sir Thomas Overbury was not there. Racked with rheumatism, he was unable to leave his room.

Everywhere was an air of conviviality and good-fellowship. Gentry in their carriages, yeomen and farmers and merchants on horseback, exchanged quips and laughter with each other and with the great mass of the poorer sort who had come on foot. Bets were offered and taken on the usual chances in the event to come—whether or not the criminals would confess, whether they would die game and how long it would take them to die. The holiday atmosphere was heightened by the fact that the landlords of the inns within reasonable distance had brought as many barrels of ale and cider as they could spare, knowing well that their patrons would be willing to pay for the drink a price which would recompense them for their pains.

The arrival of the condemned, surrounded by their fellow-townsmen, introduced a new element into the merrymaking. It was not only the gratification of the curiosity of those who had never seen the Perrys and the general sense that the climax of the proceedings was now approaching, but the intrusion of a local rivalry—a rivalry of unadmitted prides. The other towns and villages were proud that they were free from the notoriety which Campden had achieved; and, provoked by this subtle self-righteousness, Campden suddenly became perversely proud of the Perrys.

So it was that in the preliminaries of death they were unexpectedly encouraged by their townsmen. The gibes and curses which had accompanied them up the hill were heard no more. An obscenity from Job Stiles was checked by Tom Barnes's fist—to the general satisfaction of the bystanders. Only Edward Harrison stood unbending in his hatred, and though that right was, within limits, conceded to him, it was not approved.

In the crowd he had no companions but Ambrose Frewen and his daughter. Marjorie had let it be known that her attendance put the utmost strain even on her affection. 'Nothing,' she said, 'could make me go to that vile thing, if I had only myself to consider; but it is my father's duty to be there and it is my duty to be with him.'

The three were standing near the gallows when Marjorie, who in spite of her suffering was looking round with a wide-eyed curiosity, asked the meaning of the fire which was being lit under a wheeled copper cauldron.

'That's to heat the pitch,' her father explained.

'What do they want pitch for?'

'It's to pour over John Perry's body, so that his wicked carcase will last for a warning,' said Edward, in a voice deliberately loud enough for John to hear.

For a moment, it seemed that he would have the effect he desired, for there was a flash of ungovernable fear in Perry's eyes as he turned to look at the fire. But old Matthew Polegate, the baker, called out quickly: 'Never mind that, lad. You'll be dead and feel nothing of it.'

'Thank you, Matt,' said John, recovering himself, 'though I'm sure that'll disappoint Mr. Edward.'

The Perrys, taken down from the carts, were left for a moment together while their guards were summoned to assist with the placing of the ropes and the ladders. In the brief privacy, before the bystanders broke in on it, John whispered: 'Forgive me, mother!' Richard protested: 'No! No! She can't. We can't.' Joan, looking from one son to the other, smiled at Richard. To John, with a face grimly set, she said: 'You did what you thought right, son. It's past mending now.' But she forgave him with her eyes.

'For the last time, now that you tremble on the very brink of Hell,' said the Vicar of Campden, 'I charge you to confess to your crime.'

A great shout from the crowd of 'Confess! Confess!' was followed immediately by a profound silence in which no word might
be lost. But none of the Perry's spoke. The only voice was that of
Marjorie Frewen, who said: 'The witch has cast a spell on her sons.
Why don't they hang her, and then, perhaps, they'll speak?'

Though she was speaking in a conversational tone to Edward so
that her suggestion was heard only by those in their immediate
neighbourhood, the tenor of it was soon carried in ever-widening
circles to the very edge of the crowd and soon the murmur of
discussion gave place to another roar of 'Hang the witch first!'

The guards, who had brought John to the foot of the ladder,
paused.

'The witch! The witch! Take the witch first,' chanted the crowd.

The Sheriff, sensing the atmosphere, nodded to the hangman and
the guards, who thereupon took John back to where, by their
coffins, the other two were standing, and, in his place, brought
Joan forward.

'Good-bye, sons,' she said as she left them. 'Keep faith—both of
you.'

At the foot of the ladder, the Vicar again asked if she had anything
to say.

'I'd like to die with my back to Campden,' she said. 'That's all.'

'You're afraid to look on the place where your evil flourished?'

'Have it as you will, Parson,' said Joan, 'but let me do as I ask.'

There was that in her tone which made the Vicar suddenly cold.
Not much over thirty and with no desire himself to meet
death, he remembered his father-in-law, the Reverend William
Bartholomew.

He called to the crowd: 'The witch refuses to speak, but she is
willing to die with her back to Campden. We can take that as a
confession that she fears to look on the scene of her wickedness. Is
it agreed?'

'It is contrary to the warrant,' shouted Edward.

But he was overruled. The chorus of 'Agreed! Agreed!' and the
nod of the Sheriff gave Joan her last wish. The hangman's assistant

moved the position of her ladder and when Joan climbed it and stood impassively while the rope was adjusted to her neck, her sons noticed that she was gazing not at them but far beyond to where in the distance she could see upon its hill the tree-ringed circle of Seven Wells.

The ladder was kicked from under her. For a moment her feet jerked feebly in that last hopeless dance on air till Tom Barnes came forward, pushed aside the guard and, with his blacksmith's strength, pulled her legs firmly downwards to give her, in mercy, the quick death which the law would not.

Richard started to cry as his mother died. Not until he and John, noosed, stood side by side on their ladders with her corpse between them, swinging in the wind, was he able to master his emotion and, with a return of that patient, brute endurance of his, face the onlookers calmly.

'Confess! Confess!' they yelled.

'I've nothing to confess,' he said. 'If I knew anything I'd tell you now. Can you doubt it? But I've nothing to say but what I've said all along. I don't know what happened to Mr. Harrison. Nor did my mother. There's no blood on her hands or mine. It's my brother here. He killed her; he's killing me. By lies. Tell them, John. Tell them we're innocent of blood.' Then as he turned to see his brother's surly, dogged look, his voice rose to an hysterical shriek. 'Tell them, blast you! Tell them, you bastard!' He spat in his brother's face.

The crowd laughed with delight. 'Answer him,' they shouted

John merely said to the hangman: 'Can't you get it over?'

'Tell them, John,' said Richard, whimpering now, 'for God's sake, tell them!'

'Tell them—*what?*' He looked his brother full in the eyes. 'You know quite well, Dick, there's nothing to say.'

The effect was extraordinary. When Richard turned his face back to the crowd in front of him it was as one hypnotized—an impassive mask with only the lips moving, repeating endlessly: 'Nothing to say, nothing to say, nothing to say, nothing to say, nothing . . .'

The repetition was strangled in his throat as, suddenly, they pushed him off the ladder.

John, left alone, called out: 'Now, what is it you want me to say to you?'

Once again in monotonous unison they chanted: 'Confess! Confess!'

For the last time, more incongruously now than ever, John flung back his head insolently. The back of his neck chafed on the rope, but if he felt it, his expression gave no hint of it. His face wore only the old half-contemptuous, half-commanding look.

'Confess to *you?*' he said. Then, unexpectedly, as a child tired of a game, he laughed and said: 'Why not? Why in the devil's name not? Listen, then. We're all innocent. I don't know any more than you what became of Mr. Harrison.'

'You lying swine,' said Edward. 'You murdered him.'

'If you know he's dead, Mr. Edward, it's more than I do.'

'Tell us more, John,' said Tom Barnes.

'He'll tell us nothing but lies,' said Edward.

'All I tell you is this—you'll hear something some day, I've no doubt.'

After this he refused to utter another word and, at the crowd's bidding, the hangman's assistant turned him off.

Tom Barnes came forward to do for him what he had done for his mother, but, led by Edward, the spectators yelled: 'No, let him dance,' and the officers, willing to please them, barred Tom's way.

John Perry took ten minutes to die.

Nine days after the hanging, on a midnight without a moon, there were visitors at the gibbet. Neither party knew of the other's presence, and it was, as it happened, unfortunate for Marjorie Frewen that Edward Harrison was first on the scene.

Since John Perry's death, Edward had luxuriated in an almost-forgotten sense of security. Whether in fact John had known that he was a thief, he could never be certain, but he believed that he, as well as William Harrison, had strongly suspected it. Now, with his father gone and Perry dead, there would be none either to credit or to suggest that it was he who had stolen the £140 that February morning a year ago.

He had not, indeed, meant to steal it; nor was he in any way implicated in the attempted robbery from outside. But as he had been first on the scene and for five minutes alone in the room, he was in a position to discover that nothing in fact had been taken by the intruders who, possibly, had been disturbed by the signs that the 'lecture' in the church was over. Quickly he had slipped two bags of gold into his pockets.

As he had calculated everyone assumed that the money had been taken by whoever had forced the window, though, in the following weeks, something in his father's manner whenever the robbery was mentioned made him suspect that William Harrison at least was unconvinced by the simple and obvious explanation. This, though irritating, did not worry him overmuch. But when John Perry had confessed that Richard was the thief and that the money was buried in the Perrys' garden, he had experienced something like panic. While he was superintending the digging up of the garden for what he knew not to be there, question after question teased his brain. Why had John gratuitously confessed on oath a palpable falsehood? Was it the beginning of an attempt to implicate him in his father's murder? Or was it merely an insolent warning to him that he knew the truth at least about the money and might at any moment divulge it? The more he pursued these speculations, the more incomprehensible and dangerous John's conduct became, nor was he able, since he knew him so well, to take refuge in the comfortable assumption, widely held, that Perry was mad.

Now that the danger was over and the riddle beyond answering his theft took on another complexion. During his nine days of safety he had faced himself and recognized that the unpremeditated action had changed his life. The gold was a foundation on which he could build. Till then he had been dependent on his father with no prospect but that of succeeding, on his death, to a modest inheritance—to be shared with his brother—and the life of a country steward. Now he would devote himself to amassing a fortune

which eventually should give him the power and splendour of a
Baptist Hicks.

Already, in the few months he had held his father's office, he had
extorted from the tenants, by way of increased rents and arrears, far
more than he need render to the Lady Juliana. The £140 was almost
trebled. He had discovered also that with the change of government
and redistribution of estates and property, there were many of his
Gloucestershire neighbours who might be prepared to pay handsomely for silence about their part in the Civil Wars and their
conduct under the Commonwealth. In some cases, it might be even
a matter of buying their lives and freedom. Among his father's
papers he had found many items of interest which he intended to
put to their full use. And now John Perry should give him another
aid, a rare and unrivalled aid, to his goal.

Though he knew that, by tradition, the 'Hand of Glory' never
failed, his modern sceptical disposition did not intend to trust to
this. First, he would experiment with it, with no felonious intent,
on the occupants of his own household. Were it unsuccessful, he
could throw it away; but nothing was lost, except a little time and
an infinitesimal risk, by procuring it for the test. He minimized the
risk as far as he could by telling the family he would be away for
two nights on business in London. Actually he stayed there only one
night. Then, with a new cloak and hat purchased there, he rode back
to Gloucestershire taking care not to enter the district where he
might be known by sight till well after dark. It was, indeed, nearly
midnight before he reached the gallows.

'The Hand of Glory,' as all thieves and murderers well know, is
the right hand of a murderer, severed just above the wrist. Into the
fingers of the dried hand are fixed five wicks, made from five locks
of the murderer's hair and dipped in fat from his body—which can
usually be collected from the ground beneath the gibbet. When a
'Hand of Glory' is lighted and set in a house, a spell is cast on all the
occupants, so that the possessor of the Hand may do with impunity
whatever he pleases.

It did not take Edward long to take from the body of John Perry, swinging in its skeleton of iron, the portions he needed, but he had only just let himself down from the cross-beam, clutching a handful of hair which the pitch had not stiffened, when he heard in the distance the sound of horses. Unafraid of the dead, he was in terror of the living. To be discovered would be to lose everything. He leapt on his horse and rode furiously not back to Campden but down the hill to Broadway.

The newcomers were Marjorie Frewen and Job Stiles. Job did not relish his errand, but Marjorie had offered such handsome payment that it was against his conscience to refuse. Besides, it would only be a matter of minutes to open Joan's grave at the foot of the gibbet. They had not, as he had noticed at the time, buried her deep, and the earth was not yet trodden hard. If Miss Marjorie wanted to ease her conscience—and, as she insisted, all Campden's—by making certain that Joan had indeed the witch's teat, she was welcome to look. He need not and did not intend to.

From her horse, Marjorie watched, with strained, feverish eyes, as he opened the grave and forced back the coffin-lid.

'You can do the rest, Miss Marjorie. I'll not touch her,' said Job, as he withdrew into the deep darkness outside the circle of light from the lantern.

'Thank you, Job. I'm not afraid.'

Just as she was about to dismount, a great gust of wind suddenly shook John's body and made it swing violently to and fro on the gallows. The horse took fright at the movement and plunged madly forward, so that Marjorie was struck by the full force of John's legs backward into the grave beneath. As she lay there, her cheek beside Joan's cold face and the blood from her gashed forehead streaming over them both, a piece of splintered bone from John's severed wrist fell and stabbed her eye

'Job!' she screamed. 'Job, help me!'

But Job had taken to his heels, nor would a fortune have brought him back. She had no comfort but John dancing above her and Joan's sightless eyes looking up.

When dawn broke the watchman found her crouching in the Market Hall in Campden High Street. The only words she said were: 'The gallows! the gallows!' She was quite mad.

They took every care of her that tender solicitude could devise. 'Poor Miss Marjorie,' they said. 'So sweet and tender a soul should never have gone to the hanging.'

CHAPTER XVI

Release

WHEN SCHOFIELD RAN THROUGH IBRAHIM'S OPEN DOOR AND fell unconscious into William Harrison's arms, he disappeared completely from the life of Smyrna. That evening, when he did not return to the Quarter, Bayning and Pentlow, accompanied by the most trustworthy of the Janissaries, made their way up to the physician's house to enquire what had become of him. Ibrahim's surprise when he heard that he had not reached home was only equalled by his anxiety for his guest's safety; and this was followed by a torrent of self-reproach that he had not himself accompanied him back to Frank Street.

He sent at once for 'Boll,' who—he explained—had been his escort, and in a series of quick gestures asked for an account of the matter. While 'Boll' wrote busily on his tablets, Ibrahim said: 'When he got back he said nothing to me, so I thought naturally he had seen your friend safely to the gate. I liked the young man. I found him very interesting in the talk we had when he returned from the lotus tree. I cannot believe that evil can have overtaken him. If it has, I shall never forgive myself. Our Turkish hospitality will be shamed for ever.'

Pentlow and Bayning murmured a conventional protestation that he must not take it so to heart.

'Boll,' it appeared from his account, had seen Schofield almost to the gate of the Quarter when his charge had insisted on dismissing him because he wanted to wander for a few moments in the bazaars near the gate. 'Boll' had offered to stay with him, but Schofield had been adamant that he wished to go alone and that he was in no danger since for one thing he was in Turkish clothes and for another he was within a stone's throw of Frank Street. 'Boll' had foolishly accepted this reasoning and left him there.

Ibrahim, when he read this, dismissed the old slave with a fierce gesture which boded 'Boll' no good and assured his visitors that he would be suitably punished for his remissness.

'Since he is a countryman of ours,' said Bayning, 'I should esteem it a favour if you would spare him that. No doubt he was acting in good faith and there was much reason on his side.'

'I agree,' said Pentlow. 'What's done is done. Our friend was perhaps a little ignorant and headstrong. I spoke to him about it myself. We can only hope that he will turn up in the morning.'

'If by some perversity of misfortune he does not,' said Ibrahim, 'I will, if you will allow me, use all my influence to have a thorough search made. In that, I think I might succeed better than you.'

But Schofield did not turn up, nor were the English Consul's efforts, aided by Ibrahim's, of any avail in tracing him. He had disappeared as completely as if the earth had swallowed him up. The days became weeks, the weeks months, and the search was tacitly abandoned. Hope also was abandoned when, one day among the bazaars, one of the merchants discovered a tailor offering for sale a magnificent *usth-kurbi* of scarlet and gold which he·thought he recognized. He returned to fetch Nicholas Leate to come and look at it to put the matter beyond doubt. There was no doubt.

'I told him it would end in St. Veneranda,' said Pentlow.

'I should have felt happier if it had,' said Bayning. 'At least we should know he was dead.'

When Schofield came to himself once more, he found himself in bed in Ibrahim's house, watched by a Turkish servant.

'What has happened?' he asked; but the Turk shook his head in incomprehension and went out to fetch the physician.

To him, Schofield repeated his question.

'What I intended should happen,' said Ibrahim.

'But why? . . . I don't understand . . . You surely . . .'

'It is better for you not to try to move yet. You are still weak. To-morrow I will have you taken out to my house on my cotton plantation in the country. You will soon get strong there.'

'And then?'

'Then I shall use you as a slave on the plantation,' said Ibrahim, and left him.

In the year that followed, Schofield saw Ibrahim and Harrison again only once, in circumstances which he did not wish repeated. Ibrahim had spoken the truth at least when he had told Bayning and Schofield at dinner that he employed 'Boll' in his laboratory. It was only occasionally that Harrison was sent into the cotton-fields and then as a punishment, since the heat and the continual stooping made it for him a long agony. Usually, as a refinement of mental cruelty to crown his physical exhaustion, Ibrahim then sent him into Smyrna with the cotton, ostensibly in charge of the others, but in reality watched by the foreman, Wrenshaw, a renegade Englishman who had 'turned Turk,' to see that he gave no sign that he was other than he appeared—a deaf and dumb slave devoted to Ibrahim.

On this occasion, however, Harrison had been sent into the fields to work with Schofield, not as a punishment but as a trap. Ibrahim wished to see whether, left alone, he would speak to him. Harrison, who had been given to understand that both Ibrahim and Wrenshaw were in Smyrna, fell into it. But they had only time for a few quick sentences.

'You *are* William Harrison of Campden?'

'Yes. And you have come to look for me?'

' "My lady"—and Joan Perry.'

'I knew during that dinner. So did *he*. . . . Courage, my friend. Look!'

He moved away from Schofield, who looked up to see Ibrahim and Wrenshaw coming toward them from the house.

'Teach him discretion,' said Ibrahim; and Schofield found himself helpless in Wrenshaw's grip, while he watched Ibrahim with a swing of his arm which, despite his age seemed still powerful, drive his fist full in Harrison's face. As Harrison fell dazed and sobbing on the ground, he drew his stiletto, and made as if to stab him. The Englishman held up foolish, feeble hands, in an instinct to ward off death. The gesture seemed to restore Ibrahim's self-control. Deliberately, but with disdain rather than anger, he stamped on the prostrate body, then ordered him to get up and, seizing him by the scruff of the neck, pushed him, stumbling in front of him, back to the house.

Wrenshaw also took Schofield back and had him bastinadoed.

It was Wrenshaw who made his captivity a nightmare. The work itself became a monotony which, since Schofield was strong and healthy enough, had an almost soothing effect on him. It became a rhythm which, exhausting his body to a natural tiredness, liberated his mind. Accustomed to his hermit-life at Bolton, he welcomed the isolation which the barrier of language imposed between him and the other workers in the fields. What he dreaded was Wrenshaw's words.

For Wrenshaw was no ordinary renegade. He had 'turned Turk' not, like so many unfortunate captives, from the fear bred by intolerable compulsion, but from conviction. He hated the Christian faith, not as some apostates—such as the Janissaries—hated it, as a natural self-justification of their apostasy, but intensely and from within. He was proud of his own intellectual powers and the idea of God becoming man—and a Jew at that—had irritated his reason even when he had been, nominally, a Catholic. 'Childish and superstitious fables,' he explained, 'which priests tell the credulous for their own advantage. Now, in Islam, we have nothing of that. We worship the One God in His majesty, as He should be worshipped.'

The consequences of this belief, which flattered his intellect, showed themselves in the conditions of Turkish society, which suited his ambition. He was never tired of extolling the merits of the political and social system of the Turks. There, under the Sultan, everyone was equal and everyone had the same chance of greatness.

The great Vizier, Kiuprili, had been a cook; and his case was typical. There was no privilege of birth, either from family or wealth, as there was in the decadent and degenerate West. No son could succeed his father to titles or offices. If he was worthy of them, he must win them for himself in open competition with all his contemporaries. It was this, Wrenshaw insisted, which lay at the root of the greatness of the Turks. It was only a matter of time before they subdued Christendom and imposed on it the rationality of their religious and secular rule. In a year or two—even, perhaps, this year—the sacred standard of the Prophet would again be unfurled and the still unchecked and unsurpassed armies of Mohammed would sweep to Vienna and beyond on the next stage of the conquest of the West.

Surely Schofield would 'turn Turk'? It was no disgrace, but an assertion of intellectual and political maturity.

On severely empirical grounds, Schofield did not think so. He remembered that he had been told in the Quarter that the great Vizier Kiuprili had killed, for arbitrary reasons of his own—though it was announced as for the security of the state—36,000 people in five years.

But considering the relationship at present existing between himself and Wrenshaw, he deemed this argument inexpedient and said nothing. In fact, it would not have worried Wrenshaw if he had mentioned it. The man was a fanatic and, like his kind, was impervious to any appeal to his venerated canons of reason which in any way disturbed the deep emotions on which his fanaticism was founded.

It was this strain in him which made him wish to convert Schofield rather than to try to intimidate him into apostasy. Not that, since his nature had in it a strong tinge of cruelty, he altogether omitted the more obvious pressures. He hinted that Schofield might, at any moment, be sold to the galleys; and described in detail that life which only the strongest survived and, in surviving, learnt to pray for death. At times, when the fancy took him, he added another threat: 'If we can't make you a Moslem in your mind, I assure you that we are very well able to make you a eunuch in your body. The ceremony is public—and interesting.'

The result of these intermittent conversations, which depended on Wrenshaw's caprice, was to make Schofield, in the long days among the cotton, reflect on matters which he had never taken so seriously before. It was the image of the little Capuchin which was most often in his mind. He saw now what Father Gabriel meant. With his mind and will, he was prepared to endure any torment rather than renounce the Faith which, until his slavery, he had hardly believed he believed. He hoped, if the test came, that his body would not play him false.

In the spring of 1662, a week or two before the time for sowing the cotton, Wrenshaw sent for him and told him that he was to see Ibrahim again. 'He has not told me what purpose he has in mind, but I trust that your stubbornness has wearied him and that I am to be allowed to have my own way with you, at last.'

Bracing himself against the possibility, Schofield asked if he was to go down to Smyrna alone.

'Your master is not in Smyrna. He has been here for some weeks, but has kept his room. Come with me.'

Ibrahim was lying on a couch in a room opening out of his laboratory. In the year since Schofield had last seen him, he had come to look as old as his years. He was a tired old man of eighty-seven, with not long to live. Harrison was standing by him, holding his silver bowl, unafraid, now, of any violence.

When Wrenshaw had left them, he spoke in a voice so feeble that it was hardly above a whisper. It was Harrison he addressed.

'For me the end is not far now. Matters are over between us. You can go. You have paid something of the price. And take him with you. You too'—he turned to Schofield—'have paid the price for your meddling.'

'And this?' Harrison held out the silver bowl.

'Take it with you. It may get you a passage home.'

'Come along,' said Harrison to Schofield.

'You mean—we are free?'

'You have three days,' said Ibrahim. 'I shall live that long. I cannot answer for Wrenshaw after that. And remember this. I have already told "Boll" '—he smiled as he mentioned the name for the last time—'that you will be watched. He knows that is not an idle threat. If you enter the Quarter or speak to any of the merchants or make yourselves known to any of the English there, you will find yourselves back with Wrenshaw. Now go. Neither you nor I have much time.'

It was not until they were three miles on the way to Smyrna that they eased their pace sufficiently to begin a conversation.

'Yes, yes,' said Harrison, in reply to Schofield's request, 'I will explain it to you. But first tell me how is John—John Perry?'

'I did not see him. Only his mother. And that was eighteen months ago.' And he gave Harrison an outline of the happenings at Campden, as far as he knew them. 'I only hope they are still alive.'

'Yes, yes. They must be. It would be too cruel. They must be safe. At least, John.'

'It was for his mother's sake I came to Smyrna. If any harm has happened to them, surely it is John's fault.'

'I understand why he did what he did. So will you when I tell you. He has kept faith. But I knew he would. You see, he is my son.'

CHAPTER XVII

★

Theft and Restitution

THE STORY AS WILLIAM HARRISON TOLD IT WAS A PIECEMEAL affair, subject to digressions, repetitions, interruptions and explanations; but here it will be more convenient to tell it in a direct fashion, not, indeed, adding to what he said, but ordering it.

It had all started, as the old courtier had told Schofield, in Dominic's House, fifty years before, when Sir Baptist Hicks had been summoned by the old Earl and asked to undertake a dangerous but lucrative mission to Smyrna. At the time Hicks was sixty and of a character more complex than was understood either by the courtiers who hated him as 'Shylock' or by his tenants at Chipping Campden who loved him as a benefactor.

Lowly born and with what little money the family possessed devoted to the education and equipment of his elder brother Michael, he had been apprenticed to a silk mercer. Here he had become a veritable model of industry and trustworthiness; his thrift verged on avarice; his observation of the world, through those cold, steel-blue eyes, at times even shocked his master by its cynical shrewdness. He saw that money meant power and that most men could be induced to part with it by appeals to their vanity or their affections. First, with careful deliberation, he set about subduing, quietly but relentlessly, those possible sources of weakness in himself. He meditated daily in his youth on the story of Esau, who, because he was tired and hungry, was induced to sell his birthright for a meal. For a time, he even voluntarily went hungry himself and worked his body so hard that at night he could have fallen asleep on the stairs up to his room, so that, if Esau's temptation ever arose in his life, he would have hardened himself to defy it. Then, sure of himself, he cultivated every art which would enable him to play on the weaknesses of others. The result was that, when he eventually succeeded to his master's business, he was already the most successful merchant in London. He could buy cheaper and sell dearer than any of his rivals. The flattering charm with which he sold unwanted goods at a high price to an unwilling customer was equalled only by the pitiless hardness with which he exacted payment for them. At the root of this hardness was contempt for those less disciplined in their desires than himself. By the time that his brother Michael became Cecil's secretary and gave him opportunities at Court, he was ready to grasp them and become as successful a usurer as he was a merchant.

Yet, since human nature is so complex a thing that it will not suffer violence to be done to it without taking revenge, he became increasingly a prey to emotions he despised. Outwardly he conformed to whatever religion happened to be in the ascendant, because it was expected of him and was good for business, but he had no strong beliefs of his own. Born in the extreme year of the Protestant Reformation under Edward VI, he was baptized a Protestant; but when he was a child of two, Queen Mary came to the throne and, with her, the Catholic religion came back again. Hicks's parents conformed willingly and, in his most impressionable years—till he was nine—he was brought up in the Faith and went regularly to Mass. Then came Elizabeth and Protestanism once more; and in his adolescence and early manhood, he was taught to look on his childhood's practices as reprehensible and superstitious—something not to be spoken of. During his apprenticeship, he discovered Mammon for himself, and ceased, from that point, actively to believe in any other god. Yet, impervious to religion, he could not escape superstition. Despising it, he yet yielded to it more and more. He would only trade on certain days and when certain private auguries were auspicious. He was careful to watch for the new moon. Sometimes he would choose his silks not for their quality but for certain correspondences of colour.

His rational and practical self, it is true, prevented him from running to extremes. He did not consult necromancers, in spite of his occasional wish to do so, partly because he told himself they were charlatans, partly because he feared to put himself in their power. But as he grew older, this side of his nature became by imperceptible degrees stronger. After he had passed fifty and knew it unlikely that he would have a son, he became more and more dissatisfied. The accumulation of wealth had become automatic and he no longer had any pleasure in it; and he was satiated with the kind of power it gave. His superstition increased as his interest in the getting of money lessened. The harder and colder and more successful he appeared outwardly, the more uncertain and bewildered he, in fact, became.

Thus, when Dominic sent for him and broached the matter of procuring the Silver Bowl from Smyrna, Hicks was ripe for his suggestions. The money and the honours he was assured were in themselves a bait less certain than Dominic had assumed. It was the thing Dominic had feared would be an obstacle which turned out to be the main inducement.

For Simon Forman insisted that everyone concerned with the bringing of the Bowl should be an Initiate. (Dominic himself had been made one years before, though at that time he meddled little with it.) And at the same time Simon refused to allow any existing member of the Cult to be used on the mission. He was aware that he might be committing sacrilege—as he understood it—and he was unwilling to involve anyone but himself. He would not call on the least of those owing him allegiance to give him obedience in a matter where he had no right to demand it. But if men could be found who would freely undertake a mission of whose risk they had been warned and who would also submit to a ceremonial oath of secrecy, then he would vindicate the power of the Craft, whatever price he himself might have to pay.

Yet, though all that Simon stipulated was initiation into the very outermost circle, Hicks, when it was put to him, showed no opposition to being drawn in as far as possible. Indeed, he welcomed it. It was a liberation of his secret desires, an ordering of his nature so that the two strains in it no longer conflicted but supported each other, a new adventure and a rediscovered zest for one become tired and sterile. As an old man of a more conventional temperament might take a young, new mistress, so Hicks embraced the Cult.

Both Dominic and Simon, however, pointed out to him that, at sixty, however firm his intentions and invaluable his knowledge of Smyrna, it was doubtful whether his ability matched his will. For this, there was needed someone much younger—and someone, moreover, who could not be traced. Bluntly, Hicks was too old and too well known. Had he in his employ some young man who could be trusted with the matter? As it happened, he had. Young William Harrison, who was twenty, was devoted to him, bound to him both by interest and affection. Harrison was an orphan whom Hicks had taken at a very early age to sweep his shop and run errands and generally serve as a drudge in return for a mere pittance and a roof. Observing him carefully and finding there a nature in many ways not unlike his own, Hicks had given him opportunities of better service of which Harrison had taken advantage. As he grew to manhood, Hicks trusted him increasingly and actually experienced, as far as it was possible for him, a certain affection for 'young Will.' The lonely youth returned it and regarded Hicks both then and all his life almost as a father. He would be the ideal man for the mission. He was young, strong, shrewd beyond his years, with no attachments except to Hicks. As for initiation, Hicks was certain that Will would do whatever he wished, more particularly as they would be entering the Cult together. And if it was necessary that he should disappear into obscurity once his mission was accomplished, Hicks could hide him in the heart of the countryside in charge of the new house he intended to build on his recently-acquired estate at Chipping Campden.

So it came about that William Harrison was sent to Smyrna to find and bring back the Silver Bowl. Simon, of course, in common with the Arch-Priests of other countries knew its presumed hiding-place—in the ruined Tomb of Polycarp on Mount Pagos, in the inner chamber, under the seventh stone of the northern wall. Given this knowledge and Hicks's introduction to various merchants, as well as unlimited money for bribes or necessary payments, the undertaking was less formidable than it at first sight appeared. Among the residents of the Quarter, there was always one, if not more, whose interest was in the antiquities of the place. Harrison, under an assumed name, was to seek him out and, under cover of a scholarly expedition, gain access to the Tomb. The Turkish authorities were not likely to object to such a thing done openly. If they did, they could be bribed—though it was imperative not to offer too high a bribe lest their suspicions should be aroused. That Harrison might appear what he seemed—a wealthy eccentric young scholar—Dominic instructed him in classical lore and gave him two books to study on the voyage.

Everything fell out as was planned. The only difficulty Harrison encountered was that of being left alone for a sufficient time in the ruined Tomb. This he solved by making a last expedition by himself on a working-day when he knew no merchant would accompany him and by dismissing the Janissaries who were his guard for two or three hours—a course to which they had no objection.

He returned safely and speedily with the Bowl to England and delivered it to Hicks, who gave it to Simon.

In the years that followed, Harrison seldom left the security of Chipping Campden. Though the theft of the Bowl apparently aroused no repercussions in Smyrna, both Hicks and he thought it wiser that he should remain in obscurity, as Simon had ordered. On the other plane, there were repercussions enough. Four days after Simon had used the Bowl in the preparation of the love-philtre for the enchanted paper and the nutmeg, he died, as he realized he must. Gresham who, inheriting the Bowl, was indiscreet enough to test its power, followed him two nights after he made the foolhardy experiment. The others who had been involved in the affair, were brought to ruin and death. But Hicks prospered and Harrison was safe enough. If they had to pay, the payment was postponed. Meanwhile, at Campden, they continued—Hicks enthusiastically, Harrison more soberly and obediently—to play their part in the Cult.

Partly as a reward for his services, partly as a recognition of his newly-discovered interests and abilities, Simon appointed Hicks as Devil of the Campden coven, which was re-formed and given the privilege of being a coven of seven—which meant that they could order their own affairs with a greater freedom than was permitted to the ordinary congregation. They were bound to consult the Arch-Priest only on the matters of the highest importance. One of the members of the coven was the mother of Joan Perry, who dedicated her daughter to the Cult when she was fourteen. Joan, in the beauty of her girlhood and the soft ripeness of her womanhood, was for years the cherished darling as, in her age, she became the feared oracle of the circle which, at the four great Sabbats, met at Seven Wells.

It was in the orgy at one of the May Eve meetings, which was attended by all the covens in the district, that Harrison at last exercised his rights over her and, by so doing, became the father of John. But by that time Hicks was dead and Harrison was Devil in his place.

Hicks in his last years had become more and more absorbed in the Cult. His interest showed itself not only in his study of the lore in books—he had bought a large part of Dominic's library—but in a kind of amused perversity by which he persisted in leaving what could only be described as clues in obvious places. The very motto he adopted on his ennoblement—*Nondum metam:* 'Not yet the goal'—had an alchemical significance which it was difficult to escape. The Eastern *motifs* with which he embellished his mansion might be innocent enough, since all men knew of his trade with the Levant; but the eight minaret-like chimneys on the Banqueting Houses were an invitation to discovery even more obvious than his indiscreet jest with the pulpit which he presented to the church,

on whose panelling was the design of clusters of eight grapes over a
bowl. Though the carving was clumsy, the shape of the bowl—like
the middle of an hour-glass, with the base matching the bowl in
reverse—was sufficient to betray the secret to those who knew.

Hicks's final invasion of the church was one which he was unable
to achieve till after his death. He determined that the Sacred Bulls
should have their place there. In his lifetime he had seen to it that
the pensioners in his almshouses should wear a silver stag's head on
their coats. This could be explained easily and conventionally by his
crest—for the stag's head had for centuries lost its original significance as the Horned God of the Cult. But it was the unequivocal
Bulls whom he wished to honour. In defiance of heraldic usage, he
adopted two rampant bulls (the bull is usually *passant* or *couchant*)
as the supporters of his arms, had them sculptured with care during
the last year of his life and made Harrison promise that when the
great tomb he had planned in what had once been the Lady Chapel
was erected, his arms, with the bulls, should immediately so be placed
on it that all coming into church should be able to see it. It was to
the Bulls not, as once, to Our Lady that they should lift their eyes.

Meanwhile, slowly but certainly, unknown then to Harrison, a
train of events was forming which was to shatter his rural peace.
In the first place, the Bowl was in Gloucestershire, no further away
than in the Overbury house at Bourton-on-the-Hill. It lay there,
undisturbed in a lumber-room, unrecognized by anyone, for forty
years.

Gresham had, in fact, put it with those other lesser things which
he had given to Weston with instructions to bury them deep in the
earth. He had judged, whether wisely or not, that this was the best
course to take, since he had no means of returning it to Smyrna and
did not wish to leave so dangerous a legacy to his successor. But
Weston had disobeyed him and kept the Bowl—unaware of its
nature but certain of its value merely as silver—depositing it, with
certain letters and other documents as well as some trinkets which
Overbury had asked him to guard for him, in a trunk in the cellar

of his son's shop. This son, William, who was a haberdasher at the Sign of the Beaver Hat without Temple Bar, was at first implicated in but later exonerated from the Great Oyer of Poisoning; and, when his father was arrested, had refused Anne Turner access to the trunk. After his father's execution, he had desired to make what restitution he could and sent Overbury's effects to his father, Sir Nicholas Overbury, at Bourton. He assumed, as in the circumstances was natural, that the Bowl was Overbury's. Sir Nicholas did the same and gave it, with other trinkets and jewels, to his wife. But Lady Overbury, who was inconsolable for her eldest son's death, sealed them all in a box, saying she never wished to look on them again, and put the box in a lumber-room at the top of the house. Here it remained after Sir Nicholas and his lady were dead and the house passed to the second son, Giles, and, when he died without a son, to Giles's younger brother, Walter. Nor did Walter explore carefully that corner of the lumber-room, which he had associated with his mother's habit of storing a variety of useless or out-of-fashion odds-and-ends which she thought might one day be found useful.

Thus, when Walter died and the house was left to his son, Thomas Overbury the younger who was then on his travels, the Silver Bowl was still in its hiding-place awaiting its eventual rediscovery.*

It was not, however, from anyone in England that the impulse to rediscover it originated. It was from Ibrahim Paschazadé, the Turkish physician in Smyrna who, learned in alchemy of the school

---

* This, undoubtedly, is the true history of the Bowl. Some confusion has arisen because of the strange circumstance which attended the execution of the Lieutenant of the Tower for his part in the murder of Overbury. At the same minute and hour that he was turned from the ladder on Tower Hill, a silver bowl which he had presented to his fellow-commoners at St. John's College, Cambridge, fell from its shelf and was broken to pieces. This fact—which is on record—has led some to suppose that this was the Silver Bowl itself. But that it could not be so is obvious when it is remembered that the bowl given at St. John's was in their possession years before the Bowl was brought to England for Simon's use. Nor would the Silver Bowl itself have broken.—H. R. W.

of Avicenna, was making deep experiments in his search for the Elixir of Life. He, too, no less than initiates of the Western Cult, was aware of the existence of the Bowl and its reputed hiding-place in Polycarp's Tomb; but since the Tomb was practically at his door he saw no reason to disturb it until his experiments had reached a stage where the Bowl's potency would become a necessary factor in the final preparation of the Elixir.

When this time came and he went to the Tomb in search of it, he found that it had gone. Moreover, the condition of the ground and the stonework convinced him that its absence was not due to any misinformation about its hiding-place but because someone else had taken it. He had no clue to Harrison's expedition, since he was himself in England at the time, and, in fact, the ship taking him and his fellow-Turks back to the East had crossed that in which Harrison was returning from Smyrna with the Bowl. But he set to work patiently and without exciting suspicion to try to discover who the thieves might be.

By its nature, such an enquiry took some years, and it was not until he had eliminated from his suspicions all his fellow-practitioners in the Art in and about Smyrna that he turned his attention elsewhere. The story of Harrison's expedition came to his notice, apparently casually, when he was entertaining some of the English merchants, who happened to include the archæologically-minded one with whom Harrison had stayed. When Ibrahim had steered the conversation on to the subject of the antiquities of Smyrna, this merchant volunteered the information that Harrison (whom he knew as Bolland) had been particularly interested in Polycarp's Tomb and had spent some time examining it and making sketches of it. Bolland was, if he remembered aright, a student who had not long left Oxford. He had not heard from him since.

With this clue, Ibrahim himself set out for England once more, but in spite of all enquiries failed to trace either 'Bolland' or the Bowl. He did, however, get near to the truth by guessing that the affairs connected with the murder of Overbury—which were still discussed and talked of, though the famous trial was now years old—were the most likely to be connected with the theft. The deaths of Forman and Gresham were public property and Ibrahim knew quite well who Forman was.

He made the acquaintance of William Lilly, a popular astrologer, in the hope that he might learn something; but he soon discovered that Lilly was merely a charlatan making money out of the credulity of the public and was not even aware that such a thing as the Silver Bowl existed.

Ibrahim returned to Smyrna no nearer his goal than when he left it, except for a suspicion—and Wrenshaw. For Wrenshaw, a hard, discontented young man who had failed to become either a soldier or a scholar or a trader, had fallen under Ibrahim's spell and would listen for hours as he talked of the wonders and opportunity of the East and the might of Islam. When Ibrahim determined at last to go home, Wrenshaw begged that he would take him with him. He had a little money of his own, so he would be no charge on Ibrahim; and, if Ibrahim was willing to employ him, he would gladly spend all he had to get to the land of opportunity. Ibrahim, who decided he might be useful, took him.

Back in Smyrna, Ibrahim continued with his experiments as best he could without the Bowl—and, indeed, gained some success in them since, when he entered his eightieth year, he looked little more than sixty and felt younger. He had not, of course, abandoned his interest in the whereabouts of the Bowl. and assiduously cultivated the English colony in the hope that some visitor from England might make some chance remark to supply him with a clue. None did. Affairs in England—the Civil War, the execution of King Charles, the dictatorship of Cromwell—were of a complexion that put altogether out of countenance the court scandals of the reign of King James.

Then one day Ibrahim's growing desperation (for now, over eighty, he had come to consider the finding of the Bowl a matter of life or death) suddenly chimed with a coincidence to which he attached a disproportionate value. Mr. Thomas Overbury, fresh from his travels in India and Persia, visited Smyrna.

As soon as he learnt this, Ibrahim sent an invitation to his host in the Quarter saying that he would be honoured if they would accept his invitation to a feast, and, in the course of it, learnt that Overbury was on his way home to take up his inheritance at Bourton in Gloucestershire where he had succeeded to the property of his father and both his uncles. Of the murder of his elder uncle, he knew very little, but personally was of the opinion that in spite of all that had been made public there were still things that had not come to light. When he got home he was determined to spend what time he could spare from his duties as a magistrate in trying to unravel the mystery.

After he had gone, Ibrahim sent for Wrenshaw and told him that he was sending him on a difficult and confidential mission to England. He was to follow Mr. Thomas Overbury and settle himself in the neighbourhood of Bourton in Gloucestershire. Here he was to insinuate himself into the confidence of the countryside so that he might be in a position to hear every rumour and observe local happenings, with a view to learning anything which Mr. Overbury learnt about events connected with the murder of his uncle. The pains he took might be quite without result. Ibrahim warned him frankly that the chances of success were less than one in a thousand. He would not reproach him if his efforts were abortive, for, in sending him at all, Ibrahim was acting on the slenderest of clues, even, possibly, on nothing but an intuition. If, on the other hand, he was successful, everything that Ibrahim had should be his on his death.

His task was to trace the whereabouts of a silver bowl which had been stolen by an Englishman named Bolland—whom, also, he could try to find, if he wished, though Ibrahim had himself failed to do so. If it chanced that the recovery of the bowl was possible, he was to procure it by any means he could, including, if necessary, murder. If he merely heard of the bowl but found the getting of it beyond his powers, he was to return to Smyrna for further instructions. There were no other Englishmen whom Ibrahim could trust sufficiently to send with him, but he could, if he liked, take with him two Turks, both skilled in assassination. Also, he would be liberally supplied with money with which he could hire what service he needed in England.

Wrenshaw undertook the adventure with alacrity. It satisfied all sides of his nature and even the reward, which was substantial enough, was no greater inducement than the opportunity to prove his abilities and, if necessary, wreak some destruction among his countrymen whom he now hated almost to the verge of insanity.

At the close of the year 1659, therefore, there were undercurrents in Chipping Campden and its neighbourhood which were not suspected by the majority of its inhabitants. In Bourton, there was some good-natured talk about Wrenshaw, a returned soldier who had settled down there as a cobbler because, people said, he had been beguiled by a wench who was in service up at the House. But most of the conversation was about the return of 'Mr. Thomas' and how strange he was after his travels and whether he was likely to get a knighthood now that there were rumours that the King was coming back again.

And in Chipping Campden no one paid any particular attention to 'old Mr. William' and his servant, John Perry. They had too long been taken for granted. None could know—for he gave no outward sign—of the inexplicable fear and gloom which had taken hold of Harrison. Nor, though they assumed his domestic comfort left something to be desired, could they divine that his only happiness was in the mutual affection between himself and the servant who was his son.

The occasional appearance of two Turkish mendicants in the neighbourhood excited no untoward surprise. Turks and Moors were often found in the workhouses and on the roads. The Vestry accounts of Campden themselves bore witness to the charity which was dispensed to these pathetic alien beggars in a strange land. And since it is an English habit to assume that all foreigners with dark skins look alike, no one noticed that the Turks they saw from time to time begging their way between parishes not only resembled their predecessors, but were, in fact, the same two.

And that Overbury should, in time, become a close friend of the Harrisons was merely something to be expected in the ordinary course of events in rural society.

But beneath these surface simplicities lay a very different reality. The bond which bound Overbury to Harrison was stronger than that of social courtesy or neighbourly friendship. For while in Italy on his way to the East, he had been persuaded to become an Initiate. It was represented to him that in journeying to lands where strange and extraordinary magic was prevalent, it was mere prudence thus to equip himself; and since he had no convictions one way or the other and a very lively curiosity, he had consented. On his return to England, he had visited the Arch-Priest, who had put him in touch with Harrison as the Devil of his local coven.

The members of the coven, at that time, were, in addition to the three Perrys and Overbury, Reed of Campden, Daniels of Ebrington and the daughter of William Curtis of Charringworth. The coven was less active than it had been in the days of Hicks's rule or even in the earlier days of Harrison's. Until the advent of Overbury, indeed, Harrison had become more and more isolated, discussing things privately with John and instructing him, but finding no one with whom he could talk about the higher mysteries and the meta-physical theories behind them, as once he and Hicks had talked week by week, far into the night.

Nor had he the solace of Hicks's books. These had been burnt in the deliberate conflagration of Campden House. This fire, itself, he saw not as a tactical move on the part of the Royalist com-mander so much as part of the working-out of the decree of Fate that everything that Sir Baptist had striven to build should be destroyed. Not only was there no son to inherit the title and estates, but both the great houses were gone—this by wilful destruction, that in London by confiscation—in less than twenty years. These reflections added to the sense of doom under which he laboured.

Then, suddenly, shattering what little peace he had left, Overbury came to him twelve days after Christmas bringing with him the Silver Bowl.

When he discovered it with his uncle's things in the lumber-room, Overbury had no idea what it was. He thought, as his grandfather had thought, that it was merely one of the dead man's possessions; and he brought it to show Harrison as a curiosity and to ask his opinion on the representation of the Nemeseis and other hieroglyphics which decorated it. He thought Harrison might have some clue to their origin and meaning. In the circumstances, there was no reason why Overbury should not know the truth, but Harrison told it to him less in the spirit of a hierarch instructing a neophyte than of a terrified old man appealing for comfort to one younger and stronger.

Overbury gave him what comfort he could, but, though he perceived Harrison's fear, he was unable fully to understand it. The properties of the Bowl, potent though they obviously were, were not magic in the sense that the vulgar would understand the term. It was a bowl and nothing more—an inanimate thing with no life or will of its own. The danger that might be inherent in it derived from the purposes for which it was used, from its part in the pattern of the wills and desires and knowledge of those who used it. That in its long life it had acquired *mana* of its own could not be gainsaid; but this could affect no human being one way or the other as long as that being's will was unconsenting. A child could have used the Bowl for a toy and come to no hurt—and it had lain harmless enough for four decades in the lumber-room at Bourton.

But this, which was true enough, was no comfort to Harrison, though it might solace Overbury, who was uninvolved. To Harrison, the reappearance of the Bowl there in his room in Chipping Campden was as the trump of an apocalyptic judgment. It drew to a head all his vague fears and justified them. It was a demand for payment, long overdue and not to be evaded. For a moment he wondered if he had more than that night to live.

The terror passed. Facing it, he found his courage returning. His mind began to busy itself with the practical details for dealing with this new situation. The first and obvious fact which presented itself was that he could take no action at all on his own responsibility. He must consult the Arch-Priest. The second was that, until that could be done, the Bowl must remain in his keeping. To that extent he was responsible. Overbury agreed and left it with him to put in a place of security.

Wrenshaw, however, also knew about the finding of the Bowl. He heard of it almost immediately from the girl who worked in Overbury's house. Since Overbury's exploration of the lumber-room was no more than an episode in 'the master's pernickety way of tidying things up,' there was no secrecy about it. Mrs. Overbury had, indeed, sent the girl up to bring down a selection of stuffs of various kinds which she was going to sort out to see if any were worth keeping and while there she had noticed—as the thing that interested her most—a pile of trinkets and jewellery with which was a silver bowl. In her evening visit to her lover, she prattled about the simple events of her day as she was accustomed and as Wrenshaw always encouraged her to do. With considerable self-control, he let the discovery pass without remark and only much later said casually that if the trinkets in the lumber-room were of no use to Mr. Overbury, he would like, were it possible, to buy one of them for her. He had saved a good deal of money—though he had no wish for the inquisitive folk in Bourton to know this—and what better way could he spend it than in buying something to decorate so adorable a little wench? Mr. Overbury would doubtless be selling to a dealer. He would be pleased to give an equal price. As for the little bowl she spoke about, he might like to buy that for himself.

The girl soon discovered, from conversation in the servants' hall, that the trinkets were valuable family heirlooms. Wrenshaw was disappointed, but promised, when he next visited London, to bring her back something which should please her as much as any of the things she had seen. The bowl, he supposed, was an heirloom too? The girl did not think so, as Mr. Overbury had taken it with him on his last visit to his friend, Mr. Harrison—Lady Juliana's steward—at Campden. As a gift, probably, for, as far as she knew, he had come back without it. But there was no sense in bothering about that. If Wrenshaw wanted a bowl, he could pick one up anywhere. Wrenshaw agreed, dropped the subject and started to make love to her even more skilfully than usual.

Wrenshaw, in his subsequent visits to Campden to explore the land, moved with such extreme caution that no suspicions were aroused. Not even Harrison, who was in a state of feverish vigilance, saw anything amiss. It was not any particular fear but an inevitable caution which made him decide that he could not absent himself from his home to visit the Arch-Priest without bestowing the Bowl in a place of more safety than was afforded by his own treasure-chest. One night, he and John Perry stole quietly from the house and took it up to Seven Wells where they buried it safely in a spot they could remember.

Thus when Wrenshaw made his attempt at theft on that market-day morning in February when Campden was attending the 'lecture' in the church, he found no trace of what he sought. But he remained obstinately of the opinion that the trail from Overbury to Harrison was the true one. He decided that, though he could not repeat the tactics by which he had gained knowledge of Overbury's household, the principle of seducing or suborning a servant was the most satisfactory. In this case, the servant must obviously be John Perry. His one conversation with John, over ale in the *Eight Bells*, had, however, convinced him that here was a servant both faithful and discreet, and that, if he wished to get the truth out of him, he would have to resort to stern measures.

Again he laid his plans carefully and again they miscarried. The two Turks were to kidnap John at dusk one evening when no one was about, take him through the fields into the open and deserted country where by the threat of death and the application of certain tortures in which they were skilled he should be made to reveal any secrets to which he was privy.

The failure on this occasion was due to the over-enthusiasm of the Turks who, fearing they had been seen, neither withdrew nor waited till John had left the Court Garden for the edge of the fields, but attacked him when he could both defend himself and call for help from passers-by. They disappeared quickly enough as soon as the alarm was raised and were not seen again in England. John's 'two men in white' vanished as if they were indeed the myth that some thought them.

Wrenshaw's failures were, however, successful in one thing. They thoroughly alarmed Harrison. He was now convinced that the whereabouts of the Bowl were known and that attempts, increasing in desperation, would be made to get it. Perry's description of his attackers left no doubt that they were Turks and, from that knowledge, Harrison assumed that the origin of the attack lay in Smyrna. It must also be the work of someone who knew what the Bowl was. This involved a double danger—danger to the Bowl and danger to the Cult. The witch-mania was still at its height, and the discovery of the coven would be as disastrous as discovery of the Bowl.

Harrison did not dare again leave home. His visit to the Arch-Priest at the beginning of the year had been unsatisfactory. The Arch-Priest had been as much at a loss as himself to know the proper course to pursue, for, in his mind, the general question immediately arose as to whether, now that this great Hallow had been taken from the guardianship of the Turks, it ought not to remain in the West. He would have to put the matter to the Great Coven, which met under the presidency of the Supreme Hierarch, the Devil of the West, at Midsummer Eve on the Brocken. Meanwhile, he assured Harrison, the Bowl could stay where he had put it at Seven Wells. He was to come again for further instructions at the end of June.

At the end of June, however, Harrison decided that it would be inadvisable for him to leave and as Overbury was travelling up to London innocently and openly enough to receive his knighthood, he entrusted to him the task of explaining the situation at Campden to the Arch-Priest and of bringing back the decisions.

The decision was that the Bowl was to be returned to Smyrna

and that it must be taken by Harrison himself who had stolen it. Also, since hostile forces were aware of Harrison's possession of it and might make plans for continued attacks, Harrison's absence was to be made attributable to his presumed death.

By August 16th—the night of the full moon—the plan was ready to be put into execution. At midnight, in the presence of the coven at Seven Wells, the Bowl was to be solemnly unearthed; orders given, and Harrison's successor ceremonially appointed. The evidence of supposed death had already been decided upon and 'my lady' sent, days before, to pose as the gleaning-woman who should find and bring to light the hacked and bloodstained effects of the 'murdered' man. Harrison spent the afternoon visiting two other members of the coven—Daniel at Ebrington and Curtis's daughter at Charringworth—to explain to them individually the facts of the case. He considered it advisable that the official proceedings at Seven Wells should be as brief as possible. The pretence of rent-collecting made it easy for him to visit them without suspicion; the twenty-three pounds which he did in fact collect from Plaisterer would provide not only independent evidence of the ostensible reason for his movements but also a credible motive for an attack on him by some wandering marauder; and his expedition enabled him to speak to 'my lady' on his way through the field in which she was gleaning.

There was no way, however, by which he could speak to the Campden members of the coven without the risk of arousing suspicion. John Perry, of course, knew everything, but not Joan or Richard Perry or Will Reed. It was therefore decided that he should meet them in the middle of the Conygree at nine o'clock. John was to see Richard in the morning—a meeting of brothers which would pass unnoticed even if it took place in the High Street—to inform him of it and Richard was to tell his mother. As for Will Reed, he was to meet John at a quarter to nine in the fields and John was to bring him into the Conygree.

The one drawback to this plan was that Mrs. Harrison might

become alarmed when Harrison did not return from his visit to Charringworth and Ebrington and send Edward and the servants in search of him. On balance, however, this was a lesser risk than Harrison's return. It might be impossible for him to leave the house again without engendering doubts which would ruin the whole plan. To guard against mishap, John was to stay within call of Mrs. Harrison, so that he, rather than Edward, would be sent in search of Harrison if she became alarmed; and, by meeting in the Conygree, they were at least near enough to the house to improvize some course of action should it become imperative.

In the event, in spite of Mrs. Harrison's sending John in search of her husband, it was not from this source that obstacles arose. It was from Joan Perry, who was vehemently opposed to the entire project. In the Conygree she argued with Harrison that things were best left as they were. Though she would not—and when it came to the point did not—violate her oath of obedience, she made every use of her right of discussion and of the personal prestige she had acquired within the coven to plead for a reconsideration or at least a postponement of the plan. Let the Bowl remain where it was. Let a petition be sent to the Arch-Priest pointing out that Seven Wells was at least as holy a place as the hillside tomb in the East and as the Hallow had come there by chance and not by any deliberate intention there could be no harm if it was enshrined there. More, it would bring great glory to Seven Wells. On the other hand, this dangerous act of restitution might well destroy not only Harrison himself but all of them.

Her outlook was, no doubt, a narrow one. She was too much influenced by local pride and personal affections. She did not want Harrison to go into danger. Even when he explained that the worst that could happen to him would be more welcome than the guilt and heaviness and fear under which he was now labouring, she was not reassured. And, on general principles, there was much to be said for her point of view. But as it was not that of the Great Coven it could not be adopted. She persisted, nevertheless, not only in the Conygree, but at midnight, at Seven Wells, before them all.

Richard, as was expected, agreed with her; but John, when he was made Devil and invested with power to be exercised during Harrison's absence, told her kindly but with authority to hold her peace. She winced, but accepted her son's order.

The choice of John as regent in Harrison's place was inevitable. Even Overbury, who for many reasons was the only other eligible candidate, admitted, and even urged, this. In matters of the Cult he promised to obey and advise John, and, should anything happen to him in Harrison's absence, to take his place, even in spite of difficulties which might arise because of his public office as magistrate.

Everything having been duly concluded with the appropriate ceremonial and prayers, the company dispersed to their homes, except Harrison and John who stayed for a little at the circle. For one thing, there were matters concerned with the Wells themselves which Harrison wished to explain to John alone. For another, the Wells was the place where the two men whom the Arch-Priest had appointed as his guard to the coast were to meet him at two o'clock.

It was here that Fate or Chance or Misfortune intervened and altered not, indeed, Harrison's arrival in Smyrna but his manner of getting there. For the horse of one of the men who was to guard him cast a shoe and it was not until nearly five that they arrived. Harrison had already dismissed John, refusing to allow him to wait more than a few minutes after two lest the arrangements in Campden should miscarry and assuring him that the men would eventually appear. From the height of Seven Wells under the moon they watched the mist over the valley and knew it a danger to swift travel. If it explained the lateness of the escort, it also suggested urgency for John's departure. Father and son took their leave of each other with a long embrace and in tears.

When the escort arrived, it was already dawn, and in the dawn, as Harrison rode with them through Bourton, Wrenshaw saw him.

After the failure of the Turks to kidnap John Perry, Wrenshaw had decided to take even more drastic measures. He sent the Turks home with a message to Ibrahim reporting that he was on the track of the treasure and that he hoped soon to return successful. He went with them—though not, of course, openly—to Deal to arrange their passage and while there was impressed by an encounter with a press-gang. He discovered that not only were there the officially encouraged press-gangs for the navy, but there were private companies of desperate men ready enough, for sufficient money, to 'spirit' anyone away. He got in touch with the leader of one of these gangs and explained that he was a trader who knew the slave-markets of the East and would pay handsomely for a certain work he required done in Gloucestershire. After some haggling over the price and a delay necessitated by the collection of trustworthy rogues and their introduction into the neighbourhood, everything was ready for the last attempt. The leader was himself living with Wrenshaw, in the guise of a friend of his soldiering days; and the rest were within easy reach.

Thus when Wrenshaw suddenly saw Harrison and his companions riding through Bourton in the dawn, it was not a difficult matter to compass the kidnapping. Leaving the leader to collect the men and follow with all speed, Wrenshaw himself started in pursuit. He could hardly believe his luck, for he had not intended to make his attempt till at least a week later. When the three were eventually attacked and taken prisoner, he found that his luck was even greater than he had supposed. He took the Bowl and with it hastened ahead to Deal, leaving the others to bring Harrison and his companions by slower and more careful stages. He saw no reason why he should not in fact sell them in the slave-market in Smyrna. It would be safer than killing them, as well as more profitable.

Once in Smyrna, he sent them to await purchase and himself hurried triumphantly to Ibrahim with the Bowl; but the old physician, when he heard the circumstances, went down to the market immediately and bought Harrison for himself.

As Schofield was aware of most of the circumstances of Harrison's two years captivity, there was no need for him to dwell on that part of the story. Harrison probably owed his life, as he certainly now owed his liberty, to the fact that he had immediately told

Ibrahim the truth about the whole matter and confirmed it by giving details of his original theft. He pleaded with Ibrahim to allow him to return the Bowl to Polycarp's Tomb, even if that restitution meant his death. Ibrahim was thus convinced both of his honesty and his place in the Cult; and, though the Eastern and Western forms of the Craft differed considerably and in points were at enmity, no member of the one would willingly be guilty of the blood of an initiate of the other.

Yet, short of death or actual torture, Ibrahim treated him with a malicious cruelty. He continually jeered at him for a fool at being outwitted by Wrenshaw and encouraged Wrenshaw to recount again and again how it had been done. He insisted that he should appear a deaf-mute and threatened torture if any of the English who visited the house suspected that he was anything else. 'Boll' was never allowed to be absent from these meals, so that the prospect of freedom was continually hardly more than a sentence away—the sentence that he would never dare to speak. He had seen some slaves who had been tortured.

The replica of the Bowl, which Ibrahim had had made by the most cunning silversmith in Smyrna, had a double purpose which Harrison now that he was free recognized. He had thought at first that Ibrahim's order that he should never be without it was merely à perpetual reminder of his folly. But latterly Ibrahim had sometimes given him the real Bowl and himself used the replica, and the copy was so perfect that only Ibrahim knew which was which. Now, with a silver bowl in his hands and the memory of Ibrahim's words: 'It may get you a passage home' in his ears, he did not know whether he held the replica or the Hallow.

'I should not let that trouble you,' said Schofield decisively. 'Let it pay for your passage, whichever it is. Enough payment has been made for it.'

On the outskirts of Smyrna, Schofield left him. There was, he explained, nothing more that he could do in the case. If Harrison wished to return the bowl to Polycarp's Tomb, that was his affair. For himself, he had an account of his own to settle.

CHAPTER XVIII

Nine Days' Wonder

CHIPPING CAMPDEN LAY SWELTERING UNDER THE HEAT OF another August when William Harrison came home. The Street, under the sun of the early afternoon, was almost empty. It was harvest-time, and those who were not in the fields were resting. Some children were playing, sailing paper boats on the trickle of water by the roadside. Job Stiles's young assistant strolled, whistling, with a plank on his shoulder over to the *George*. In the distance, a traveller turned his cantering horse into Tom Barnes's smithy. There was no one else to be seen or to see the return of the ghost.

It was unlikely that Harrison would have been recognized even had anyone met him. He had aged far more than the two years which the calendar chronicled. The jauntiness had given place to a stoop and a lagging step. His skin was so dark that he might have been mistaken for a foreigner. His clothes, once so neat and carefully tended, were ill-fitting and ragged. In place of his little cane was a stout, gnarled stick on which he leant heavily.

Yet, as he surveyed the Street, it seemed to him that he had never been away. Nothing but himself had changed. It was as if he had awakened from a strange dream and was now on his way home to tell John about it. His wife would nag him, as usual, and ask him why he was late and upsetting her domestic arrangements. Edward would remark to her across him that old men never knew when it was time for them to retire from their work. . . .

As he turned up Church Street, the church clock struck two. The meal would be cleared away by now. . . . Outside the Perry's

cottage, a woman he did not know was washing one of the windows
Surprised, he spoke to her.

'You will pardon me,' he said, 'are you a friend of the Perrys?'

She turned fiercely on him: 'I don't know what right a stranger's
got to insult me or what it's got to do with you. Or'—suddenly
suspicious—'was it you that threw the mud?'

'Mud? Of course I didn't throw any mud.'

'Well, someone did. And it's a shame and a scandal the way they
persecute an honest body just because we live in this house. It's in
my mind that someone here teaches the children to do it. If I could
only catch 'em, I'd wring their necks, I would. This is the third time
this week.'

'But the Perrys——?'

'What about them?'

'They're not—they're not here any more?'

'Look you here'—the woman turned threateningly, as if she was
about to hit him with the cloth—'you're an old man, but that's no
reason for me to let you taunt me.'

'I assure you, nothing was further from my mind. You see I'm—
I've been away for some time and I was wondering what had
heppened to the Perrys.'

'You must have been a long way away if you don't know.'

'Yes, I have been.'

'I thought everyone would have known of the hanging. Last
spring. For murdering old Harrison. You can see John still swinging
up there on the gibbet.'

Harrison dug his nails into the palm of his hand; and, with the
other, clutched more firmly at his stick to keep himself from falling.
He thought his heart would stop as the blow he had half expected
yet told himself was impossible fell at last.

The woman noticed nothing. She continued to chatter, more
amiably now, as she finished cleaning the mud off the window. 'No
one in Campden would take this cottage. That's how we got it.
We lived over at Moreton and I wish we were back there. But my
husband wanted to work at the mill here. Restless sort, he is; always

wanting a change. This cottage was empty and we're not superstitious so we took it. Mind you, I wouldn't have done, if I'd known
the bother it was going to be. And it's not even cheap. He promised
we could have it cheap—Mr. Harrison that is—but we were no
sooner in and knew we had to stay here for a bit than he put up the
rent. Regular skinflint he is. Anyone'll tell you that. But if you lived
here once, perhaps you know him?'

Harrison had recovered himself a little. 'Yes,' he said, 'I know
him. I'm his father.'

'His *father?* But if you're his father, you must be——' She turned
to look at him. 'So *that's* what's wrong with you,' she said. 'I thought
there was something as soon as you came up asking questions.
You're crazy.'

Fortunately at that moment, Tom Barnes came out of the *Eight
Bells* opposite. His assistant had come to fetch him to attend to the
horse which had just called at the smithy and he was returning, not
without a grumble, to the work. Harrison went over to him.

'Tom—Tom Barnes, you know me, don't you?'

Tom looked down at the old man, blinked, looked again and
said: 'That I do—or so I think I do. You can't be a ghost, 'cos I don't
believe in 'em; and the ale's not so strong that I'm seeing things; so
you must be old Mr. William, that you must, though I'll be danged
if I can figure out how.'

'Yes, Tom. It's me. I've come back.'

'Aye, but come back from *where?*'

'That's a long story, Tom. I'll tell you about it. I was kidnapped
and taken to Turkey.'

'Well, well, well! Turkey, was it? Not but what I can see by your
face you've been somewhere hot.'

'Is it true they hanged the Perrys?'

'That it is. I pulled old Joan's legs myself; and I'd have done the
same for John if they'd have let me. . . . And there 'tis now. That's
what he said afore he died—that we'd be hearing summat. And here
you are alive and them dead for killing you. If that isn't a wonder.
The Campden wonder.'

'Will you help me home, Tom, please?' Harrison clutched at the blacksmith's strong arm.

'Why, that I will, Mr. William, and be glad to. Take it easy.'

Over his shoulder he said to the boy: 'You go back to the smithy and tell 'em they can take their horse somewhere else. I've something more important to attend to. That I have.'

So, leaning on Tom Barnes, William Harrison went up to the Court Gate and so came home.

It was a nine-days' wonder. Not only Campden itself thronged up to the House that evening clamouring to see him, but in the days that followed crowds from the surrounding countryside, even greater than those who had witnessed the execution of the Perrys, flocked into the village. Visitors in the neighbourhood halted on their journey to turn aside to Campden to confirm for themselves the incredible tale. In Oxford, Mr. Antony à Wood noted in his diary, under the date, *Wednesday*, *August 6th*, 1662: 'Mr. Harrison, supposed to be murdered two years ago, came out of Turkey to his home in the country.' In London, it became the gossip of the coffee-houses.

As far as he could, Harrison hid himself from inquisition and the majority of the visitors had to be content to speak to those more fortunate natives—especially Tom Barnes—who had actually seen and spoken to Harrison and to hear from them the tale he had told of the circumstances of his kidnapping. In his story, Harrison had thought it wiser to adhere strictly to the truth, except in two particulars which might reveal those circumstances which must be kept hidden. He therefore altered the scene and time of his capture from the place where it had actually occurred to the vicinity of the furze-brake near Ebrington where his hat, comb and band had been 'found' by 'the gleaning woman'; and he made no specific mention of his escort until he came to the slave-market in Smyrna. This was the easier since, on his enforced journey to Deal, the party had broken up to avoid suspicion in travelling.

His account, as it was later published and as, with slightly more diffuseness, he told it at the time, ran thus:

'On a Thursday, in the afternoon, in the time of harvest, I went to Charringworth to demand rents due to my Lady Campden; at which time the tenants were busy in the fields, and late ere they came home, which occasioned my stay there till the close of the evening. I expected a considerable sum, but received only three and twenty pounds and no more.

'In my return home (in the narrow passage amongst Ebrington furzes) there met me a horseman and said: 'Art thou there?' and I fearing that he would have rid over me, struck his horse over the nose, whereupon he struck at me with his sword, several blows, and ran it into my side; while I (with my little cane) made my defence as well as I could.

'At last another came behind me, ran me into the thigh, laid hold on the collar of my doublet, and drew me into a hedge, near to the place. Then came in another. They did not take my money, but mounted me behind one of them, drew my arms about his middle and fastened my wrists together with something that had a spring lock to it—as I conceived by hearing it give a snap as they put it on. Then they threw a great cloak over me and carried me away.

'In the night they alighted at a hayrick, which stood near unto a stone-pit by a wall-side, where they took away my money. About two hours before day (as I heard one of them tell another he thought it to be then) they tumbled me into the stone-pit. They stayed (as I thought) about an hour at the hayrick, when they took horse again. One of them bade me come out of the pit. I answered they had my money already and asked what they would do with me, whereupon he struck me again, drew me out and put a great quantity of money into my pockets, and mounted me again after the same manner.

'On Friday, about sun-setting, they brought me to a lone house upon a heath (by a thicket of bushes) where they took me down almost dead, being sorely bruised with the carriage of the money. When the woman of the house saw that I could neither stand nor speak, she asked them whether or no they had brought a dead man.

They answered No, but a friend that was hurt, and they were carrying him to a chirurgeon. She answered if they did not make haste their friend would be dead before they could bring him to one. There they laid me on cushions and suffered none to come into the room but a little girl. There we stayed all night, they giving me some broth and strong waters. In the morning, very early, they mounted me as before and on Saturday night they brought me to a place where there were two or three houses, in one of which I lay all night on cushions by their bedside. On Sunday morning they carried me from thence, and about three or four o'clock, they brought me to a place by the seaside called Deal, where they laid me down on the ground. And one of them staying by me, the other two walked a little off, to meet a man with whom they talked. In their discourse, I heard them mention seven pounds; after which they went away together and half an hour after returned.

'The man (whose name, as I after heard, was Wrenshaw) said he feared I would die before he could get me on board; then presently they put me into a boat and carried me to ship-board where my wounds were dressed. I remained in the ship (as near as I could reckon) about six weeks, in which time I was indifferently recovered of my wound and weakness.

'Then the master of the ship came and told me (and the rest who were in the same condition) that he discovered three Turkish ships. We all offered to fight in defence of the ship and ourselves, but he commanded us to keep close and said he would deal with them well enough. A little while after, he called us up and when we came on deck we saw two Turkish ships close by us. Into one of them we were put and placed in a dark hole where how long we continued before we landed I know not. When we were landed, they led us two days' journey and put us into a great house, or prison, where we remained four days and a half; and then came to us eight men to view us, who seemed to be officers. They called us and examined us of our trades and callings, which every one answered. One said he was a chirurgeon, another that he was a broadcloth weaver, and I (after two or three demands) said I had some skill in physic. We

three were set by and taken by three of those eight men that came
to view us. It was my chance to be chosen by a grave physician of
eighty-seven years of age, who lived near to Smyrna, who had
formerly been in England and knew Crowland in Lincolnshire,
which he preferred before all other places in England. He employed
me to keep his still-house . . .'

The main drawback of a miracle is that it is very seldom believed,
even by those who witness it. Those who report it are invariably
disbelieved by the majority of men. Something of this quality of
innate scepticism adhered to the reappearance of William Harrison.
As it was impossible to deny that three people had been hanged for
the murder of one who was still alive, there was a growing tendency
to search for something that could be disbelieved, as a kind of
inverted compliment to the course of English justice. The obvious
thing to disbelieve was Harrison's story, which was certainly strange
and whose accuracy could not be proved.

Within a week of his return, there were several well-defined
schools of thought on the subject. There were those who maintained
that he had never been kidnapped but had disappeared of his own
volition. Of these, one party suggested that he had taken a holiday
from his wife—probably with some wench he had procured—while
another insisted that he had been indulging in nameless and pro-
miscuous debaucheries in London or Paris. When it was pointed
out that twenty-three pounds would hardly keep him in this state
of nefarious enjoyment for two years, the supporters of the theory
nodded sagely, explained that he himself had stolen the £140 which
he had blamed on undiscovered robbers and had probably also
embezzled great sums of Lady Campden's money over a period of
years.

On the other hand, an equal number of critics contended that he
had in fact been kidnapped—though not, of course, sold as a slave
in Turkey—and that the kidnapper-in-chief who had arranged the
'spiriting' was none other than his son, Edward, who wished to
enjoy his father's place. The general dislike of Edward made this,

on the whole, the most popular theory; though a minority insisted that the origin of the deed must be sought among some person or persons unknown who, for political reasons, wanted the old man out of the way because he knew too much.

The only point of agreement between the various theorizers was that the blame for the glaring miscarriage of justice must somehow be laid at the Harrisons' door. They did not, however, know that William Harrison agreed with them.

When, the afternoon he came home, he had learnt all the circumstances of the Perrys' deaths, his grief sharpened his hatred of his wife and his eldest son. He spoke once to each of them. To Edward he said: 'You will leave this house to-night and you will not attempt to see me again as long as I live.' To his wife he said: 'I shall not speak to you again, except to remind you of your part in the murder.' Then he left them and rode over to Bourton to see Sir Thomas Overbury. He must know what had happened. But, on the way, he decided to go to the gibbet to face the thing he had done.

For his anger and hatred of others was as nothing compared with that which he turned against himself. In the end, it was he and none other who was responsible. He made no excuses that the beginning of it was a mere youthful mistake which anyone, in the circumstances, might have made; nor did he plead in extenuation that he had been caught in the web of fatality. He had accepted for too long the true doctrine of the Nemeseis to find comfort in the cowardice of that imprecision. He wondered, certainly, why he who had played the smallest part in the matter and who had made at least a partial restitution should be called to pay the heaviest price. But he did not dwell on this, knowing that the way of the gods is inscrutable and seldom matches the huckster economics of earth.

That his payment was the heaviest he knew only in full force as he stood at the gallows, trying to find some semblance to the son he had loved in the shrivelled, hideous thing which hung there in its awkward chains, its eyes picked out by the crows and its right hand cut off by some obscene wanderer. Compared with this, his own death would have been nothing. For a moment he feared for his reason and no tears would come to give him relief.

But two travellers, passing by on the road, saw nothing but an old man looking with interest at a felon's corpse; and one remarked to the other that it was pitiful how old age seemed to provoke a nastiness of curiosity.

Overbury, when his servant announced that Mr. Harrison had called to see him, assumed that it was Edward and began soundly to rate the man for not immediately saying he was not at home.

'I am sorry, Sir Thomas; but this is another Mr. Harrison. An old man. Not Mr. Edward Harrison, sir.'

'What does he want?'

'He wouldn't say, Sir Thomas, except that he wished to see you on an important matter and thought you would wish to see him. He is a little shabby, sir, but I do not think he is begging.'

'Is he like—did you know old Mr. Harrison who was murdered?'

'No, Sir Thomas. I came to you, you will remember, the Christmas after that unfortunate occurrence.'

'Yes, yes, of course. I was wondering if this could be his brother. You might have seen a likeness. I don't know any other Harrisons, but you can show him in here.'

'Yes, Sir Thomas.'

Overbury was quite certain in his mind who it would be and, in the moment before Harrison's appearance was able to school himself to a seeming casualness. In front of the servant, he merely said: 'I am glad to see you, Mr. Harrison,' and offered him a chair.

But Harrison remained standing, and as soon as the door closed said tonelessly: 'Why did you let them die?'

'Please sit down,' said Overbury. 'We have so much to say. Why have you been so long?'

'I've nothing to say that matters. But you—why did you let them die?'

'I obeyed John,' said Overbury, 'as I swore to do. It was his will and his choice. But none of us knew it would end as it did. When you did not return, it was impossible to save them. Why have you been so long?'

'I was a prisoner.'

'So were we—all of us.'

Harrison, convinced of Overbury's sincerity, sank into a chair. It occurred to him, as one of those irrelevant trivialities that invade the mind even in moments of the greatest tension, that this was the first comfort he had known for two years. 'Tell me,' he said.

Overbury told him how John had feared that Joan, whose opposition to the scheme became more violent as soon as Harrison had left, would by some indiscretion betray what was afoot.

'She would never have done that—never. He could not have thought it,' said Harrison.

'Yes, he was wrong; but there is no doubt that he thought it honestly. You must believe me there. There was more colour for it than you may understand. Though it was not so much his mother herself as Richard. He had less sense than the others and was weaker. He took his mother's side and might have said something without intending it.'

'But to accuse them of murder!'

'It was to silence them, that was all. After that, nothing Richard might have said would be believed. And neither of us thought they could come to harm.'

'Neither of you?'

'Neither John nor I. He asked me about it and I told him what I believed to be true—that no one could be hanged for murder unless the body was produced. That is the law and Sir Christopher Turnor observed it. They were freed at once, because he would not try them. We knew the body would never be produced and so thought that Joan and Richard were in no danger. John knew he might have to die himself and faced it. He asked me to tell you that he did it without fear, because it would show him worthy of your love and trust. He was the greatest man I have met.'

'Thank you.' And at last, in a hurricane of grief, the tears came and the old man was eased a little.

'When they were on trial a second time, he did his best to save them. We thought you were dead and that there was no more we could do. John said he had been mad and that they were all innocent. But it was too late. And at the very end he had to act again to check Richard, who might have betrayed us all, not from malice but from foolishness. I think that was John's worst moment—to earn his brother's hatred. But there was no question of saving him. I was in court and smelt death, for all Hyde's smooth words.'

'But why were they tried again?'

'Your wife and Edward working through Lady Juliana. We could not stand against that.'

'And you?'

'In public, I played the magistrate. It was the least I could do. John, anyhow, ordered it that suspicion might be still further allayed. I think I saved them from death in Campden by arresting them on a pretended warrant. It was a risk I had to take—but in the end it did little good.'

'One last question,' said Harrison. 'Why did Joan send that young man out to find me?'

'If you had returned in time, they would not have been hanged. "My lady" brought the Arch-Priest's permission when he got news that you had disappeared in Smyrna. I did not see the man myself, but I gather he was little use to you.'

'No use at all,' said Harrison. 'It was foolish to send him. If I could have got home, I should have come.'

'And now, may I know your story?' asked Overbury.

When Harrison had told him, they fell to discussing what remained for them to do. They were all that were left of the coven. Old Daniels had died in the winter; Curtis's daughter had married and gone with her husband into Sussex; Will Reed, terrified at the happenings, had left Campden to seek work somewhere where he was not known.

'I shall not be here long,' said Harrison, 'but I have one last work to do. But I shall do it alone. I shall not ask you to help me.'

'May I know what it is?'

'To kill Hyde.'

'But how? We no longer have the Bowl.'

'It can be done without it. I think I have the knowledge, though it may take time. The spell can only be cast on one of the High Days, and at first I may fail. But you must be clear of this. I order that.'

'But is there nothing I can do?'

'I shall write you an account of these matters. Add to them an abstract of the part you played. Then see, when the time is ripe, that they are published. There is too much curiosity abroad. Three of them died to keep the secret. We must see that the secret is kept.'

During the next week, the body of John was taken down from the gallows and those of Joan and Richard disinterred from their graves at the foot of it and brought back for burial in Campden. It was considered part of Harrison's eccentricity that he insisted that they should be buried not in the churchyard but in the gardens of Campden House. This proceeding would ordinarily have provoked much opposition; but there were still those who maintained that, even if Joan was not a murderess, she was a witch and the Vicar was glad to accede to Harrison's request as a way out of an awkward dilemma.

Harrison was careful to point out the graves to his wife every day. Within six weeks, the assiduous gossip, Mr. Antony à Wood, was able to record a new sensation: 'Harrison's wife has hung herself in her own house. Why, the reader is to judge.'

The other vengeance took longer. Sir Robert Hyde was rewarded for his services by being made Chief Justice of the King's Bench. It was not until May Day, 1665, that suddenly and without warning he was struck dead while presiding over his court.

EPILOGUE

★

The Pamphlet

SCHOFIELD DID NOT RETURN TO ENGLAND TILL THE AUTUMN OF 1676. He arrived in London, his hair prematurely white and lacking his left arm, but contented and at peace with himself. For he had taken revenge for his slavery and had found a faith for which he had been willing to die.

What Wrenshaw had told him during his captivity—that the Turks were preparing for a final onslaught on the West—was no idle boast. The blow fell soon enough. The Sultan declared war on the Emperor, and the young Kiuprili, who had succeeded his father as Vizier, advanced at the head of an army of 120,000 men, 123 field-pieces, 12 heavy battering cannon, and 60,000 camels. No such armament and no such danger had been known for a century when Solyman the Magnificent had conquered eastern Europe and the drums of Lepanto had sounded the last Crusade. The West seemed lost. Against the Turkish flood, which engulfed the land from Adrianople to Belgrade, from Belgrade to Budapest, from Budapest to the banks of the River Raab, the last barrier to Vienna, there were a mere 6,000 Christian troops, under Count Raymond de Montecuculi. Even when the echo of the crusading call roused the quarrelling monarchs of the West and Louis of France sent 4,000 men to join Montecuculi, the odds were such that defeat seemed a certainty.

There, by the banks of the Raab, under the monastery of St. Gothard, the little army, outnumbered by twelve to one, awaited the Turkish advance across the river. And Schofield was with them

—a mercenary soldier once more, but with a new spirit. He found he could echo the ingenuous prayer of John Spork—the 'Austrian Ajax'—who commanded the Christian cavalry, as he prostrated himself bareheaded on the ground in front of his men and prayed aloud: 'O, Mighty Generalissimo, who art on high, if Thou wilt not this day help Thy children the Christians, at least do not help these dogs the Turks, and Thou shalt soon see something that shall please Thee.'

He could not know—though he might have guessed—the scorn with which Kiuprili contemplated his adversaries. Seeing the hairless chins and powdered perukes of the elegant Frenchmen, the Vizier asked contemptuously: 'Who are these young girls?' But he saw clearly enough the result when the 'young girls,' laughingly answering the Turkish cry of 'Allah! Allah!' with 'Allons! Allons!' charged and drove the Turks back into the river.

In that battle, which saved the West, Schofield lost his arm and accounted it a little thing to give.

Though, in the perspective of after-years, St. Gothard was seen as the decisive encounter which marked the beginning of the Turkish end, it was to those concerned in it merely a breathing space. The fight continued and in the years that followed Schofield campaigned, now with Montecuculi, now with the other great Christian leader who arose, Sobieski of Poland, until age and failing health convinced him that his usefulness as a soldier was over.

Now he was back in London—a new and unfamiliar London—which was rising on the ruins left by the Great Fire. In his wanderings in it, rediscovering what there was of the past, exploring the present, he came to a little bookshop in the Strand, by St. Clement's Danes, which he knew of old. Here the title of a new pamphlet caught his eye: 'A True and Perfect Account of the Examination, Confession, Trial, Condemnation and Execution of Joan Perry and her two Sons, John and Richard Perry, for the supposed Murder of William Harrison, Gent.' He bought it at once and made his way to the nearest coffee-house where he might read it undisturbed. The

sub-title told him in epitome what he wanted to know: 'Being one
of the most remarkable occurrences which hath happened in the
memory of man, sent in a letter (by Sir T. O., of Bourton, in the
county of Gloucester, knight, and one of his Majesty's Justices of
the Peace) to T. S. Dr. of Physic in London.—Likewise Mr. Harrison's own account, how he was conveyed into Turkey, and there
made a slave for above two years; and then his master which bought
him there, dying, how he made his escape and what hardship he
endured, who at last (through the providence of God) returned to
England while he was supposed to be murdered; here, having seen
his man-servant arraigned (who falsely impeached his own mother
and brother as guilty of the murder of his master) they were all
three arraigned, convicted and executed in Broadway-hills in
Gloucestershire.' *

Harrison had arrived home too late, then. . . . The Perrys were
dead. . . . And with them the secret of the matter. . . . Sir T. O. was
obviously Overbury. . . . If Overbury and Harrison had written
this together, it must represent what they wished to be made known.
The facts would be there, but the truth assuredly not. . . .

As he read of the events of the night of August 16th, 1660, as they
had been represented by John Perry, of the trial and execution of
the three, he caught something of the past in which he had so
strangely become involved; but he found he could not re-live its
emotions. Believing what he now believed, he was self-reproachful,
neither that he had failed to save Joan, nor that he had tried. That
was how things had fallen out.

He returned, as so often in memory, to the wisdom of Father
Gabriel. However mistaken, deluded, sinful, the 'Old Religion'—
the Craft of the Wise—might be, it was nearer the truth than the
new, cold heresy of belief in man's equality and God's remoteness
which, even though the Turks were defeated, was creeping in other
forms over the West. There might be mercy for the Perrys, for
surely they, in Father Gabriel's phrase, were 'poor mistaken
visionaries who, in their own way, were humble before their

* The pamphlet is quoted in full in Howell's 'State Trials,' Vol. XIV.

distorted image of the Creator.' Schofield made a prayer for the repose of their souls. . . .

He continued reading and passed to Harrison's account of the matter. He admired the ingenuity with which he had handled his 'abduction,' he guarded reference to 'the man, whose name (as I after heard) was Wrenshaw.' The part of the history in which he had shared and Harrison's difficulties in getting home of which he knew nothing had an interest of another kind.

' . . . it was my chance to be chosen by a grave physician of eighty-seven years of age, who lived near to Smyrna, who had formerly been in England, and knew Crowland in Lincolnshire, which he preferred before all other places in England: he employed me to keep his still-house, and gave me a silver bowl, double gilt, to drink in; my business was most in that place; but once he set me to gather cotton wool, which I not doing to his mind, he struck me down to the ground, and after drew his stiletto to stab me; but I holding up my hands, he gave a stamp and turned from me, for which I render thanks to my Lord and Saviour Jesus Christ, who staid his hand and preserved me.

'I was there about a year and three-quarters, and then my master fell sick on a Thursday, and sent for me; and calling me, as he used, by the name of Boll, told me he should die and bad me shift for myself. He died on Saturday following, and I presently hastened with my bowl to a port almost a day's journey distant; the way to which place I knew, having been twice there employed by my master about the carriage of his cotton wool. When I came thither I addressed myself to two men who came out of a ship of Hamborough which (as they said) was bound for Portugal within three or four days. I enquired of them for an English ship; they answered there was none; I entreated them to take me into their ship; they answered they durst not, for fear of being discovered by the searchers, which might occasion the forfeiture, not only of their goods, but also of their lives. I was very importunate with them, but could not prevail.

'They left me to wait on Providence, which at length brought out another of the same ship, to whom I made known my condition, craving his assistance for my transportation. He made me the like answer as the former and was as stiff in his denial, till the sight of my bowl put him to pause. He returned to the ship, and after half an hour's space, he came back again accompanied by another seaman and for my bowl undertook to transport me; but told me I must be contented to lie down in the keel and endure much hardship, which I was content to do to gain my liberty.

'So they took me aboard and placed me below in the vessel in a very uneasy place, and obscured me with boards and other things, where I lay undiscovered, notwithstanding the strict search which was made in the vessel. My two chapmen, who had my bowl, honestly furnished me with victuals daily, until we arrived at Lisbon in Portugal, where (as soon as the master had left the ship and was gone into the city) they set me on shore moneyless to shift for myself.

'I knew not what course to take but, as Providence led me, I went up into the city and came into a fair street; and, being weary, I turned my back to a wall and leaned upon my staff. Over against me were four gentlemen discoursing together. After a while one of them came to me and spake to me in a language that I understood not. I told him I was an Englishman and understood not what he spake. He answered me in plain English that he understood me and was himself born near Wisbich in Lincolnshire. Then I related to him my sad condition, and he taking compassion on me, took me with him, provided for me lodging and diet, and by his interest with a master of a ship bound for England, procured my passage; and bringing me on ship-board, he bestowed wine and strongwaters on me, and, at his return, gave me eight stivers and commended me to the care of the master of the ship, who landed me safe at Dover, from whence I made shift to get to London, where, being furnished with necessaries, I came into the country.'

To this, the publisher had added a note: 'Many question the truth of this account Mr. Harrison gives of himself and his transportation, believing he was never out of England; but there is no question of

Perry's telling a formal, false story to hang himself, his mother and his brother: and since this, of which we are assured, is no less incredible than that of which we doubt, it may induce us to suspend hard thoughts of Mr. Harrison till Time, the great discoverer of Truth, shall bring to light this dark and mysterious business.'

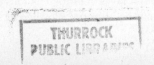